Blood Tells No Lies

By

Giampiero D'Angelo

© Copyright 2022 by Giampiero D' Angelo. All rights reserved.

It is not legal to reproduce, duplicate, or transmit any part of this document in either electronic means or printed format. Recording of this publication is strictly prohibited.

DISCLAIMER

This is a work of fiction. Names, characters, places, and incidents either are products of the author's imagination or are used fictitiously. Any resemblance to actual events or locales or persons, living or dead, is entirely coincidental.

DEDICATION

Dear Family,

Like my life, I dedicate this book to you.

To my wife, Christa.

To my son Albert, his wife Laura, and my grandchildren Vienna and Emilia.

To my son Stephen, his wife Nicole, and my grandchildren Leo and Celia.

TABLE OF CONTENT

Disclaimer..iii

Dedication..iv

Prologue 1

Chapter 1 Wedding Bells 6

Chapter 2 A Revealing Reception................................15

Chapter 3 Planned Mistake..25

Chapter 3 Wine and Blood at Lunch 37

Chapter 5 A Walk in the Park 48

Chapter 6 The Promise..51

Chapter 7 Just a Card Game 65

Chapter 8 The Trip 71

Chapter 9 Landing in a New Country 79

Chapter 10 Confusion 85

Chapter 11 Still Confused..94

Chapter 12 First Impression 100

Chapter 13 Speeding Can be Costly..........................118

Chapter 14 Beautiful Narrow Streets........................129

Chapter 15 At this Time of the Day 141

Chapter 16 A Stranger in the Room 155

Chapter 17 A Tour 158

Chapter 18. A Needle in a Haystack 169

Chapter 19 Reflection of a Tour 171

Chapter 20 Food Clears The Mind 176

Chapter 21 A Napkin Saves the Day 185

Chapter 23 An Evening to Remember 192

Chapter 23 Realization 200

Chapter 24 A Palace 207

Chapter 25 The Note 211

Chapter 26 A Mother's Help 227

Chapter 27 Be Nice 235

Chapter 28 Busted 236

Chapter 29 Heaven Laughs too 249

Chapter 30 Pizza Puts Everything on Hold 254

Chapter 31 The Search Continues 262

Chapter 32 Waiting For a Guest 267

Chapter 33. Limited Confessions 268

Chapter 34 Your Ride is Here 277

Chapter 35 Luca 282

Chapter 36 Rest in Peace Pops 292

Chapter 37 Open your eyes 297

Chapter 38 Leaving Town 301

Chapter 39 Seeking Home 306

Chapter 40 Settling the Scores 312

Chapter 41 The NewYork Exhibition 317

Chapter 42 Corleone calling 336

Epilogue 339

Acknowledgement 343

PROLOGUE

The town was blanketed by a hot, thick air that was often prevalent in this part of the country. Yet, to Franco, Teresa, and Luca, it was a welcome relief from the stagnant, smoke-filled air inside the only cinema in town. In 1972, Corleone, Sicily, was not precisely the party town of Italy's biggest island. It was made bearable once the theatre, the only one within 50 kilometers, added an element of prestige that the town appreciated over the establishments of the neighboring municipalities provided.

As the three friends leisurely walked up the cobblestone street discussing the movie they had just finished watching, a movie that Luca believed would have a negative effect on their town, but Teresa and Franco believed that the movie would put Corleone on the world map. Franco suddenly stopped and grabbed Luca by his shoulders.

"Perhaps this movie will also curtail the activities of the Mafia," he told him with a straight face.

Knowing Luca's connections with said organization, Franco turned to Teresa and then back to Luca and waited for his response with bated breath.

"Perhaps," Luca said after a few moments of serious contemplation.

After exchanging a few silent looks, they burst out laughing at the absurdity of their comments. It wasn't until Teresa snaked her arms around their waists that the group realized that they had stopped. Her arms had guided them towards the main piazza. Their laughs and conversations bounced off the walls as they continued their trot.

Regardless, there were some aspects of the movie that they never agreed on. But they reached commutuality regarding the quality of the movie. It was established that the acting was fantastic. Apolonia's father resembled Teresa's father, and they also shared similar values. If they were ever to visit America, New York's Little Italy and Mulberry Street, where the movie 'The Godfather' was filmed, would be on their bucket list.

Their conversation deviated and jumped from one topic to another. They were always like this. How could they not since they were born only days apart.

The three had always been close, but the relationship between Franco and Teresa was special, almost magical. As babies, barely half a year old, the only way to calm their temper was to lay them in the same cot. There, twisting and turning similar to a fire left unattended, the babies would wail. It wasn't until the mothers rested their waddled bodies together that their cheeks had dried. Wails would turn to giggles, and the two would babble in an instant. It was as if the two had sensed each other's aura.

Many labeled the event as a magical spectacle. Their mothers attempted to rest other children in the carriage with them, but this used to further upset the two children, and the mothers were forced to separate the children again. It was only when the two rested alone in the same cot that life seemed to have gained peace, and this is how they grew up, always joined at the hip.

This extraordinary relationship between the two had never faltered. Even the introduction of adolescence, a confusing, stressful transitional stage in their physical and psychological development, did not alter this extraordinary connection. In fact, their commitment was further forged in steel, thus beginning a natural progression in their life-long relationship.

As they walked, each absorbed in their own thoughts, a confident and cerebral young man was busy fighting against his emotions. Franco, who was perhaps the brightest, wondered why his anxiety was rising with the oncoming date of his wedding.

He reasoned that it was not nervousness, for the only time he had felt a little anxious was when he had to ask her father for her hand in marriage. But that experience turned out to be a rather pleasant one.

"The Gods," Teresa's father had responded, "Had already decided long ago that you two should be together. Who am I to tempt the Gods?"

What he was currently feeling was not anxiousness or nervousness. It was something else, something that the simple act of holding her hand had heightened. For sure, the mere touch of her hand always swelled his heart, but as the wedding date was coming closer, this ordinary show of affection was also swelling something much lower on his body.

"Anticipation!" he said aloud, happy that he had figured it out.

His sudden verbal outburst caused Luca and Teresa to turn to him. "What?" Teresa asked Franco.

"Nothing," he responded, shaking his head, "I was just thinking about our wedding," he added, smiling at her.

"Yes, me too," she said, smiling back.

Teresa knew Franco better than himself. She had noticed his emotions fluctuating from irritable to easy-going and back to irritable in a span of minutes. She had also noticed that as the wedding day was getting closer, he had been holding her hand a little tighter, hugging her a little longer, and kissing her with a little more greed.

"Yes, it is anticipation, my love, but not for our wedding. It's for our wedding night!" She thought, letting out a little laugh.

"What are you laughing at?" Franco wanted to know.

"I'm laughing with the angels, my love," she responded, drifting back into her own thoughts.

Although her love for Franco was no less intense, she was more pragmatic. Her goal was to give him a home filled with love and laughter. To create a Heaven where all his day's problems and stresses would vanish as he walks in the front door. Knowing his intentions, she was positive that in a town full of young men talking about leaving Corleone behind, Franco's intelligence and level-headed thinking would ensure that he would accomplish this. It is here, in this dream of a location, that she predicted they would forge a safe and long life together; besides, she too felt the swelling.

"I'm glad I have you as my friends," Luca said, bringing the other two back into the real world.

"Luca, what a beautiful thing to say," Teresa answered, kissing his cheek.

"Thanks," he said, wondering if someday he too would project the same happy aura that surrounded his friends at the moment.

Realizing that, unlike his friends, who knew they would be together before they could talk, he had played the field, not allowing himself to fully commit to any relationships, afraid that he could never reach the happiness that he was now seeing.

Until recently, he must admit, when the baker's daughter caught his attention and that emotion shielding armor that he had protected for so long had started to dissipate slowly.

He had mentioned this to Franco, Teresa, and his cousin Mauro, with whom he had a friendly competition for the attention of some of the young women in town, but for some reason, he couldn't confront her.

When it comes to Laila, his mountainous confidence faded into a valley of self-doubt.

Continuing their leisurely stroll, they approached the town square, where a couple walking toward them interrupted their solitary inner observations. Recognizing the couple, Franco quickly looked over to Luca, whose face confirmed his suspicions.

The next few minutes would be crucial for their future. However, it would not be Franco's action in the next few minutes that would forever change their life. It would be the actions of one of the three friends in the next few days that would result in Franco never seeing his beloved Corleone again.

CHAPTER ONE
Wedding Bells

Present Day

The camera and a strategically placed hand hid the yawn. Instinctively, Luke knew that his brother Sal had noticed. Confident that he had taken enough pictures of the wedding couple and anyone else remotely associated with the wedding, he ignored this certainty and continued to wander, aimlessly taking pictures of things he found interesting.

Luke admitted that Our Lady of Pompeii Church, located on Carmine St., in Manhattan, had elegance. Constructed in the late 1920s by Matthew Del Gaudio, the ten large marble columns leading to an arched ceiling adorned with colorful paintings depicting various religious themes, combined with the twelve built-in semi-circular windows on either side of the church emitting natural light, would normally be a photographer's ultimate dream. But for Luke, a multi-potential photographer whose true love was portraits in natural settings, this church lacked depth. He believed a well-taken portrait, ugly or beautiful, would reveal both the subject and photographer's soul, and as beautiful as this church was, Del Gaudio's soul did not reveal itself in the architecture. The talent and genius of the man were clear, but his soul and the mysteries of this religious edifice stayed hidden behind the marble pillars and concrete walls.

Franco decided that taking a picture of this stagnant old lady would not disclose any secrets, so he moved on in search of an interesting face. First to grab his attention was a man that he recognized to be one of the limo drivers. In his mid-thirties, the combination of a handsome face, wavy chestnut brown hair, and a tailored black suit that failed to hide his superb physique made the man look more like a strip-a-gram than a chauffeur. But none of those things motivated Luke to snap a picture. No, it was the man's eyes that had captured his interest. The pale green eyes were not focused on the couple getting married or the church's magnificent stained-glass windows, which Luke noticed for the first time. The eyes appeared to be focused on the confessional booth.

Changing his position, he zoomed in until only the man's eyes filled the frame. Positive that the man would give him what he wanted, he slowed down his breathing and patiently waited. Suddenly, the man shifted his eyes slightly and fleetingly looked directly into the camera. The glance was quick, but Luke was quicker, capturing the exact moment the man revealed his soul.

"Got ya!" Luke thought as he moved on in search of his next subject.

He looked around to search for another unsuspecting subject waiting to be captured by him but faintly heard someone call his name. It was Lisa, a beautiful and witty twenty-seven-year-old photographer. He decided to ignore her and resume his hunt, albeit he noticed how her heavily tattooed right arm made her look marginally unbalanced, something that Luke thought matched her mental state.

Lisa, unaffected by Luke's usual reaction to her wishes, followed him. Frustrated at not being able to get near him, she called him again, a little louder this time.

Ignoring her yet again, he moved away, taking pictures of other people he found interesting. As he strolled forth, he couldn't help but think back to the man with the pale green eyes, wondering what the man could possibly want to confess that another man could absolve.

After several unsuccessful attempts, fed up with the cat and mouse routine to catch his attention without disrupting the ceremony, she looked around for an opportunity. Her chance came because of the congregation that was about to finish the 'Apostles' Creed.'

"I believe in the Holy Spirit, the holy catholic Church, the communion of saints, the forgiveness of sins, the resurrection of the body, and the life everlasting."

In perfect timing, at the end of the prayer, Lisa yelled, "Amen."

Everyone turned around, including Luke, whose eye contact with Lisa ended his false loss of hearing. Holding her arm out as a sign of stopping, she quickly approached him.

"Did you think you could ignore me forever? Your brother wants you to stop fucking around and take more pictures of the bride," she said with a look of pure irritation in her eyes.

"What's wrong with you?" He said, frowning at her, "We're in a church! And tell Sal that I've taken enough pictures to fill two wedding albums. Although these people are so dull, he'd be hard-pressed to fill a single page."

"He said that he's paying you to do what he wants, not what you want," Lisa whispered, leaning closer, ignoring his sarcasm.

Luke looked directly in the eyes.

"No, he didn't."

Lisa tried to hold his gaze but failed miserably.

"He would have if I told him what you just said," she told him, looking away.

Sal, who was a full-time videographer that specialized in weddings, baptisms, and recently more high school proms than he would like, inched his way into the muffled conversation. He looked between the both of them and sensed the tense atmosphere.

"Luke, what are you doing?" He whispered, almost cautiously as if scared of a blow-out.

"What?" Luke snapped.

"I know you're an artist," he began without sarcasm, "But please, stay focused on the wedding couple."

Avenged, Lisa stared at Luke with the 'I told you so' pose, hands crossed, and brows raised.

"I've taken plenty of pictures of the blissful couple. I think you'll be happy," he answered, ignoring her.

"I'm always happy with your work, but can you please at least make it look like you're interested. It makes it easier to get more events," Sal said, a hint of pleading in his voice.

Luke answered him with a couple of short nods.

"Okay, go. They're about to wrap it up," Sal commanded quickly.

Moving in different directions, Luke and Lisa quickly closed in on the altar and took their positions for the perfect shot. Poised to snap, they waited for the priest, who presented the newly married couple to the congregation without enthusiasm.

"Friends and family, it is my pleasure to introduce for the first time Mr. and Mrs. Baldacci."

The congregation's half-hearted claps and cheers reminded everyone that this was not new to anyone attending this wedding ceremony. Their only concern was how quickly they could get to the reception, which triggered a series of events that would go viral in any century.

Following tradition is not something that can be easily removed from the DNA of Italians. Consequently, the marginally happy couple's hasty exodus from the church to wait in the lobby for their first but not last congratulations of the day is almost comical.

Their selfish action to exit the church leaves a gigantic gap between the nimble wedding party and the slower little children and old people with canes or walkers. The usual orderly filing out is forgotten, and guests began to fill the gap haphazardly, leaving the immediate family members behind.

This did not go over well with the parents and grandparents, who started yelling at the people ahead of them. Ignored, one of the older people tried to narrow the gap by picking up his speed. He used his cane to nudge the people ahead of him instead of using it to hold himself up, disaster strikes! Like a leading cyclist's fall at the Tour de France, the old man's tumble caused the other old women and small children to fall over each other, uttering a cacophony of obscenities.

Laughing for the first time in months, the priest crossed himself as he withdrew to his chambers, holding his ample jiggling girth with both hands.

Following the priest's direction, Luke noticed an old man leaning on his cane in the front pew laughing at the priest's wiggling belly and the mayhem he left behind. The man was obviously at an impasse, for he kept alternating his attention from scene to scene, seemingly unable to decide which one was funnier. But the honesty in his pleasure was real, and Luke thankfully captured it with a well-timed shot.

Fortunately, there were no serious injuries recorded, but the mood had changed, and the wedding party is forced to prematurely make their way to the waiting limos.

Busily packing up his equipment, Sal ventured a glance over to Luke and Lisa, who now performed a harmonized ballet of photography. However, while Luke was snapping pictures of the wedding guests and party, Lisa was snapping pictures of Luke. Shaking his head but not surprised, Sal approached Lisa outside the church.

"Okay, Lisa, start packing up. I'll finish here."

"The reception better have good food, Sal; I'm starving."

"We'll be there in a couple of hours; can you last that long?"

"I'm a woman. We can all last more than a couple of hours," she said, raising an eyebrow. "It's you guys that can't last longer than it takes to make instant coffee."

"Christ, Lisa," Sal said, frowning, "you're in front of a church!"

"What is it with you, Cassaro brothers, and your frowning?" she asks, frowning.

"What?" Sal said, shaking his head.

"Never mind," she answered him, shaking her own head.

"Just keep it down!"

"Speaking of keeping it down," Lisa purred, trying to keep her eyes on Luke as he passed by, shaking his head.

Once again, she looked away. She had never been able to look at his hazel eyes and not look away. The only person in the family without brown eyes, Luke had always attracted attention, but for Lisa, it was the complete package that had fascinated her all these years. At slightly over six feet, his fit body moves with graceful power as he lures his camera to do his bidding in capturing the moment.

Following him around the room with her eyes, Lisa laughed at herself as she cursed Luke's camera for hiding his ruggedly handsome face.

"Jesus, Lisa, he's your cousin," Sal said, noticing her stare. "Besides, he's got a girlfriend."

"First, he's my second or maybe third cousin, but more importantly, what makes you think she satisfies him?" Lisa replied, keeping her eyes on Luke as she walked away, leaving Sal again shaking his head in disgusted amusement.

After taking the last few shots, Luke finished his own packing and joined his brother.

"I'm done, Sal. I'll head on down to the reception hall. You guys ready to go?"

"Yes, just about. Lisa is putting the gear in the car. We'll be right behind you."

Before Luke walked away, Sal called him back, "Listen, Luke, thanks, you got me out of a jam."

"Hey, what are brothers for," Luke said, giving him a friendly slap on his shoulder.

Sal held Luke's forearm, stopping him from leaving.

"I'm serious, Luke. You're too good a photographer to waste your time with this shit! I really appreciate you being here." He reached over and hugged him.

Luke returned the hug, slapping his back a couple of times.

"Sal, you say that every time I do this, and that's about three times a month!" Luke joked. "Plus, I don't mind; it keeps me sharp."

"Bull shit! I know you do it for me, and I love you for it," Sal disagreed. "Besides, having you here is like Michelangelo painting my bedroom ceiling," he finished, laughing at his own joke.

Both smiling, they started for their cars, but halfway there, Lisa pulled up, leaning out of the car window.

"I'm going. You get a ride with Luke," she yelled, leaving the brothers speechless as they stared at Sal's disappearing SUV.

CHAPTER TWO
A Revealing Reception

The New York Botanical Gardens had been, arguably, the most sought-after destination for a wedding reception in the United States. Certainly, for the New York area, there was no argument. The 250-acre estate's lush gardens with its many secluded enclaves offer even the most discriminating photographers many settings to challenge their creative nature. But perhaps the most difficult part, Luke reconfirmed, was choosing the perfect location from the plethora of amazing possibilities. As Luke took his last few shots before moving on to the reception hall, he was once again reminded of his brother's genius in picking the perfect location. After nodding to Sal that he had yet again chosen wisely, he made his way over to the hall to take some preliminary shots prior to the guests' arrival.

As Luke entered the hall for the first time, he was astonished at the beauty he found. Decorated in fine white and grey table coverings and napkins, with an oversized champagne glass, each filled with different flora from their private gardens as a centerpiece, the Garden Terrace Room created a stunning setting. But the focal point and the signature shot was, without a doubt, the flawlessly set head table that acted as the perfect foreground to the three huge floor-to-ceiling windows topped by a half-moon window with nine cutups. Now empty, Luke wondered if the expected guests would spoil the pristine postcard image. Surprisingly, the arrival of the invitees did not lessen the splendor of the hall, and Luke, Sal, and Lisa took some of the best shots they had ever taken.

Having enjoyed a well-deserved rest and great food, after dinner and before the dancing and speeches began, the trio was free to do their own thing. Sal worked the room for future business, Luke examined the room for interesting faces he would have loved to photograph, and Lisa, finally having satisfied her restless, selfish stomach, relentlessly hit on Luke until the speeches began, and she went back to concentrating on her job.

Now that the speeches were over, the crew freeform shot around the room. Undeterred by his earlier spurns, Lisa resumed her attack on Luke. Once again, repeatedly rejected but still highly aroused, she finally gave up on Luke and scanned the room for an alternative target. The best man did not know what hit him, only that he found himself under a well-hidden garden canopy enjoying the fruits of this sensual woman's skills. Sated, she re-entered the hall, closely followed by the best man, who Luke noticed was wiping his eyes. Strutting to her table, she picked up her camera and slowly walked to a mystified Luke.

"I made him cry!" she said, sauntering away backward to the beat of the playing music and blowing Luke kisses.

Turning his back on the oncoming flying kisses, he spotted the best man now smiling and shaking his head, leaving Luke unable to decide whether the man was happy or confused; regardless, he readied his camera for the shot that came within seconds of this instinctive action.

The rest of the night progressed as expected. Now, late into the night, with remnants of guests scattered around the hall like discarded toys in a child's playroom, their lackluster dance moves, if any, no longer motivated the tired live band, that at most had three or four songs left in them, Luke, in a semi-trance, drained and inattentive took a few more uninspired pictures of some kids that still had the energy to run around and seemed like the only bright spots in this dull procession.

"Okay, let's wrap it up. We've taken enough pictures and video; let's meet at my house on Tuesday, 10ish, Okay?" Sal asked, snapping Luke out of his trance.

"Morning?" Lisa wanted to know.

"No, night, you can show up in your sleazy clubbing dress and a bottle of Vodka while we edit our work," Luke said with a little more bite than he wanted.

Unresponsive to the finger Lisa just flipped him, he turned to his brother and hugged him.

"Later, I love you," he told him.

"Love you too. Don't forget lunch at mom's tomorrow."

As Luke turned to leave, Lisa, obviously wanting a kiss, blocked his way with her arms wide open, her head tilted upwards, and her eyes closed. Looking at Sal, Luke gave him a wry smile, then patted Lisa's shoulder and walked away.

"You don't know what you're missing, cuz. I'm so good I would make you cry too!" she hissed, following Luke with her head.

Stopping a few feet away, Luke turned to face her.

"I'm no best man," he said stoically.

"Neither was he," she said, motioning with her head to the best man, who was slumped in a chair with his head down as one of the bridesmaids consoled him with her hand on his shoulder.

"But his girlfriend will be happy with his improvements," she added with a crooked smile.

"Congrats! Miss sex therapist of the year!" He reached for her and gave her a body-hugging kiss on her forehead.

"You missed my mouth by four inches," Lisa added coquettishly.

"I do love you, you know," he said, laughing and holding her at arm's length.

Sal, who had been watching this with silent interest, finally interjected, "I think I'm about to hurl my Brussel sprouts!"

"Fuck you, Sal; this is one of the good ones," she exclaimed, breaking Luke's grip on her shoulder. Raising herself on her toes, she grabbed him with both hands behind his neck and kissed both of his cheeks. Then thinking it over, she planted one on his mouth. The kiss was neither long nor passionate, but the softness of her lips surprised Luke, who remained frozen.

"Love you too. See you Tuesday," she softly whispered in his ear.

Wondering if indeed she would have made him cry, he took a long deep breath, rubbed his tired eyes, and watched her walking away with Sal in tow.

Happy that this long exhausting day was almost over, he walked into the large inner lobby where the bright, almost blazing light, in contrast to the muted lighting of the reception hall, caused him to bat his eyes several times. As his vision readjusted to the unfamiliar environment, he noticed an old couple waiting by the indoor fountain. The woman was sitting on a nearby couch, her walker resting patiently close by, waiting for her master's attention, while next to her, leaning on his cane, the old man stood with stoic resignation, staring into the fountain. Intrigued by the couple's soundless concentration Luke, once again reinvigorated by the possibilities this scene offers, gently laid his bags down, took out his camera, added his selected lenses, and took a few shots. Then, focusing on the face of the old man, Luke recognized him to be the gentleman in the front pew laughing at the accident in the church and decided to approach them.

Reaching them, still shooting, he saw the two carnations in the water that had grabbed the couple's attention. Uninterested in the floating flowers, Luke apologized for the interruption and asked the couple if he could take some more pictures.

Ignoring his question, the old man asked Luke to look at the flowers in the water.

"Look at this, they come together, go to where the water drops, separate and make a circle, and then, look, look, join again to start the circle all over again," he explained in a moderate Italian accent without taking his eyes off the fountain.

Luke silently watched a few more turns of the carnations, and in fact, their performance was constant.

"You're right! It's like a synchronized dance routine."

"I told you, Mary, yes, that's it!" he exclaimed, turning to his wife, "that's the right word, synchronized."

Ignoring her husband, the old lady addressed Luke in an equally moderate Italian accent.

"Yes, my husband loves the camera!"

"Sorry?"

"You asked if you could take our pictures. He loves it," she reaffirmed, pointing to her husband.

"No, I don't," he protested with a slight smile.

"Yes, you do!" she insisted, winking at Luke.

"Okay, maybe I do, just a little." He laughed, turning to Luke.

"Are you family of the bride or groom?" Luke asked, continuing to take pictures.

"The bride, she's our granddaughter," the old man answered, looking into the camera.

Luke found that asking his subjects personal questions often led to more realistic expressions and better results.

"How long have you two been married?" he asked, keeping to his M.O.

"61 years," they answered in unison.

"Wow. Congratulations."

"Yes, and in 61 years," the old man said, waving his hand from one end of the hall to the other, "I've never seen such an expensive wedding. Back in the day, you went to the Church and then celebrated at the house. No big fuss. You didn't have to sit here and wait for a ride home; half-hour, and we're still waiting," he finished, shaking his head and giving Luke a hoped-for shot.

"What house? We had our reception in a hall with 300 people," she contradicted him.

"This just seems too much."

"Relax; they'll be done in a bit. Enjoy having your picture taken by this young man. What's your name?" she asked.

"Luke," he answered, without stopping his shooting.

Although he found both subjects interesting, he was fascinated by the old man's hands. The hard, crooked, and fierce-looking fingers were a stark contrast to the fine gentle features of the man's face.

"I'm Sonny," the old man said, offering Luke his hand, "and this is Mary."

"Nice meeting you both," Luke said, accepting Sonny's hand. *"Holy shit! Are these hands ever soft! Not what I expected,"* Luke thought. Then he asked, "Sonny, do you mind if I take some close up of your hands?"

Sonny nodded his head and let out a short but loud laugh.

"These hands have worked hard for a long time; I guess a little rest posing for pictures is okay."

As Luke began to focus on his hands, Sonny looked down at him and asked him if he was Italian. Before Luke answered him, he took several more shots, shifted his stance, and took more pictures.

"Yes, I guess," he finally answered him.

"You guess? Are you embarrassed about where you come from, Luca?" Sonny asked, narrowing his eyes.

Luke sheepishly looked through his camera at some of the pictures he had taken.

"No, I love Jersey," he joked.

They all laugh.

"Very good! Comedy lifts a heavy heart," Mary said.

"Yes, and it hides deep scars," Sonny added.

The old man put his hand on Luke's shoulder. "You should never be ashamed of your roots, Luca. Roots are what keep you grounded and steady. It's your roots that will keep you standing when someone is trying to knock you down," he finished, chuckling and applying a little more pressure on Luke's shoulder.

Luke felt the physical weight of Sonny's hand on his shoulder, but what weighed more was Sonny's statement. Unwilling to discuss it, he pretended that his phone was vibrating in his pocket.

"Excuse me, I think that's my phone. Thank you both very much. I hope your ride is here soon."

"Have you ever been home, Luke?" Sonny asked, ignoring Luke's thanks and his phone.

"I am home."

"That was funny the first time," Sonny responded seriously.

Flustered, Luke awkwardly bent down on one knee and began to put away his equipment as he searched for a suitable response. Luckily, Sonny, called by one of his relatives, gave Luke a reprieve. After helping his wife up off the couch, Sonny walked close to Luke, who was still on one knee, and with difficulty, he slowly leaned close to him.

"La vita e un viaggio, chi viaggia vive due volte."

"What does that mean?" Luke asked, looking up.

"Life is a voyage; he who travels lives twice." He turned and walked away, yelling at his daughter for making him wait.

CHAPTER THREE
Planned Mistake

Purposely having parked his car at the far end of the well-lit parking lot to avoid any unsolicited interactions with liquored happy people that tend to appear after these events, he briskly walked to his car. As he reached the first row of cars, the smell of recently rejected alcohol and the sound of dry retching that preceded yet-to-come vomit made him alter his route slightly. Disappointed that a beautiful place like this must endure the weaknesses of humanity, he picked up the pace in an effort to get away.

Almost running now, his phone vibrated, attracting his attention. Slowing down, he reached for the phone, took it out, and looked down. Eight missed calls and several text messages from Tiffany caused him to swear under his breath and reluctantly dial her number. As he waited for Tiffany to pick up, he suddenly felt that he had forgotten something. With every ring, his trepidation grew to the point where, when she answered, his heart skipped a few beats.

"Where the hell were you?" Tiffany barked.

Her voice sparked his memory, and everything was clear. *Shit, shit, shit. The gala. Big mistake. Idiot!* Luke thought, closing his eyes and wishing this all away. When that failed, he invoked the most common trait men have and played dumb.

"Where am I? What do you mean? I was working, and now I'm going to my car and coming home."

"At work? You were supposed to meet me three hours ago!"

It had worked once, so he decided to try it again.

"Be where?"

"Alright, cut out the crap Luke, the gala."

"Oh, Jesus. Fuck. I totally forgot. Babe, I'm so sorry."

"You are so full of shit! You've been trying to get out of going for a month now. Plus, since when were you working tonight? I've been trying to get a hold of you for the last five hours, Luke. How could you do this?"

Luke was sure that she was now fighting back the tears but decided not to respond.

"You've only called me once today; you didn't say shit about working, and then I couldn't get a hold of you."

"It was a last-minute thing. One of Sal's photographers bailed on him, and he asked me to help him out."

"Again?" she asked, not expecting him to answer. "That's the third time this month. I know that your family is very important to you, but you can't put their needs ahead of ours. There were some very influential people there that could have helped your career, Luke. I'm trying very hard to get our lives to the next level, but you're indifferent to everything I'm trying to do. Do you even care?"

Luke continued to walk toward his car, trying to listen to Tiffany and, at the same time, come up with a good answer to her question. Before he could answer, he was distracted by a subway train passing under a lit billboard. Shaking his head, he stopped and stared at the advertisement.

"Come home to Sicily and live again." Suddenly, Sonny's face filled his thoughts, and he ignored Tiffany's question.

"Luke?" Tiffany called.

Luke stared at the poster for a few more seconds without answering Tiffany.

"Luke, you there?"

A few more seconds went by, and he finally answered her.

"Hello, Tiff? Hello? Tiff? Are you there? I'm starting to feel like you hung up on me," he predicted, stirring from his trance.

Luke looked down at his phone and closed his eyes. Then, knowing that to call her back would be a colossal waste of time because she would not answer, he slowly put the phone away.

The drive home gave Luke enough time to reflect on his mistake. *"But was it a mistake?"* He questioned himself.

In truth, he had been trying to find a way to get out of attending the gala for months, so when the call came from his brother, he did not hesitate to accept. To her credit, Tiffany had never overtly pressured him to give up or even alter his dream to exhibit his photographs at a New York City gallery. She had, in her subtle ways, introduced him to many of her friends and acquaintances, hoping that he would realize that there were other options as well. In fact, Luke's personable nature had presented him with several business opportunities, all of which he graciously declined without any resentment from the one making him those proposals.

This gala was, yet again, one of her attempts at gently guiding him into her reality. He knew that missing the gala would upset her, but her accommodating and caring nature would not allow her to be upset for long, so he thought the risk had been worth taking. Nonetheless, to hedge his bet, he stopped at a 24-hour florist to buy her a bouquet of roses.

Carefully placing the flowers on the passenger seat reminded him of the first time they met. Inhaling deeply, he could still remember the smells of that beautiful mid-spring afternoon; when taking pictures in Central Park, he noticed two beautiful young women in conversation with an older man.

Something about their actions caught my eye. After paying for the roses, I used my camera to zoom in and noticed two things. One, the women were indeed incredibly beautiful, and two, the trio kept on looking over in my direction. Suspicious, I decided to confront them. As I walked toward them, one of the women walked away, leaving the older man alone with the gorgeous woman.

"Is this guy bothering you, miss?" I asked, keeping my eyes on the man.

After a short chuckle, the beautiful woman answered.

"Actually, this man thinks you're the problem."

Taken aback, I shifted my glare between the two as she went on to explain further.

"This man is a retired New York police officer. He thinks that a young man alone in Central Park in the middle of a weekday is suspicious."

I tried to explain, but I could not find the words.

"Especially," she continued with a mischievous smile that made me feel slightly uncomfortable, "when that young man is taking pictures."

Proud of my quick recovery, I answered. "Actually, miss, I'm a professional photographer. And to be honest, I was interested in that little boy..."

"Really?" she interrupted, taking a step back.

"Funny. Not that way, watch!" I responded, then went on to explain that I was interested in the boy's covert attempts to get his mother's attention by bothering his younger sibling in the stroller.

Following the direction of my outstretched arm, they looked over to see the mother who, in a deep conversation with another woman, was ignoring her young son. The son, right on cue, reached in the stroller and hit his sibling. He began crying, forcing the mother to deal with the situation.

"How did you know that?" the young woman wanted to know.

"He's done it twice now," I explained, then noticing she was mildly intrigued, I continued. "I wanted to capture his face just before he committed his crime. But I knew if I started taking pictures of little boys, there would be more than one former cop after me. This place is crawling with retired first respondents. No offense, pal," I added, looking at the man, "thanks for your service," I finished thinking of my brother-in-law in the military and far from our family.

"None taken. It's a good place to keep sharp."

Smiling and nodding his thanks, the man moved away. He left us alone, giving me an opportunity to introduce myself and ask her the usual banal question.

"What brings you here this fine afternoon?"

Surprisingly, she didn't chastise me for asking a question she must have heard thousands of times. After introducing herself, she explained that having finished their shopping earlier than anticipated, Rebecca, her shopping buddy, suggested they call their driver. She wanted to have him pick up their parcels and meet them at the far end of the park so they could walk unencumbered. Liking the idea, she agreed.

The uncomfortable stillness that followed was elegantly broken by her reaching for the roses and slowly bringing them to her pretty waiting nose. Smiling, she asked me who the flowers were for.

"Bringing them to my mother's. I'm going there for lunch. She loves roses," I answered her as I took a rose and handed it to her.

"As do I," she had simply said, accepting the rose and confirming her interest.

The attraction had been obvious and mutual. So much so that six months ago, only two months after they met, Luke moved in with her in her Manhattan apartment with the provision that he would pay for the food and do all the cooking. The deal was a good one, and it stayed solid to this day.

As the elevator doors to their floor opened with a muted thud, Luke took a quick look at the time on his phone. *One thirty, I hope she's sleeping.*

Wishing they had changed the lock to a numbered keypad, Luke reluctantly chose the proper key, held it with only his thumb and forefinger, and lightly inserted it in the keyhole. Hoping to aid the bolt to noiselessly slide out of its strike plate, he tightly shut his eyes and slowly turned it.

Successful in his stealthy task, he gently opened the door and stepped inside. Holding the door open with his foot, so it does not shut, he reached for his equipment and deposited them in the hallway. He finally completed this delicate task which was made much more difficult because of the 'guilt gift' held in his other hand. He then turned and silently closed the door.

Proud of his 'Pink Panther' performance, Luke walked down the small corridor oblivious to his portraits and landscapes, strategically and expertly arranged by Tiffany on either side of the hallway. Looking around the corner at the end of the hallway, he noticed Tiffany reading a bridal magazine on the couch, wearing a very sexy negligée that showed off her perfectly shaped legs. He felt disappointed that he might have to continue to explain himself but then realized he would have to do it stroking those sexy legs. He felt delighted and moved toward her.

"What's this?" she said, without a smile, pointing to the roses.

"I stole them from the wedding; please don't turn me in," he said, slowly approaching her.

"Not funny," she said, turning her attention back to her magazine.

Luke bent from his waist to offer Tiffany the flowers.

"I'm sorry. I feel terrible."

Refusing the flowers, she continued looking absentmindedly at the magazine.

"I'm sorry," he repeated.

"Do you know how bad it looked to be there by myself?" She flipped the page violently. "I had to lie, Luke, and you know how I feel about lying. I had six men ask me if I was there alone, and that was not out of concern for my safety, Luke. Four of them were there with their wives!"

He looked at her with as much empathy as he could express.

"I'm sorry," is all that came out.

"Luke, there were very important people there that could have helped with your career," she finally said, looking up at him. His puppy dog eyes oozed enough remorse that Tiffany reluctantly took the flowers from Luke and smelled them. With her nose still in the flowers, she looked up at him.

"I did agree to have you meet the Grafs."

"Meet them? What for?" Luke asked, sitting close to her.

Tiffany picked a rose from the bunch and offered it to Luke. Refusing the rose, he waited for her response.

"From what I understand, they're looking for a digital production manager for their New York office. They said you would have complete artistic control and plenty of time to freelance and..."

"I don't know, Tiff," he stopped her. "A job interview? I haven't gone to one of those since high school, and that was with a pimple-faced assistant manager at MacDonald's who was younger than me!"

"That's a poor attempt at humor," she said while trying to put the rose back in the bunch. Failing, she smelled the rose put it down beside the bunch, and looked up at him.

"They've seen your work, and they think you're perfect for that position. I wouldn't say that this is a job interview; they just want to meet with you to discuss your salary, which I'm sure will be considerably more than what you're making now!"

Realizing that she might have gone too far, she apologized, offering the rose again.

"I'm sorry, Luke; you know I didn't mean it that way."

"I know you didn't, but Tiff," he said, not yet ready to accept the rose, "I don't know if I want that."

"That's the problem; you don't know what you want. I thought we talked about this."

Luke stood up and moved to sit on the ottoman directly in front of Tiffany and reached for her hands.

"We did; I remember saying that I loved photography and that I would be looking for a small studio."

Before she answered, Tiffany let go of his hands, grabbed his wrists, and brought his hands together.

"Luke darling," she began, softly kissing his hands. "You're not a studio photographer, my love. Look at your favorite portraits, the ones you love; they're all taken outdoors, in a natural setting, not in a studio." Seeing that she was reaching him, she continued. "You know that you don't really want that. Besides, they are very influential people that love the Arts. Perhaps they could help you put together a showing."

Luke looked down at their interlocked hands.

"So, I would be using them?"

Holding his hand tighter, she smiled at him.

"Come on, Luke, don't be so naive; you don't think they would be using you. These people are socialites; there's nothing more they love than to discover talent. It gives them a 'one up' on other socialites; it's a game. And Luke, they're very jealous of their discoveries. Once they commit to you, they will always back you, always Luke. I know; I come from that life."

"I know you do," Luke said and instantly regretted it.

He went into this relationship with his eyes wide open. He knew that she was wealthy, of course; she had confirmed as much when she told him that her driver was going to meet her and her friend at the other end of Central Park. Yet during their time together, she had never made him feel inferior because of his lack of wealth or social status, so his last comment was very insensitive.

Before he could apologize, Tiffany sat up and inched her face close to his.

"I'm not saying I want to go back to that life, not without you anyway." She laughed, offering him the rose again.

Luke took the rose with a smile.

"Who's the meeting with?"

"Ignat, and Steffi Graf."

"Ignat, and Steffi Graf? Will we be playing tennis after the interview?"

"Now that is funny," she laughed and then added more seriously. "Make all the jokes you want, but this can lead to better things for you, for us."

"You know what leads to better things?" he asked.

He prevented her from responding by covering her mouth with his finger and then leaned in, tenderly kissing her forehead. Facing no resistance, he moved his lips to her cheek while gently fondling her now exposed thigh. Encouraged by Tiffany's search for his lips with her own, Luke stroked her legs with added vigor.

"I knew it would come to this," she whispered, closing her eyes in anticipation of yet another skilled performance by her lover.

CHAPTER FOUR
Wine and Blood at Lunch

If the food passed around this typical Italian American dinner table at lightning speed could hear, it would be hard-pressed to understand any of the free-flowing conversations.

Reaching for the same meatball, playfully slapping each other's hands, Luke's parents, Frank and Teresa, or as everyone called her, Resa, discussed what their gift should be at the upcoming wedding of the neighbor's daughter. Sal was teasing his sister Lucy about her husband's long absence overseas, and Mikey and Dianne, Lucy's young children, were making faces at Luke. He, in turn, was doing his best to make them spill their drinks by making his own funny faces. The atmosphere was happy and friendly. But as happens in many Italian gatherings, the mood can change quickly and without notice. Which is what happened when Luke asked, "Luce, how's Bobby doing?"

The question attracted everyone's attention, and a sudden quiet clouded over the gathering. Everyone tried not to look at the two people having this conversation but could not help the want to listen in. Looking at the buffet table, where a picture of a man in uniform is displayed, Lucy answered him with a slight smile.

"He's doing great. The kids and I are flying to Sicily next month for the ceremony."

"Where in Sicily?" He inquired.

"Sigonella Air Base, close to Catania."

Shifting her focus to Lucy's response, Resa joined in with a big smile.

"Major General Rossi. Few Italian Americans reach that rank in the Army. We're all very proud," she added, squeezing her daughter's arm.

"Any news on his next posting?" Sal asked, cleaning his plate with a piece of bread.

"It's not definite, but he's fluent in Italian, so it will most likely be in Italy somewhere."

"You'll have to move," Sal said.

Lucy gave Sal a dirty look and then looked over to the children, who hadn't missed a thing.

"Ma, I'm not going!" Dianne protested.

"Ya, Ma, I'm not going," Mikey said, imitating his older sister, not knowing exactly what it meant.

Realizing his mistake, Sal silently mouthed an apology to Lucy.

"Nothing is decided yet," Lucy reassured the children.

"I don't care. I'm not going, and that's that!" Dianne insisted.

"Ya, that's that," Mikey confirmed.

Wanting to change the subject, Resa looked to Luke.

"What's the matter, Luke? You look tired."

"Really? I just didn't sleep much last night, ma."

"Are you sick?" she said, reaching over to feel his forehead.

"No! Come on, ma," Luke objected, quickly moving his head away. Sal slapped his brother on the back.

"I guess Tiffany's been keeping you up!" Sal quipped, raising his fist.

"You know Sal, you're a real pig," Resa said, trying to swat him.

"At least he doesn't change girlfriends like you change your underwear," she finished, actually landing a shot.

"What, once a month?" Lucy responded, making everyone laugh except the two children.

"Ugh! Uncle Sal, you only change your underwear once a month?" Dianne asked.

"Once a month," Mickey repeated.

"Seriously, Luke. Are you sure you're not sick?" Resa asked him again.

"I'm sure, Ma. I think I would know."

"Leave him alone. He's fine," Frank said, finally joining in.

"You've got bags under your eyes. He's got bags, Frank," Resa said, looking to Frank for some affirmation that never came.

Sal mimicked his mother. "Poor baby, he's got the bags under his eyes."

"What are you? Ten?" Luke asked him.

"You've got the Al Pacino eyes," Sal said, pointing to his own eyes.

"Al Pacino doesn't have hazel eyes," Lucy stated.

"Don't make fun of him!" Resa came to Luke's defense.

"I don't mind. I wish I did look like Al Pacino."

"Mom, who's Al Pacino?" Dianne yelled out.

"Pass the cheese," Sal asked Luke.

Luke looked at Sal and corrected him. "Pass the cheese, please."

"That's right, Uncle Sal, it's past the cheese, please," Dianne agreed.

In a formal and serious tone, Sal yielded to the pressure. "Luke, would you kindly pass the cheese, and Luke, thank you very much," he finished, raising his eyebrows.

Luke passed the cheese bowl over to Sal and gave Dianne the thumbs up.

"Where's the cheese? Who took all the fucking cheese?" Sal yelled out.

"Mom, Uncle Sal swore!" Dianne yelled.

"Hey, watch your language!" Resa reprimanded Sal and then continued. "Relax, I have more cheese in the fridge."

"Who's Al Pacino, Uncle Luke?" Dianne questioned.

"He's a famous actor."

"I never heard of him," Dianne said.

"You never heard of him? He's in 'The Godfather,'" Sal said. Then impersonating Pacino, he continued, "Just when I thought I was out...they pull me back in."

"Godfather III. Hey, that's pretty good," his father complimented him.

"Thanks, Pops." Passing the remaining pasta to Sal, Frank also quoted from 'The Godfather.' "Take the Rigatoni. Leave the spoon."

Everyone joined in the laughter except for the kids, who just looked at each other and shrugged their shoulders.

"Uncle Luke, you're my Godfather, right?" Dianne said, causing the laughter to subside.

"That's right, Di, Uncle Luke is your Godfather."

Sal patted her head, "but he's not 'The Godfather.' That's a classic movie," he finished, looking at his mother.

"You don't need to know, Dianne," Resa responded.

"Why not? We're talking about a great movie," Sal disagreed.

"I'm sick of it. There's more to Corleone than 'The Godfather,'" Resa said, obviously disappointed.

"Here we go again," Sal said, shaking his head.

"Here we go again?" Resa glared at Sal and then continued. "I don't like it, Sal. You'd think that the only thing that ever came out of Corleone was that movie and the Mafia!"

"Come on, Ma; it's the best movie ever made," Sal declared.

"You already said that!" Resa said.

"I'd rather watch 'Zootopia,'" Dianne pointed out, making everyone laugh, except for Resa, who gave Sal a look only a mother could and then patted Dianne's head.

"Good girl. Let's talk about something else."

With his head down and half-heartedly trying to hide a smile, Frank instigated. "Did you know Pacino actually has family in Corleone?"

The slap to his shoulder from his wife was quick and forceful.

"Really, Frank?"

Frank's smile widened as he kept his head lowered.

"I didn't know that," Luke said.

"Of course, you don't. You don't know shit about Corleone," Sal accused him.

"Like you do?"

The bickering went on for a while until, having had enough, Lucy and Resa began to clear the table and went to the kitchen.

Now looking directly into Luke's eyes, Sal answered his brother.

"I know that, like most of Sicily, Corleone's history has been a violent one. Conquered and liberated many times, its culture is influenced by many nations. To its benefit, I would add, it's one of the reasons they have a strong family bond, probably the strongest in all of Italy. I also know it's where your roots are, brother."

"Right, and that's why they left that great place," Luke responded, gesturing to his father.

"What's your problem, man?" Sal questioned, shaking his head.

"That's the second time in two weeks that someone has let me know where my roots are. All I know is that it's a foreign place. And yes, mom's right, the entire world only knows of it as the place where the Mafia comes from."

"What the fuck Luke!"

"Maaa, Nonna (grandmother), Uncle Sal is swearing again!" Dianne snitched.

"Sal, I don't feel an attachment to the old country. I don't feel Italian or even Sicilian; I feel American. Sure, we eat the food; keep some of the old traditions, but what else is there?"

Sal and Frank looked at each other, and then they looked at Luke.

"Blood?" they said in unison.

"Blood? Sure, there's that, and because of that, we love each other. But it's not blood that makes us who we are. Blood? That's just fluid that runs in our veins to keep us alive," Luke submitted.

Frank picked up a clean paper napkin from its holder, unfolded it, and wiped his mouth. The boys knew that their father would never give them direct advice; this action was a prelude to an anecdote he was about to share that revealed the way he saw the world, leaving it up to them to decide on the path they wanted to take. Of course, when they were younger, they would roll their eyes and make faces as Frank tried to give them some information by which they could make up their mind. As they got older, those little examples and astute observations of life became important treasures they found useful.

Slowly Frank folded the napkin to its original configuration and laid it back beside his half-empty glass of wine.

"And wine is just a liquid," he began as he twirled the glass in his hand. "But when you look a little closer, you see that wine is much more intricate, more delicate, for wine doesn't start that way. To begin, you need a piece of land, land that, by the grace of a higher power, must have the perfect soil. Here is where mortals take over."

Stopping as he often does before continuing, he took a small sip of his wine.

"Someone has to plant the grapevines; the environment has to be right for the grapes to grow; they must be picked at the right time by people that have the know-how. But that is just the beginning, for, at this stage, they are just a bunch of grapes. Now the winemaker takes over; only his many years of expertise will turn those grapes into wine. So, you see, Luke, many things can go wrong during this miraculous event, but when they go right, it becomes this beautiful wine we are sharing today."

He quickly drained the glass dry.

The boys listened in silence, for they knew that their father was not finished, and they were right.

"Blood like wine also needs a lot of factors to go right for it to develop into what we become."

"Yes, Pops, I get the analogy, but when does one's blood stop being where it comes from and start being where it lives? A few weeks ago," he continued, not waiting for his father to answer, "at one of the weddings we were shooting, I took some pictures of this old man and his wife. We got to talking, and his wife asked me if I was Italian. When I hesitated before answering her, the old man asked me if I was embarrassed of my roots." He stopped to see his father's reaction. Of course, he should have known better; his father would not react at this stage, so, silently chastising himself for the thought, he continued.

"Pops, you know I am deeply respectful of my family. But I can't say the same for my heritage. I've spent a great deal of my adult life trying to distance myself from Italian, Sicilian, or more precisely Corleonesi traditions, that frankly, I don't think I miss," he stated, taking a long breath before continuing, "not until I'm here surrounded by all of you, that is."

Luke could see that his father wanted to respond, but he was not ready to let him have the floor.

"Yes, I know that you believe that you would not have been able to achieve anything that you have without what you absorbed when you were growing up in Corleone, but Pops, everything you and mom have so graciously given us comes from this country, not Italy, plus, in reality, it's not the environment that teaches you things, it's the people that live in that environment that teach you. What you taught us, you could have taught us in any country, any world."

"You're right, Luke. We did leave that beautiful island partly because of those dark aspects that it has absorbed over its long, violent history. You're also right, as we all are, to be proud Americans because it is this country that has given us everything that we have, not Italy. But Luke, those are material things. The essence of who you are comes from the seeds that, although we have sown here, come from Corleone. Like wine, blood will always take on the characteristics of its environment, but it is up to the winemaker to bring those characteristics out as it was for your mother and me to do with our children. In those seeds or, if you like, that blood, you'll find some of the traits you are now struggling with. So, the uneasiness of your heritage comes from your ignorance of the contents of those seeds, the history of their existence, and our failure to communicate that to you properly."

"Now hold on, you have three children, I'm the only one that seems to have misunderstood, so the fault, and I'm not saying that there is a fault," he said, looking at his brother and sister, who had just joined them, "must lie with me."

"No, Pops, you and Mom did the right thing. Luke's right…."

"No, he's not, and let me tell you why. Your mother and I…."

"…Why don't you boys go out the back?" Lucy, who had joined her father's court earlier, broke their reflective mood. "I'll bring the espresso out, and you can explain, Dad."

Frank, Sal, Luke, and a shoeless little Mickey silently walked out into the backyard in a single file reminiscent of the famous Abbey Road album cover from the Beatles.

CHAPTER FIVE
A Walk in the Park

Sundays were Mary and Sonny's favorite days. Both well in their eighties, they no longer had the responsibilities that their positions once demanded. Although they loved those days, the selfish nature of time forced them to release those duties to younger and more energetic family members. But time is also a generous creature, for it gives them the opportunity to enjoy long leisurely walks after an early mass and before Sunday lunch with one of their four children.

Their conversation usually revolved around the grandchildren. Today, Mary wanted to talk about the young photographer they met several weeks ago.

"That young man at the wedding, what did you think of him?"

"What young man?"

"You know which young man. You've been telling anyone that will listen how this professional photographer was only interested in your hands."

"Oh, that kid. I think he is very confused. I noticed him at the church too".

"You did?"

"He looked uninterested in the wedding ceremony, bored maybe until he started to take pictures of that pileup." They both laughed at the memory. "But then, when he was taking our pictures, his whole face lit up. He looked like a kid in a candy store, my picture, your picture, and my hands."

He laughed, "If the boy knew the sins that these hands have committed, would he have wanted to photograph them?" He laughed harder, "He was having a wonderful time."

"I'm sure he was, but what about that attitude?"

"I just think that he is confused about who he is and where he comes from."

"You know Sonny," she said, holding his arm a little tighter, "I've noticed that some of our younger grandchildren have the same attitude. Do you think they'll eventually forget where they came from?"

Silenced by her question, Sonny reflected before answering. "I think it's inevitable," he said. Then stopping her from walking any further with a slight pull of her hand, he faced his wife. "Maybe they all need a good Italian woman to teach them," he said, kissing her cheek.

She returned the kiss saying, "God gives biscuits to those with no teeth."

Turning together, they continued their walk.

CHAPTER SIX
The Promise

Having spiked his espresso with Sambuca; something that annoyed his father, who is a firm believer that a 'corretto' (corrected) espresso should only be taken with clear grappa. Luke waited for his father's reprimand. When several silent seconds went by without one, he tried egging him on by staring at him and clearing his throat.

"Great coffee," he exclaimed, focusing on his father.

Frank was adamant that he would win this little game that Luke and his brother liked to play this time.

"Sal, your coffee, it's getting cold," Frank yelled, ignoring Luke's antics.

Determined, Luke took a sip of his espresso.

"Ah! That's sooo good!" he said, smacking his lips

"I'm glad you like it. Your mother is trying out a new brand," Frank responded, smiling.

After staring at each other with intense, narrowing eyes, they broke into fits of laughter, knowing that this one may have to end in a stalemate.

Making his way to the silent combatants after a short but very enjoyable playtime with his niece and nephew, Sal picked up his coffee, also spiked with Sambuca, and drained it.

"This is cold! But it tastes great!"

Sensing a possible restart to their game Luke seized the moment.

"I put something extra in it, Sal."

"Must be Sambuca, Luke. Good choice!" Sal declared.

"Ganging up on the old man, I see." Frank stared down at the boys. "It's not going to work. I refuse to make your day."

"Come on, Pops, you always make our day," Sal said.

"What are you, eight?"

"Ya!" Sal said.

"Mom thinks we're ten," Luke corrected him.

"Alright, kids." Frank gave in. "You know Luke," he began raising his voice and index finger slightly, "espresso should be…."

Frank was not allowed to finish. In a sign of victory, Luke and Sal gave each other high fives, yelled something incoherent, and ran off to play with the kids, leaving Frank to enjoy his coffee with a silly grin.

Before reaching the kids, Lucy called them in. When she was challenged by the kids, her request became a demand that was enforced by Sal's gentle nudges of his nephew and niece towards their mother. Watching the kids battling their mother's wishes, Luke remembered that he had not finished his coffee. As he turned to go back, he noticed his father was laughing.

"Are you laughing with the angels again?" He asked teasingly.

His father stopped laughing to look at him with a wrinkled gaze. He looked to be thinking very deeply but then shook his head and said, "That game never ends."

"There, we agree."

"What do we agree on?" Sal asked, rejoining them.

"That, the war between angels and demons will never end," Frank answered.

"What war. Uncle Luke?" Dianne asked, surprising the men.

"Hey, where did you come from?" Sal asked her, picking her up in his arms.

"What war. Uncle Sal?"

"Pops?" Sal turned to his father for help.

"Dianne, come, come to Nonno," he said, waving her to him.

Sal put her down, and she ran over to her grandfather, where he picked her up and made her sit on his knees.

"You know how angels are always around us, protecting us from doing terrible things?"

"Yes, I talk to them before I go to sleep, every night!"

"Good girl. So, you know that there are also bad angels, right? Those are angels that try to make you do those bad things."

"Like not listening to mommy?"

"That's right. Those angels are called demons, and they're always fighting with the good angels."

"I don't like demonds!"

"Demons, honey, there's no d," Frank said, kissing her cheek.

"Okay, I got to go now," she said, squirming out of her grandfather's lap and running off to play with her brother.

"Why didn't you tell her about how you need evil to have good and sadness to have happiness and so on?"

"She's seven, Sal. I had this conversation with you guys when you were in high school, and it still took you some time to understand."

"He still doesn't understand now," Luke joked, moving quickly away from Sal, expecting a playful punch.

Luke's vibrating phone saved him from Sal's retaliation. He held up a finger, read the text, and typed into his phone.

"All good?" his father asked.

"Yes, it's just Tiff; she keeps messaging me. Sorry."

"Don't apologize. How's she doing?"

"She's doing great, just busy with work," Luke answered without looking up.

Sensing there is more there, Frank gently probed his son. "Luke, is everything okay?"

"I'm in the doghouse again. It's like no matter what I do, I'm always in the doghouse. Most of the time, I don't even know what I did, but I still end up there. I'm there so often I'll need to change my mailing address soon."

"Welcome to the club," Frank said, smiling.

"She's been on my case a lot lately. She wants me to take this job at a marketing firm one of her parents' friends runs. The thing is, it'll pay twice what I make now, but I don't know, I love…."

"Still, twice what you're making now…I don't know either, Luke," Sal questioned.

Frank looked at his son for a few seconds before speaking.

"You've already made your decision Luke. But, there's something else that's bothering you," Frank stated, knowing that Luke's complaints are symptoms of a larger issue that he was having trouble figuring out.

Before answering, Luke examined his father for a few seconds, wondering if he, too, would someday be as perceptive. He had always felt comfortable confiding in his father, but this blood and heritage matter had him troubled, and he needed his father's thoughts to help him through this.

"You're right; I'm not going to take the job, she'll be disappointed, but it won't affect our relationship much. And you're also right that there is something else that is bothering me. It's this blood thing. I've spent a great deal of my life trying to distance myself from Italian, Sicilian, or, more precisely, Corleonese perceived traits because I have always felt people saw us as mobsters before anything else, and to some extent, I have been able to do that, at least when I'm not around all of you. And now, with an American girlfriend that I'm seriously considering asking to marry me, I'm still concerned about my heritage."

Seeing Sal was about to contradict his feelings, he quickly continued.

"I know she wouldn't, but I don't want any of her friends and family to ask the same stupid questions my Anglo, Jewish or Asian friends asked in university when the subject of organized crime or gang-related incidences would come up. 'Luke, isn't that right?' or 'What do you think, Luke?'"

"Mom's right, that movie is 50 years old, and people still talk about it as if it's the Bible on Corleone. Pops, you know I am deeply respectful of my family. But I can't say the same for my heritage, and if I can't respect my blood, how can I respect myself? More importantly, how can I respect my future wife. How can I make her happy if I'm not truly happy with whom I am?"

Frank stood and put his hand on Luke's shoulder. "I'll be right back."

Sal looked at his brother and squeezed his forearm. "You know, Luke, I have never felt the way you do, but I feel for you, and I do understand. Even if I tease you about it once in a while, I'll always be there for you," he said, turning and walking away before Luke could answer him.

Luke followed his brother with his eyes, wondering why he was so lucky to have these people as his family.

In his bedroom, standing in front of his dresser, Frank called for his wife to help find something.

"What, Frank? Oh! You think it's time?" she asked, seeing that what he was looking for was already in his hands.

"He is so conflicted, T, he loves Tiffany and the world that she could give him access to, but he loves his family and traditions that we have," he said, using his sweet name for her.

"Yes, he is, but we knew that this could happen, and I agree, just make sure you put everything back."

"Yes, my love," he responded as he had done countless times before.

Halfway through texting Tiffany back, his father came back, placed a small old leather coin purse on the table, and poured two espressos. When he reached for the Sambuca, Luke stopped him.

"Thanks, but this time I want grappa," Luke ordered, finishing his text.

Obeying, Franks added the grappa to Luke's coffee, then noticing that his son was still engrossed in his texting, he added Sambuca to his own coffee.

Luke took a sip of his espresso and must admit that perhaps his father might have a point when it came to coffee enhancements. Unwilling to admit it quite yet, he ignored the small purse and changed the subject.

"Hey pops, sorry to hear about your friend Andy."

"Thanks, it was unexpected."

"Did he suffer much?"

"I don't think so; the bus hit him doing 80 miles an hour!" he answered with a quick laugh.

"I thought he had cancer?"

"He did. But the bus got him first. Better this way, the insurance pays double."

"You're being awfully callous."

"It's my way of coping."

Luke thought he could see his father's eyes getting moist, so he quickly asked him another question.

"How was the funeral?"

"It was a closed casket."

"How's Maggie doing?"

"She's fine; she said that they're going to spread the ashes in his favorite fishing spot," he said, wiping his eyes with a napkin. "Speaking of ashes, I want you to make me a promise, Luke."

"Sure."

"Don't be so quick to accept, son," he warned. "Anyway, when my time comes…."

Luke started to say something, but Frank held up his hand.

"…whenever that is, I'm not talking now! I need you to spread my ashes."

"Come on, Pa." Luke laughed.

"And Luke, it has to be this one spot."

"Really! Okay, no problem, I'll…."

Luke's phone alerted him to an incoming text. "…Sorry, hold on."

After finishing answering the text, he lifted his head and pointed to the wallet.

"What's with the wallet?"

"It's not a wallet; it's a coin purse. It was given to me by your mother's father when we left Corleone," Franks explained, handing the purse to Luke.

"I want you to have it."

Luke took the coin purse and turned it in his hand several times.

"Thanks, that's really nice. But where is this coming from?"

"It has always held important things in my life, and it continues to do so. Inside is a piece of paper with directions to my spot."

"You have a spot?" Luke said with a laugh.

"I do," his father replied seriously.

"Okay, I'll play along. So, where is this spot?"

"Sicily, Corleone, to be exact."

"Right? Come on, where's this spot?"

"Seriously, look at the paper," he ordered Luke.

Not sure if his father was playing him, he slowly opened the coin purse keeping his eyes on his father. Finally, he spotted a piece of paper, took it out, and read it. "These directions are in Italian, but you are serious," he exclaimed, frowning.

"Absolutely."

"Pops, all these years, you never once mentioned about going back to Sicily. Why do you want your ashes to be buried there?"

"You're right; your mother and I rarely mention Corleone, and that is the error in judgment we made, but I think it's time to speak of it now, especially since..."

"Really, you never once mentioned going back to Sicily all these years. Why now?" he insisted.

"Two reasons; one, if you can take the time, your mother and me would like to arrange for all of you to attend Bobby's ceremony. It's not Corleone, but it should give you the flavor of Sicily."

"Pops, that's a tremendous offer; thank you, I will make sure to take the time." He hugged him, acknowledging his gift.

"Good, I'll book it next week. You'll be there for ten days, so plenty of time to visit our hometown."

"And the other reason?"

"Your mother and I will never go back, but Sicily's beauty or Corleone's complicated history has nothing to do with it. It's something much more personal, and perhaps it's time for us, I mean your mom and me, to tell you why we chose to leave Corleone when we did. I'll go get them, you..."

The incoming call stopped Frank in mid-sentence.

"Go ahead, answer," he told his son.

Luke's attitude was not a surprise to Frank; when they first came from Italy, Frank and Teresa made a conscious decision not to settle in an Italian neighborhood. Moving away from a place where the line between honor and revenge often did not exist, they did not want their children exposed to the same thing in America. They understood, of course, that the seventies were different from the forties, but some aspects of the more antique Sicilian customs are difficult to eradicate from their makeup.

Loyalty to the family, commitment to your beliefs, and love for life, qualities that are true of most Sicilians, they believed could be instilled in their children at home.

Looking back, he was sure that not revealing what he was about to reveal to his children much earlier was a mistake. But he was also certain that Luke, after learning of their reasons for leaving Corleone, would, through his lenses, understand and reveal the realities of his heritage and not the perceptions that often blur them. It might take some time, but he was equally positive that to absorb and expose those truths, Luke must experience them and not just learn them from others, including his family. Leaving Luke to his call, he stood up and headed towards the house to get the rest of the family. Halfway there, Luke called him.

"Pops, hold up. Tiff wants me to go down to her office and bring her one of her files at home."

Franks nodded his head.

"I'll go get them; you were going to tell us why you..."

"Later. Go!" Frank interrupted, making his way back to his chair.

"There's plenty of time to talk about that. Just tell your mom we'll talk next Sunday."

"I have some time."

"No, next week is fine. I'll just leave you with something to think about. Only your blood can answer all of those questions you have and don't be afraid, Luca," he said, using his Italian name. "Blood tells no lies."

"Let's talk now, I..."

"Luke, go. We'll talk next Sunday," he said, sitting back down to finish his coffee. "And Luke, that picture of the old man at the wedding you sent me. A masterpiece! You're a talented and passionate photographer. Don't ignore that gift!"

Luke looked at his father for a few moments, then quickly hugged him tightly.

"Thanks, that means a lot to me. I love you, Pa."

Frank nodded his head as Luke walked away.

"Love you too, son," he said softly.

CHAPTER SEVEN
Just a Card Game

Caffé Ruggiero's small patio, a highly sought-after tourist location in Corleone, Sicily, was completely full. Therefore, the four men occupying one of the tables playing scopa, an Italian card game, appeared to be a poor use of the bar's resources. It was not. The players, in fact, formed a symbiotic relationship with the café, for they received espressos, cold drinks, and wine from the bar. In return, the bar attracted more tourists who had been directed there by tour companies and guides to experience the languid life of the Sicilian population.

The card players required no acting; they were doing what the people of this town had been doing for centuries. Their emotions were genuine because the games were real. From time to time, the players would change, but the card games went on. Occasionally, when a fourth player was needed, they would ask one of the tourists to join them. But they would first ask the potential player some questions to make sure that he was a competent scopa player, for they took their game very seriously.

Today, the tourists were lucky as they were witnessing the A-team of scopa players working their trade.

Having just finished a hand, one of the players took a sip of wine from the small Italian stemless wine glasses, slammed the glass down without spilling any of the wine, and passionately argued with his partner and one of his opponents about the inadequate playing of the previous hand. The fourth player, having stayed away from the heated dispute, causally took a long drag of his cigarette, blew the smoke away from the other three, placed the butt in a wooden bird's mouth that was mysteriously standing beside him, took a sip of his own wine and began to shuffle the cards.

"Did you see that, hon?" asked a forty-something man who was taking photos or videos like many of the tourists. "That's so cool!"

The man's wife, dressed more for a cocktail party than a leisurely walk in a Sicilian town, shook her head and, in a condescending tone, answered her husband.

"Smoking in a restaurant? Who does that any more?"

The husband inched closer to his wife and whispered in her ear.

"You f'n kidding me, Alice? Do you have to find fault in everything you see? Why don't you go for a walk and see if you can find any other social mores these people are breaking?"

His wife turned and, without a word, started walking down the street. Turning his attention back to the game, the tourist noticed a beautiful young woman walking by.

"Good morning, miss Alessandra. Come sit, take Carlo's spot. He knows nothing about scopa." One of the players called her over in Italian.

"Go fuck yourself. What do you know about scopa?" Carlo was quick to respond.

Wishing he had done better in his high school Italian, the tourist put his phone away and concentrated on the conversation that was quickly escalating into an argument again.

"One thing is for sure, it's better to look at Alessandra's beautiful face than your ugly one," the player joked.

"We all agree there!" Carlo added with a laugh.

All laughing now, Alessandra kissed him on the forehead.

"Always the gentleman Pasquale, but I have work to do."

"Come on, just one hand. I'd like to win once in a while!" Pasquale pleaded.

Alessandra looked at Carlo, who stood up and held the chair for Alessandra.

"Please, make him happy. I'm tired of listening to him."

"So, turn down your hearing aid!" the smoker joined in after removing the cigarette from the bird's mouth and took another drag. "Why don't you be a gentleman and offer Alessandra a bitter instead of that chair?" he added, laughing.

"Thanks, it's a very tempting offer, but I have to reopen the Historical Building. I'm late as it is," she declined, placing a gentle hand on Carlo's shoulder, who was forced to sit back down.

"How are things over there?" Carlo asked.

"Same as always, most of the questions from the tourists are about the Mafia," she responded in a more somber voice.

There was a sense of sadness as the card players all fell silent. Not wanting to change the mood permanently, she continued.

"Not to worry, gentlemen. I'll never stop fighting for the real Corleone. After all, someone must educate the tourists," she finished, looking and smiling at the man who was obviously listening to their conversation.

"Not too much education, I hope," another player cautioned.

Alessandra looked at the man, narrowed her eyes, shook her head but decided to remain silent.

"What? Did I say something wrong?" the man asked, putting his cards down on the table. "This town depends on those tourists. If they want to come here because of the Mafia, let them," he reasoned.

"Sure, Antonio, but don't you want them to leave with a different impression of what this town has to offer?" Alessandra asked him.

"Why are you even answering that idiot? His interest in our history goes as far as his deepest pocket," Pasquale accused him.

"Don't be such a hypocrite, Pasquale; those tourists put two of your children through college," Antonio responded.

Having heard this discussion before, Carlo shook his head and looked at Alessandra.

"Alessandra, you've done a lot for our town already. Thanks for trying to keep everyone honest."

"Not enough, Carlo," she said. Then, turning to the tourist, she asked him in English what had attracted him to Corleone.

"The movie, I guess," he responded honestly, nodding his head and smiling at her.

"Thanks." She smiled and then turned to the players to translate. "There you have it, gentlemen. The movie. Someday, I hope that my efforts will have tourists flocking to Sicily and Corleone, not for the

Mafia connection that the movie made popular, but for the rich history and beauty that it offers."

"You're well on your way to doing that. Your mother tells me you have a special project in mind," Pasquale said.

"I do, but I'm a long way from telling you about it," she responded with a sneaky smile.

"Okay, okay, let us know if we can help," Carlo said.

"I will. Have a good day, gentleman," she said, giving the tourist a final nod and smile.

The tourist watched Alessandra closely as she walked away and entered the Corleone Historical Building. Looking in the other direction, he spotted his wife sitting on a bench near a fountain rubbing her foot with one hand and holding her shoe, which was now missing a high heel, in the other. Heading for the Corleone Historical Building, he decided that a lesson in Corleone's history and beauty was preferable.

CHAPTER EIGHT
The Trip

Moving from side to side, Luke sat restlessly in his airline seat. Conversely, the box on the window seat next to him rested motionless, comfortable with the weight of Luke's reassuring hand resting on its top.

A flight attendant approached Luke with the usual friendly but uncommenting smile.

"I'm sorry, sir. You'll have to store the box in the overhead compartment or under the seat in front of you. I can also keep it safe for you at the front of the plane."

"I've tried, the overheads are full, and the box doesn't fit under the seat."

"It will be safe with me at the front." She smiled with honesty as Luke reluctantly released the box to her.

Attempting to relax and not think about his upcoming task, he pushed the release button and leaned as far back as he could. The minute change in the angle of his seat was marginally less uncomfortable, but he closed his eyes anyway, hoping that sleep would sweep his thoughts away.

The attempt was a complete failure. Closing his eyes placed him right back in the cold, sterile room of the hospital's morgue.

It was a useless attempt; I could no more console Sal than I could find solace within me.

At one point, I could no longer take in enough oxygen to support my legs. Feeling that I was close to fainting, I quickly left the room to find the nearest exit in a panic. I remember stepping outside and inviting the cool raindrops to hit the back of my head as I doubled over with agonizing sorrow. Immediately realizing that this was not helping, I straightened and allowed the fresh, cool air to swiftly enter my lungs and bring some life back into my body.

Even now, my memories of that day are so vivid that agony shrouds me yet again. The day when my brother and I had to identify our father's body

His memory was so real that the same constricting feeling once again began to take over his body. Suddenly, a gentle touch on his shoulder shocked him back to reality. A quick, noisy long double breath and a rapid blinking of his eyes eventually revealed the figure of a dwarf pointing to the seat next to him.

"I'm very sorry to disturb you, but I believe that's my seat," she said, smiling.

"Yes, of course, sorry," Luke apologized, straightening a little to allow the woman to pass.

The lady sat and made herself comfortable before addressing him.

"I hope I wasn't the cause of that labored breath."

Feeling uneasy, Luke squirmed slightly in his seat as he searched for the right words to answer her. Recognizing his discomfort, the lady laughed aloud.

"I'm sorry; I have a wicked sense of humor. I know I wasn't the cause; you did the double breath thing before seeing me. But I think it was worth it, for me anyway." She laughed again, then a little more seriously, she added, "I'm sorry, I'm Sarah," she apologized, offering her hand and a generous smile.

Finding her smile contagious, he smiled back, shaking her hand.

"I'm sorry about that. I was in another world. Nice to meet you, Sarah. I'm Luke."

"What world was that, Luke?"

Taken a little aback by Sarah's forwardness, Luke answered her vaguely. "I was just reliving a stressful moment."

"How so?" she asked.

Luke would not ordinarily reveal his thoughts to someone he had just met, but for some reason, her persistent directness felt genuine, and he was comfortable sharing something this intimate with her.

"I was thinking back when my brother and I had to identify my father's body at the morgue. At one point, I had to get some fresh air."

"And thus, the great big breath you took as I interrupted. I'm sorry for your loss. When did your father pass away?"

"Four days ago."

"That's very recent."

"Yes, I didn't stay for the reception after the cremation; I took the first available flight out." Her silent but inquisitive look prompted him to continue, "My father made me promise to bury his ashes in his hometown. I just want to get it over with," he said, shrugging his shoulder and smiling at her.

"A little angry, are we?" she asked, holding his look.

"You don't miss much, do you?" he questioned back, still smiling.

"That's what I do."

"What do you mean, that's what you...."

Stopping mid-sentence, he followed a passenger walking by and staring at Sarah. "…there are many people coming around here; I know it's not for me. I would say they're being rude, but the look on their faces would suggest otherwise."

"Yes, I think some of them recognize me. I've written some books and articles."

Luke looked at her a little closer, and he suddenly recognized her from a picture in a book that Tiffany read often.

"Sarah, Sarah Leone? Shit! Sorry I didn't recognize you, Dr. Leone. Your picture on the book is a little different."

"That's all right. Please, call me Sarah. You must be talking about my second book; I was going through my blond phase when I wrote that one. That is very observant. What do you do?"

"I'm a photographer. Do you mind if I take a few shots of you? My girlfriend is a huge fan; she will be ecstatic."

"That would explain your sharp eye, and no, I don't mind if you take my picture."

"Thanks. So, what brings you here, Sarah?" Luke asked, sticking to his M.O. of asking questions as he took pictures.

Before Sarah could answer, a flight attendant interrupted them.

"Excuse me, Mr. Cassaro?"

"Yes."

"You've been bumped up to first class. Please follow me."

"Pardon me?"

"Yes, Captain Amato has arranged it. He apologizes for not personally greeting you. He will most definitely see you when we disembark. But he hopes this will make amends," she finished, holding his eyes.

"I really don't understand, plus I'm fine here. This young lady and I are having a very nice conversation."

"Luke, don't be silly," Sarah told him. "Take the offer. It's like winning a lottery."

"Actually, Dr. Leone, I know that you never fly first class, but the seat next to Mr. Cassaro is yours if you like."

Before she could refuse, Luke answered for her. "She'll take it." He then turned to Sarah and added, "I'm not moving if you're not."

"Hmm, a moral dilemma," she stated, looking intensely at Luke for a few seconds. "Alright, I'll break my own rule."

The move was quick and effortless for them. First-class in the new Alitalia Boeing 777-300ER had several choices of seating arrangement;

Luke and Sarah were directed to seats 3E and 3G in the middle aisle. Slightly angled inward for ease of conversation, they were commonly referred to as the "honeymoon" seats. Settled in with a perfectly chilled glass of prosecco accompanied by a selection of antipasti, ranging from bruschetta to cheese and fig jam, they resumed their conversation.

"I don't like being in business class, let alone first class. I feel that I'm taking away a seat from someone that could use the room. I'm perfectly comfortable in the economy; I don't think it's very ethical," she said, physically referencing her body size with her hands.

"Ethical? I think you and my father would have gotten along very well."

"Really? How so?"

"He was an ethics professor at Columbia University." They both laughed at the irony.

"And you think he would agree with me?" she asked.

"No, I think he would say that it's not the size of your body that should determine whether you should fly business class or economy. It's the size of your bank account that should determine that. But he would have loved to debate it with you, plus he would have explained it much better."

Sarah delayed her response as she eagerly eyed the smoked tuna and citrus salad appetizer placed in front of her. Then, looking over to Luke's appetizer of traditional Sant'Angelo salami with vegetable compote, she wondered if she had made the wrong choice. One taste of the tuna, and she decided her choice was correct.

Since they both ordered the same first course, a beautifully prepared light tomato, capers, olives, and tuna sauce on a bed of Liporata-style short pasta, there was no need for their taste buds to be envious of each other.

Simultaneously taking a breath and patting their stomachs, they looked at each other and laughed. As the attendant approached, they quieted their laughter into a slow chuckle.

"Your seconds will be right out," the attendant stated, instigating an immediate restart of their laughter.

For the second course, they selected different dishes. Sarah had chosen a Cacciatore style chicken supreme with chicory, olive flan, and roasted potatoes. After a long self-debate, Luke decided on the swordfish rolls with capers from Pantelleria, rosemary potatoes, and Sicilian caponata.

They talked about their lives for the better part of two hours, completely satisfied, agreeing that the amazing Italian dinner would surpass many of the finest Italian restaurants in New York. Sometimes superficially, other times explicit enough to make Luke feel that Sarah understood his feelings more than she was letting on. They exhausted most topics that strangers would not have remotely discussed. Silently agreeing to refrain from any further conversation, sleep took over their private worlds.

CHAPTER NINE
Landing in a New Country

Gently awakened by the pleasant voice of the head flight attendant announcing that the descent to Rome's Fiumicino airport had begun, they smiled at each other as they each accepted a small hot moist towel and a complimentary toiletry bag.

"I think I will go and freshen up," Sarah announced.

Left alone, Luke reviewed the shots he had taken of Sarah during this flight. The pictures were good but not exactly what he was looking for. So, on her return, he asked her if he could take more pictures.

"Sure, but while you're doing that, what did you mean when you said I have an astonishing ability not to miss much?"

"Right, I did say that. When I said that I left right after the cremation because I just wanted to get it over with, I thought I sounded frustrated. But you recognized it as anger," Luke submitted, taking more shots of Sarah. "You were right! I remember standing in front of the casket with my brother Sal beside me. I looked around the room, and all I saw was this pained look of sorrow on the faces of the people there. What was odd was that our family, I mean the immediate family, all had distinctive looks." He stopped, put his camera down, and looked at Sarah. "My mother looked sad, my brother looked confused, and my sister and brother-in-law looked distressed. But the reflection looking back at me from the shiny silver corner of the casket was anger, and I was.

I remember thinking, *I can't believe it, Pops, for a fucking Vespa? Why couldn't you just let him go? What were you thinking, chasing that thief down the street for a ten-year-old Vespa?* So yes, I was angry. I know he loved that motorino. Mom told me he went everywhere in the neighborhood with it. He would often forget things on purpose, just to go back to the store. But it was still only a Vespa. So, you are right, Sarah. It wasn't frustration that made me book the flight; it was anger," he finished, exhaling.

"That was not hard to figure out, Luke. Without a doubt, the easiest diagnosis I've gotten right. But Luke, anger is multifaceted; sometimes, it reveals itself through a single unexpected incident; other times, it is much deeper than that. Earlier, you mentioned that, unlike the rest of your family, you have some reservations regarding your Sicilian heritage. Even though, at times, you enjoy participating in your Sicilian traditions. Perhaps you're angry because your father's untimely death has hampered you from reconciling that conflict. But your anger will not disappear by burying the ashes; you need to understand that anger. While I think you're well on your way to doing that, I hope this journey will complete that process and ease your pain."

Acknowledging her acumen, Luke nodded his head in agreement as he blankly stared into space. Unaware of the landing and taxiing to the gate, Luke was shaken back to reality by the ping of the seatbelt sign. As they prepared to disembark, Luke looked over to Sarah and asked, "How will it do that?

"Do what?"

"This journey. Ease my pain. I'm here for only three days."

"A lifetime can happen in a second; in three days, the whole world can change. And don't forget to enjoy this country; it has a lot to offer."

"Really?"

Sarah looked up at him with reprimanding eyes and then inclined her head slightly as she seemed to be contemplating something.

"Come on, Luke, You're not that ignorant of the art, history, and love of life, just to mention a few of the things that this beautiful country has to offer," she said.

"I'm going to Sicily, remember?" Luke said, trying to be funny.

"It doesn't change what I said. It probably amplifies it!" Sarah responded, ignoring his lackluster attempt at humor, and walked ahead of him to the exit.

Prior to disembarking, the captain greeted him with an extended hand.

"Thank you for flying, Alitalia. I hope you enjoyed your flight."

"Yes, I did, very much. And thank you for the upgrade."

"It's a very small favor, Mr. Cassaro. I have relatives in Corleone," Captain Amato replied with a big smile.

Luke nodded and walked off the plane, wondering how the did captain know his name and that he was going to Corleone, but the thought was fleeting as he sped up to reach Sarah. She's a quick walker, but Luke's long legs gave him the advantage as he reached just behind her in no time.

"Sarah," he called.

Sarah turned and slowed her walk, allowing Luke to come and walk beside her.

"I just wanted to tell you what a pleasure it was spending the night with you."

"I'm sure your girlfriend would love to hear that!" Sarah responded with a quick laugh.

"No, she would not. But she'll understand when I give your very special note to her."

Sarah smiled, and then, a little more seriously, she looked into Luke's eyes.

"You're a fine young man, Mr. Luke Cassaro. It doesn't take a tiny psychiatrist to tell you that. It's plain to anyone that meets you. Without any hesitation, I believe that you will achieve what you're looking for. We both know it's somewhere in there." She reached up to touch his chest, and surprisingly, her hand was cold, so much so that Luke felt it seeping through his shirt.

"Thanks, Sarah. I think I will stop pretending to read your books and articles. Instead, I will read them for real."

"You might not like what you read, Mr. Cassaro. And please send me some of those photos you took of me."

"You may be right, but I'll read them anyway. I will also send you some of my photos; hopefully, you'll like what you see, Ms. Leone."

"If you're half as talented as you are pleasant," she said, laughing and reaching for Luke's extended hand, "I will love them."

"By the way, you never did tell me what you're doing here," Luke asked her.

"I'm receiving a lifetime achievement award from the AILA."

"AILA?" Luke said in a surprised tone.

"The Association for Italian Living Abroad," Sarah elaborated.

His brows rose, and his eyes widened in surprise, "Wait! You're Italian?"

"Born in Milano, grew up in Jersey. I'm a proud American Italian Jew." She smiled.

Holding his hand a little tighter, she pulled him closer and reached up to kiss both his cheeks in farewell.

"I have your number; I'll call you," she said, walking away.

CHAPTER TEN
Confusion

Da Vinci International Airport in Rome was loud, crowded, and disorganized at the best of times. Today it was exceedingly so. For Luke, who was desperately trying to get to the gate on time for his connecting flight to Palermo, it was a nightmare. Hot, thirsty, and upset at not having the time to take some exquisite shots of the people around him, he forced himself to focus on his target. Fortunately, the directional signs were in Italian and English, making it easier for him to navigate as he quickly read one of them to realize that his destination was only two gates away.

As he approached the gate, he saw the attendant standing behind the counter. He also noticed that the counter is void of any passengers. Hoping that he was not too late, his breathing quickened. His heart raced as he switched his grip on the box to an under-the-arm football hold. Like a running back, he picked up his speed, dodging slower passengers along the way as he slithered past them.

Only yards away from his goal, a mother blocked his way as she pushed a carriage with a young child in tow. Anticipating her speed and direction, he leaned slightly to his right to fly past her. What he did not expect was her older child's cry.

"Mom, we're going the wrong way!" He shouted suddenly.

The family came to a sudden stop, forcing Luke to swerve to avoid a collision. Stopping a few steps away from the family, he turned to make sure that they were okay. They seemed to be fine, but they were also in an obvious state of confusion. He looked toward his destination and then looked back to the family. *Shit!*

He quickly turned toward the family and asked, "Ma'am, what gate are you looking for?"

"B11," the woman answered, still confused.

"Your son is right. That gate is the other way," he said as he thumbed towards the direction B11 was.

The mother thanked him profusely and then turned the carriage on a dime and headed the other way, dragging her son behind her. Luke did likewise and continued toward his destination, this time running.

Panting as he arrived at the gate, he decided that regardless of his poor Italian, he would politely greet the agent.

"Buongiorno," he said, handing her his ticket.

Obviously not impressed with his attempt to speak Italian, the agent answered him in English.

"Yes, good morning. How may I help you?" She asked with a polite smile plastered on her face.

"Sorry, the airline made a horrible mistake. They put my bags on the wrong baggage claim belt. I thought I wasn't going to make it!" He explained, reverting to English too.

"I'm sorry, but there is no more room on this flight. It is completely booked," she apologized, without looking at the ticket.

"What?" He looked around for some imaginary help that never came. "I don't understand. This is a connecting flight."

"I'm very sorry, sir," she apologized again, handing him back his ticket.

"How is it possible? I waited for them to find my baggage for almost an hour, and now you tell me that the flight, which is a connecting flight, is no longer available?" He asked, quite shocked at the way the events were unfolding.

"I'm sorry, but you will have to reschedule your flight. All the passengers have boarded. Perhaps I can help you make other arrangements, please, your passport," she said, holding out her hand.

Luke reached in his bag and handed her his passport.

"Please, miss, there must be a mistake. I did everything right. Why should I have to pay for the airline's incompetence?" He tried once more to plead his case, praying that maybe there was a quick solution to his predicament, that he couldn't just see it yet, or at least he hoped so.

Finally, looking at the passport, the agent quickly looked up and then rechecked the passport.

"Give me one second, please," she said with a very big smile.

Luke's hopes grew as he saw the agent having an animated conversation with one of her colleagues. She pointed to his passport several times; each time she did, her supervisor looked up at him. After reviewing the passport for several more seconds, the supervisor reached for a phone, said something quickly that Luke could not understand, and waited. After several anxious seconds, the supervisor smiled at Luke hung up the phone, and, along with the other agent, cautiously made his way back to him.

Before addressing Luke, he cleared his throat.

"Sorry for the delay, Mr. Cassaro. My name is Arrigo Ferri, I'm the supervisor here, and I have been able to clear you for boarding. Business-class, of course, window or aisle?"

"What?" Luke asked in a confused haze. Had his prayers been answered that quickly?

"Would you like a window seat or an aisle seat, Mr. Cassaro?" the supervisor asked again with a smile.

"Aisle, please. What just happened here?" He asked, not quite believing if whatever was happening was real or not.

"Nothing very serious, sir. There was a misunderstanding. It was our fault, and we apologize for the inconvenience."

Luke accepted his boarding pass and walked away, shaking his head. *What a country!*

Walking down the passenger boarding bridge towards the plane entrance, Luke, a little confused but feeling extremely lucky, noticed an extremely upset young lady walking towards him with an attendant close behind.

As he approached the entrance to the plane and crossed paths with the lady, he heard her shouting at an attendant escorting her out, "I don't understand. My father will hear about this. He's the head of security at this airline, for Christ's sake!"

"Then I'm sure he'll understand," the attendant responded as they walked past him, not even the slightest bit bothered by her empty threats.

Understanding what had just happened, he stopped and questioned the accompanying attendant.

"Hold on. I'm not comfortable with this, she..."

"Please, Mr. Cassaro, do not concern yourself with this. Like my colleague says, her father will understand, and so will she when we explain it to her," the attendant replied in a no-nonsense tone.

"But..." he tried again, but before he could say anything, the attendant looked at him exasperatedly, which made him clamp his mouth shut.

"Please, we do not want to delay the flight any further," the attendant said, spreading his left arm out and gestured him to enter the plane.

Surrendering, he finally entered the plane, where a smiling flight attendant greeted him.

"Mr. Cassaro, right this way, please."

Luke walked behind her to his seat.

"Thank you," he said as she walked away.

A young man in the seat next to his was looking out the window. From Luke's vantage point, he could see the man's profile, and it reminded him of a young Daniel Craig.

"Buongiorno," he said, trying his Italian again.

"Buongiorno," the man answered, turning to face Luke.

The change in the man's appearance was staggering, for the handsome left side of the man's face disappears and was replaced by an ugly, scarred side. Starting just above his eyebrow, the red scar ran down the entire right side of his face, made a left turn just below his lip, and finished at his right ear, forming the letter J.

The man laughed, saying, "Don't worry, man, everyone has that reaction. But yours is a little different. Your look is one of interest, not disgust." Then extending his hand, he introduced himself. "My name is Larry Laurence. Lorenzo to be exact."

"Hi Laurie, I'm Luke," he answered, vanquishing the residual uneasiness of his prior confrontation.

"You're quick!" Laurie said with a smile. "So, this flight is very short, Luke. Why don't I start?" He didn't wait for approval. "My name is Larry. I like Laurie actually; I think I'm going to start using it, do you mind?" Again, not waiting he continued. "I'm 35 years old and bi. I'm not attached now, although I have some prospects. I have my own travel agency, specializing in wine tours, and I'm here scouting the Sicilian area for appropriate destinations. This," he said, pointing to his face, "and the amputation of my left leg were the result of a car accident. A semi lost one of its tires and hit my car's windshield, causing a terrible accident. I was in the hospital for two months and then at a rehab center for another three." He looked at Luke for a few seconds, then finished, "I am happy!"

Reflecting on his conversation with Sarah, Luke wondered if he had a sign on his forehead saying, 'I'm approachable, stranger. Tell me your life story.' Regardless, in a world where spin is valued more than the truth, the man's attitude was refreshing. His boldness and frankness impressed him to the point where he felt comfortable revealing himself to this stranger.

"I'm a relatively healthy 33-year-old heterosexual from New Jersey. I'm here to bury my father's ashes, as I promised him I would. We are a family of Italian Americans with roots in Sicily. My family is proud of their Italian roots. I'm just proud to be American. I would not be going to Sicily if it was not to fulfill that promise. I am a professional photographer and I'm very much intrigued by your disfigurement. I would love to take your picture. You have an amazing personality that reveals itself on both sides of your face," Luke finished, offering Laurie his hand.

"Wow! I thought I was blunt," he said, shaking Luke's hand.

"May I," Luke said, pointing to his camera.

"Of course. Start with my best side," Laurie responded by turning his scar side towards Luke.

"Perfect," Luke agreed as he began to take shots of the young man.

It only took a few shots for Luke to realize Laurie's exceptional photogenic qualities. What struck him the most, however, was the contrast and contradictions of the miss-matched sides of Laurie's face.

Where the intact left side reflected an image of handsome indifference, the scarred right side radiated pure empathy.

Entwined between the light and friendly conversation, the shooting continued until, with a slight bump, the plane touched down at Palermo's Falcone Borsellino Airport.

"That was fast!" Luke said.

"It always is when you're having fun! Thanks for the enjoyable conversation, Luke. One thing I want to tell you, though. I'm a proud American just like you, but "Chi si volta, e chi si gira, sempre a casa va finire."

"You've got to be kidding me! You too?" Luke groaned.

"What do you mean?" Laurie asked with a confused frown on his face.

"It's just that a lot of people lately have been telling me these Italian proverbs."

"I won't be the last," Laurie predicted as he exited the plane.

Luke reached for the box and exited the plane a fair way behind Laurie.

"Laurie!" he yelled.

"Yes?" Laurie turned but continued to walk backward.

"What does it mean?"

"No matter where you go or turn, you will always end up at home," he translated. Then pointing to the box, he added, "I'm sure your father thanks you for that. I have your number; I'll contact you when I'm in New York in two weeks."

"Okay, great. I'll be looking forward to it!" Luke said to no one as Laurie had already turned the corner. *"There's going to be a full house when I get home."* He thought.

CHAPTER ELEVEN
Still Confused

It is strange how a simple object of technology can have command over one's temperament. The comment was referencing a particularly scorching summer day when the air conditioner was facing difficulty and standing in a long line-up to get your rental car becomes an unpleasant experience. The situation becomes irksome if you are waiting in a tight, crowded space.

The Falcone Borsellino Airport.

As mentioned above, due to the scorching temperatures, the musk and sticky odors from all the packed bodies emanated in the dense air. It amalgamated into an acrid scent that entered Luke's nostrils, much to his regret. Hoping to rectify the unsightly problem, Luke attempted to breathe through his mouth, but that amplified the profound effect on his senses. Therefore, the net result of his effort caused him to taste the ammonia-tinged scent on the back of his tongue.

To distract his reeling mind, he forced himself to focus on his surroundings, noting and observing who would be fit to serve as a subject behind the lens of a camera. Then suddenly, from his right peripheral, an attractive middle-aged woman passed him down the corridor with three swiveling men in tow. Curious, he focused on the three men and the woman and noticed their eyes had a knowing gaze.

The woman was aware that she was being watched, and the men were conscious of that awareness as well. It is in that mutual understanding of his subjects that Luke's creative juices began to flow, composing and framing the three within his mind. The woman would be in the foreground, a head-on shot to capture her emotions while creating the illusion of mystery with the three men in the background. Still, he couldn't help but remain agitated, he had already been waiting 45 minutes, and a quick look over to the counter did not raise his hopes that his turn would be coming soon. Although he desperately wanted to reach for his camera, his lack of energy was suppressing this desire. This self-induced personal emotional tug-of-war lasted long enough for the counter to clear; ceasing the chance, he walked up to the counter before it could be occupied again.

"Hi," he said cordially.

The attendant had ignored him, so he pressed further, "Hi. Are you going to help me?"

"Yes, I can, sir, but we did not call you up. You'll have to wait behind the yellow line until we call you," he informed Luke without acknowledging his presence, resolute in his request.

"But I'm next in line," Luke pointed out to the attendant with a smile, attempting to drop his defenses by being tolerant.

"Yes sir, of course, but we have paperwork to finish before getting to the next customer. Thank you," he said, pointing to the yellow line behind Luke.

Luke exhaled in frustration and returned to stand behind the yellow line.

"They told me they are not ready for me; I must go behind the yellow line, so here I am," he explained to the next person in line as he stopped to stand in front of him, his sour emotions clear on his features.

"Cretini." Luke recognized the curse, the man behind him spat idiots under his breath.

"Si." Luke agreed, replying in his mother tongue, Italian. It was done to redirect the man's anger away from him, hoping that the man was upset at the rental company instead.

As he turned back to face the counter, his name was suddenly announced, for which he was grateful.

"Il prossimo, per favore." (Next, please.)

It was an invitation for Luke to step up; he shook his head and stepped up to the counter

"Hi, it's my turn now, is it?" he attempted to strike at his funny bone with a sarcastic joke.

"Yes, of course, I called next," the attendant responded with a smile. "Okay, let me see your passport and driver's license, please."

As the attendant inspected the document, Luke observed that he had the same look as the agent at the Alitalia counter.

"Mr. Cassaro," he said, clearing his throat. "My apologies, please right this way."

Curiously looking around after the abnormally quick service, he decided that silently following the attendant would be in his best interest. The movement of the attendant became suddenly swift; it became challenging to understand his motives, but he found peace in silently following his steps.

"Mr. Cassaro, next time, just come to the front of the line and ask for me personally. My name is Valentino."

"Thank you, but I tried to..."

"Will this car be suitable for your trip, Mr. Cassaro?" Valentino interrupted to cover his mistake.

"Yes, that would be fine," Luke laughed, "but I ordered a subcompact. That," he said, pointing to the car, "is a Mercedes convertible!"

"Yes, a GTC Roadster of course."

"But I paid for a subcompact," Luke said with a big smile.

"Yes, but you have been assigned this GT. No extra charge, of course," Valentino answered whilst handing Luke the keys, after which the man was no longer seen, for he had made a hasty exit.

It was quite odd.

Before Luke entered the car, he took several breaths. *What is going on here? Upgraded three times in a matter of hours? I wonder if Sal has anything to do with this. Nah, he's still pissed at my quick departure. Or maybe mom? I don't know, but I need to find out. I think I'll call home as soon as I check in at my hotel.*

Entering the car, his eyes were introduced to the most incredible car interior he had ever seen. Suddenly, as he reached for the steering wheel, the feeling that perhaps there had been a big mistake engulfed him. Assuming that a frazzled Valentino would be stomping through the airport door screaming at him to leave the car, he hastily tapped the directions in the car's GPS, popped it into drive and quickly drove away while keeping an eye on the rear-view mirror, hoping that it would remain void of any human figure.

This looks simple enough; E90, SP4, and I should be in Corleone in about one hour and fifteen minutes.

Navigating through traffic was not an issue for Luke, and now that he had the wheels of the GTC Roadster in his palms, he had trouble finding a stable enough speed. Once he entered E90 for the first time, he spotted a straightaway down from his position. The GPS estimated the length to be about two kilometers; hence, he took a quick scan of his surroundings and decided to open it up. In less than 500 meters, the GT reached approximately 180 km/h but slowed it to 150 km/h upon feeling uncomfortable.

Once he was cruising comfortably, Luke felt comfortable enough to examine the car's interior. The soft black, red-trimmed leather woven throughout the plush fabric, combined with the Burmester High-End 3D Surround Sound system, was enough for Luke to consider the car the best and most expensive vehicle he had ever been in, let alone driven. But his favorite feature, by far, was the climate-controlled Saddle Brown, Macchiato Beige body contouring pilot seats with stitched decorative inserts.

Upon settling in, the constant purring of the engine coupled with the fast-moving lush green countryside began to overwhelm his senses with a feeling of inner peace. Nonchalantly, he stroked the Mercedes logo embellished on the passenger seat; it was a peaceful habit of his which was unfortunately broken by the onset of the peripheral areas of the town. The interchanging steep and gradually winding roads forced him to slow down to drown to respect the topography. Slightly disappointed at the reduction of his speed, he negotiated the GT convertible past a collection of streets and laneways that, although well marked, were written in Italian, and he could not decipher them. He decided to rely on the GPS, and it took little time for him to arrive at his destination. He was a little saddened that his drive had ended; he missed the soft, warm breeze caressing his face alas, he had a day to look forward to. So, he took a final, deep breath and confidently parked in front of his hotel.

CHAPTER TWELVE
First Impression

(Day One)

Like the majority of the institutional buildings, private or city-owned, Corleone's Historical Building was a two-story converted warehouse.

Recently renovated, the upper floor that once housed uncut flour from the mill was now a Bed and Breakfast with three separate units. Spacious and uncluttered, each unit had its own bathroom, air conditioning, and a balcony furnished with a bistro table and two chairs.

Some would say their establishment held the best accommodations in town.

The lower level of the building was divided into three sections, front, middle, and back. The kitchen, though small, was well equipped with the latest and best appliances. It helped the chefs to prepare and serve American-style breakfast to the guests. There was a wide array of options one could choose from the menu, ranging from Eggs Benedict to Southern Style Creamy Grits with Cheese.

The middle part was where the B&B reception and the breakfast/café areas were located. Here you found three small tables for two and two larger tables for four that were set daily with care and pride by Maria, the cook, and Maria, her helper or server.

As for the façade of the building, it was the most extensive section in a multi-functional zone that served as a library/museum, information center, and Alessandra's office.

The space's design was made to include the Historical Society with the B&B accommodations; this space was separated by a beautiful ornate iron gate that was retracted when the Corleone Historical Building was open.

Initially, it was owned by the Orsini Family; this ideally located warehouse was renovated to run it as a hotel. However, fate intervened as it often did in this part of the world.

Just before the renovations could finish, Mrs. Orsini fell ill.

Despite the numerous doctors who were called in to help, Mrs. Orsini was not getting better. Her health was failing fast; hence Mr. Orsini made a 'deal with God', and within the hour, Mrs. Orsini recovered with no sign of ever contracting an illness. And so, discussion regarding this miracle was often discussed but never substantiated.

The Orsini family felt obligated to donate this newly renovated site to the Church. After graciously accepting the donation without question or verifications of the miracle, the Church entrusted the operation of business to the historical society, or more precisely, Alessandra.

As the general manager and sole full-time employee of the historical society, she was the head of operations of many establishments, including the B&B, librarian, curator of the small museum, and operator or guide for the tourists in the area. Of course, any profits were shared equally between the church and the historical society.

Returning from her morning tour Alessandra re-opened the building. As she straightened some brochures on the shelf, she shivered from the cold, artificially controlled by the ventilation system.

I can't understand this love affair with cold air? she thought to herself after shivering for the umpteenth time. Determined to introduce some warmer air into her environment, she moved to open the front window opening them to allow the warm breeze to circulate in the room. She already felt at peace.

When she turned the crank, she noticed a young man getting out of a car. She had stopped for a while, observing the stranger; hence she noted the box he carried in one arm and the rest of his baggage. He held it so reverently that the woman could tell that the box had some sort of importance to him.

The man took a few steps and then readjusted his baggage to avoid spilling over. Gently placing the box on the car's trunk, he moved what looked like a camera bag from his left shoulder to his right, allowing him to carry the box with his freed, unoccupied right hand.

Somehow having noticed her, he stopped mid-action and waved his hand, forwarding a friendly greeting. This act caused the box to slide off the trunk, but since he was focused on her, the world behind him went ignored. To avoid the impending disaster, the woman began to alert him of the box by waving back fervently and pointing at the box behind him. He was a bit disoriented at first, but eventually, interpreting her signals therein, the man went into recovery mode. Right hand releasing the suitcase and the camera bag sliding off his shoulder, the man pirouetted with such grace that would make Baryshnikov green with envy; he successfully caught the box.

As the man turned to claim his accolades, she shook her head and turned away.

He attempted to decipher the need he felt to wave to the beautiful young lady in the window for a bit. Harboring the uncertainty and his belongings, he began the walk to the hotel before sneaking a peek back at the window that suddenly looked unwelcoming. Disappointed that the striking young lady did not appreciate this amazing act of balance and agility, Luke continued his sulking walk to the hotel. However, his disappointment is short-lived as the four men playing cards outside a nearby café clapped and howled their appreciation, so he displayed a tentative bow before entering the hotel's premises.

Back inside the Corleone Historical Building, Alessandra doubled over with laughter. The scene she witnessed was, in fact, very comical, and she must admit that she was very impressed with the young man's recovery abilities.

Then realizing where the man parked, she became agitated, "Can't he read signs; the parking lot is just behind the Hotel," she said to herself, her voice reverberating in the empty room.

Like the Corleone Historical Building, this hotel had been newly renovated. Although small, the front desk was flawlessly decorated, thus visually inviting to one's eye.

'Not what I expected.' Luke said to himself as he walked up to the counter, remembering his last conversation with his friend Vic.

"*Ya man, we went all over Sicily. Palermo, Agrigento, Marsala, Taormina, depending on your budget, you can stay in luxury hotels that'll cost you over $1500.00 a night and B&Bs for as little as $50.00 a night, but some of those you have to share bathrooms,*" *Vic told me laughing. He then said to me that since he was never in Corleone, he could not help me with that, but to be careful anyway because some of the pictures they use in brochures can be misleading.*

And he had been careful. Surprisingly, there were many hotels and B&Bs to choose from. However, since the prices were within his price range, he decided on the newest hotel. Now, as he slowly looked around, he silently agreed with Vic that the pictures on the web do lie. Albeit, for him, the pictures did not do justice to the hotel.

Carefully placing his bags beside him on the floor, he brushed himself up and walked to the receptionist area to address the clerk.

"Hi. I booked a room here. Luke Cassaro," he said clearly, observing the man behind the desk with mild interest.

The man smiled, responding to the new client politely, "Good day, Mr. Cassaro; we've been expecting you. Welcome to Hotel Boni." Turning to his workmate, the attendant waved to him, gardening his attention, thus motioning him to the front desk.

"Fernando, please mind the desk."

Fernando, clearly this man's junior, nodded his head and stepped behind the counter. Once the man had taken his position, the senior employee stepped up to the traveler, a spring evident in his step.

"My name is Vincenzo; I will help you, Mr. Cassaro," he said, reaching for Luke's bags.

"Oh no, that's okay; really, it's not necessary," Luke protested, hurrying his speech along with his bags, catching one in his arms before Vincenzo could.

The man looked perplexed by this behavior, to which he finally commented, "Please, I insist."

Luke, feeling that he had offended the man by accident, finally nodded and ended his insistence.

"Thank you, but I'm going to hold on to this," he said, securing the box within his hold.

"Yes, of course," Vincenzo replied, picking up Luke's bags. "Right this way."

Luke followed the clerk to an open elevator that was clearly added as part of the renovations. The only safety equipment he saw was the brass railing that only went up halfway.

The clerk noticed Luke's slight hesitation and reassured him, "I assure you Mr. Cassaro; this is quite safe."

Stepping into the lift, Luke moved to the furthest possible corner, to which Vincenzo smiled and shifted the brass lever from the stop position to up.

Silently and smoothly, the elevator whizzed past the second and stopped on the third and final floor. Fishing out a small fob, Vincenzo placed it close to a small rectangular box on the side of the wall activating the front doors causing them to slide open automatically.

Vincenzo graciously invited Luke to step outside the contraption after stepping out himself. Luke noticed the subtle act and felt gracious that Vincenzo had felt the need to comfort him, so accepting Vincenzo's invitation, he followed him into the suite. He was immediately astonished at the size of the room. Enormous by any standards, Luke's attention was immediately drawn directly ahead, where at the far end of the room, he saw a set of double glassed doors leading to the balcony. To the left was a king-sized brass canopy bed positioned on an elevated platform and decorated with shear white drapes, drawn open and tied to the four posts. The bed itself was flanked by two white lacquer nightstands that, like the matching six-drawer double dresser standing on the wall next to the bed, were trimmed with brushed brass.

Shifting his gaze to the right side of the apartment, he saw a small glass-top table and four chairs next to the balcony doors. Further in, the room is furnished with a couch and chair that match perfectly with the room's color palette of the room but in Luke's opinion, they would be very uncomfortable to sit in.

Vincenzo drew the matching drapes of the balcony and opened the doors to the outside.

"This is the balcony. I think you will enjoy the view, Mr. Cassaro." Vincenzo stepped up to Luke's side, noticing his fascination with interest.

"Thanks, Vincenzo; this is a wonderful room."

"Prego. This is your fob," Vincenzo said, holding it up to his field of vision.

"It will open your front door and the minibar, which is fully stocked. The air conditioning," he continued after opening the bar fridge, a procedure done regularly to give assurance to the customer, "Can be adjusted from the wall unit located just to the right side of the front doors. You can also open it with your cell phone along with access to our web site," he finished, handing Luke the item in question.

"Really? How does it do that?" Luke fiddled with the fob, turning it in his hand before looking at the hotel employee curiously.

"Simply access our site. You will be prompted to enter a code or hold the fob close to your phone or computer, and you'll gain access."

"That's amazing!" Luke answered enthusiastically, his fob now tucked away safely in his pocket.

"Is this system not available in the United States?" Vincenzo asked, narrowing his puzzled eye.

"You know I don't think it is; at least I've never seen it," Luke responded, examining the fob.

"Yes, it's a fascinating tool and very effective. The bathroom is just through that door; would you like me to show you?"

"No, that's fine. I'll look later."

"The closet is just to the left of the bed. You'll find the safe there as well. Your fob can also be used to access the safe in this room, or you have the alternative of using the keypad to enter your own combination." Taking a step back, the man had neatly tucked his luggage in the corner before saying his adieu, "If you need anything Mr. Cassaro, please, anything, we are more than happy to help."

Luke would have prefered if Vincenzo would have stopped addressing him as Mr. Cassaro, but something told him that this man would be uncomfortable with that. After all, it was the nature of his job, so he decided to let it slide.

"Actually, do you know where I can buy some cigarettes?" Luka asked before Vincenzo could take his leave.

The man took out a pack of cigarettes from his pocket and handed it to him without a word. Luke took one cigarette and tried to return the package to Vincenzo, who refused it with both hands extended.

"No, please take the whole thing," Vincenzo spoke, his generosity evident in his tone.

"No thanks, one will do for now," Luke retorted, trying to hand the pack back.

Vincenzo placed a lighter next to the fob on the table and smiled.

"No, no, please Mr. Cassaro, I insist. It is our pleasure."

"Thank you." Luke capitulated, extending his hand for the other man to shake it.

Vincenzo looked from Luke's eyes to his extended hand; he hesitated slightly before finally shaking it.

As Vincenzo walked to the front door, Luke called to him again. "Sorry, Vincenzo, can I ask you something?"

Vincenzo stopped and turned to face Luke, signifying his undivided attention. "Of course, Mr. Cassaro."

"I did pay $150.00 per night to stay at this hotel, right?"

"Yes, sir. That is our regular charge."

"That is extremely low for a room this large and beautiful," he said, looking around the room.

"Mr. Cassaro, we have two of these rooms in the hotel. They are identical rooms on each end of the hotel; you have been assigned this one."

"But this can't be $150.00 a night."

"No, but it was not booked, so we decided to have you stay here. No additional cost, of course."

Vincenzo walked to the front door, but before he could cross the threshold, he turned to the new guest and smiled before officially greeting him

"Welcome to Corleone," he said before closing the doors with both hands.

"Hold on, Vincenzo. This is for you." Once again, Luke reached out to Vincenzo, but this time he pressed a 20 euro bill into his extended hand.

"No, thank you Mr. Cassaro, that will not be necessary."

Vincenzo was frazzled at the gesture, but he remained cordial. Finally, he bade Luke adieu by closing the doors of his room, leaving Luke to his thoughts and a rejected 20 euro note.

Luke stared at the closed door for a few seconds, shaking his head. *Man. This country's confusing. They either treat people like dirt, or they treat you like a prince. I don't get it.*

Once he was calm and comfortable, he decided to take a shower. Upon feeling the heat, he frantically took his sweaty clothes off and headed for the bathroom, intending to relax right after.

"Wow!" he said upon marveling at the beautiful interiors of the bathroom.

Two matching pedestal sinks and mirrors stood guard on each side of a door found at the far end of the space. In the middle of the room was a rectangular depression with a rim about six inches high on three sides; the fourth side was open with steps leading to the bottom of the pit. Ignoring the door between the sinks, he stepped to the bottom of the pit; now naked, he spun about in the depression slowly as if calculating something in his mind.

The depression was about four feet deep, with seven jets on each side. *'Now what?'* he said to himself, wishing that he had taken Vincenzo's advice when he offered a brief bathroom tour.

'There's only one way to find out.'

He headed for the controls located at the far end and moved the marbled inlayed lever marked 'doccia' (shower) to C, hoping that the C stands for 'caldo' (hot), a word he recognized. Immediately, three glass partitions and a raindrop shower head begin to drop from slots cut in the ceiling. The water was at a perfect temperature that Luke welcomed by closing his eyes, tilting his head towards it, and catching the falling droplets in his opened mouth.

After a long and necessary shower, he stepped out of the bathroom as a new man. Especially after the massage he received from the falling droplets of the shower, he felt rejuvenated. He changed into shorts and a t-shirt, picked up the pack of cigarettes and lighter, and walked out onto the balcony, where the activity below was surprising. Men, women, and children of all ages were leisurely walking about, sitting in the piazza having animated conversations or enjoying their beverages at one of the busy bars around the area. Everywhere he looked, he saw happy faces.

Slightly to his right, a beautiful young girl was hanging out her clothes to dry. She noticed his presence, so she looked up at him and waved. Enticed by her friendly demeanor, he threw the cigarettes and lighter on the bistro table he had just noticed and walked over to his camera bag. Choosing his most expensive camera, he walked back out and took several pictures of the girl.

An older lady walked into the scene; Luke assumed her as the younger girl's mother because she took down the recently hung clothes and turned them inside out before hanging them again. She did all this while continuously yelling at her daughter in Italian.

Intrigued by the mother's passion and her daughter's nonchalant expression, he alternated his viewfinder between his subjects until he captured the two emotions simultaneously.

"Perfect!" he said a little too loud, garnering the mother's attention.

"Perché stai scattando le foto?" (Why are you taking pictures?) she turned her ire to him, yelling at his actions

Defensively, Luke pointed to his camera.

"Mi scusi," (I apologize) he said in Italian and then added in English, "Can I take your photo?"

"Che?" (What?)

"He wants to know if he can take your picture," the girl translated to her mother.

"No!" she told her daughter. "What's wrong with this guy? He should want to take your picture, not mine!"

"I'm sorry, mister, but she said no," the girl translated to Luke in perfect English.

"Tell her I'm a professional photographer from New York, and I find both of you interesting subjects. I want to take a few more pictures, please."

The daughter translated his request to her mother, to which she responded with a curt shrug.

"We don't mind," the younger girl responded to him with a smile, positioning herself with her mother.

His phone rang before Luke could take a shot; the ringtone pierced the hubbub of the noise around him, forcing him to pick up.

"Hello?" he answered in a rush before deciding to put the phone on speaker.

"Hey, bro."

"Sal! I was just about to call you. What's happening? You still upset at me?" he asked, expertly realigning the frame with his subjects, taking quick shots as the conversation continued.

"Na, I know why you left so quickly, plus I'm up to my neck with work; I wouldn't have been able to come anyway. So, how you doing?"

"Great, and you, Mom?"

"I'm doing great, but Mom's not too happy with you. Pissed at you for not calling her."

"Didn't call? I just got in. Two minutes ago," he lied through his clenched jaw, "Jesus!"

"You know how she is. So, is everything okay? How was the flight?" Luke heard some interference from the other side, assuming that his brother was in the middle of his work.

"I'm glad you asked, Sal." Meanwhile, Luke resumed taking shots of the two women and began to recount his experiences of the last 14 hours, starting from the upgrade to first class. Part ways through, he noticed that the women were now posing, and he lost interest.

Raising his hands and the camera, he thanked them in Italian.

"Grazie, signore." As he slipped the camera away, he resumed his recounting until he talked about the present.

"You had nothing to do with this, right? Or Mom, did she pay for all those upgrades and all?"

"I wish I could take credit for that, but I can't, and I don't think Mom did either. Maybe you just got lucky," he suggested.

"No one gets this lucky. I'm telling you this is weird, and it's making me a little uncomfortable."

"You're there for a shitty task. Maybe it's Pops making it up to you or not; either way, enjoy it while it lasts."

"I am enjoying it so far. But Sal, this is a confusing country. I just finished taking a shower in the most amazing modern bathroom, but people are still hanging clothes on outside lines. Interesting, isn't it?"

"Very interesting. Especially how you did all of those things within two minutes." He heard Sal chuckle, to which he only shook his head and sighed.

"Very good! Inspector Clouseau," Luke responded.

They shared a laugh, and then Sal continued with another question, "Just one more thing, Mr. Cassaro. Who were you thanking?"

"I took pictures of this lovely older lady and her beautiful daughter. I will say no more until I speak with my lawyer or my mother," he continued to jest, to which the brother seemed to be immune as his answer was short but warm.

"I'm afraid they're both not here."

"Great! Tell her I'll call tomorrow, 10 am her time." Unknowingly, Luke hummed, but his thoughts were disrupted by Sal's otherworldly view of his intentions

"Hey, don't get in trouble taking pictures of young girls. You'll come back married!" The two brothers shared another laugh; Sal's voice was loud enough to be heard from the outside, where Luke had finally slowed his laughter to broken huffs. "From my vantage point, it wouldn't be a big sacrifice."

"Should I tell Tiffany to take the next flight out?" Sal said, laughing aloud.

"Not just yet, but keep her number handy."

"I have it on speed dial," he answered, continuing his laugh.

"Okay funny man, talk to you soon. Love you."

"Love you too."

Before going in, Luke took one last look at the two women who had apparently finished their chores and were now heading back. Looking back at Luke, the young girl, making sure her mother was not looking at her, gave him a very sultry smile and blew him a kiss.

"I think I'm starting to like this country," he said, smiling to himself.

CHAPTER THIRTEEN
Speeding Can be Costly

It was early in the afternoon, and unexplainably Luke did not feel tired. After reviewing his latest shots and deleting those that felt unmoving to him, he went out on the balcony to observe the countryside. Its serene beauty so entrapped him that he decided to go for a country joy drive.

Before leaving, he carefully tucked the urn away in the safe of his room for which he used his fob. Upon use, the safe opened automatically, but he noticed that the box would not fit in the space and, therefore, he must first remove the urn. It did not take him time to complete the task; hence once he felt satisfied, Luke picked up the pack of cigarettes and took one out.

It had been over 10 years since he had stopped smoking, but occasionally, he still felt the desire to hold the filter within his fingers. He could only cope with this craving by purchasing a single pack and discarding all of the cigarettes until the package was devoid of its contents. In the beginning, he was discarding a single pack a day, but decades later, one pack lasted for months.

He had no idea why this ritual of his works, only that it did, and he was not willing to change it now.

So, falling onto his alternative habit, he walked to the bathroom, opened the door between the sinks, for this was the location of the toilet, and tossed the cigarette in the bowl and looked for the flush handle. Unsuccessful in his attempt, he unworriedly assumed that the toilet had an auto flush function.

After taking a couple of steps, he realized that he had yet to hear the sound of the flush. Turning back to the toilet, he was puzzled to see that the bowl was devoid of the cigarette and water. Flabbergasted, he shook his head, grabbed his camera, and walked out.

He was still shaking his head once he approached Vincenzo behind the front desk in the lobby. "Vincenzo, I need to ask you about the toilet," he said slowly and deliberately, unsure how to formulate his sentence.

"Is it not working, Mr. Cassaro. I can have Fernando take a look at it."

"That's just it; I don't know if it is." Luke rubbed at his temples, not quite sure of what he had witnessed.

"I'm sorry?" Vincenzo's brows were knotted, his professional visage dropping a little.

"I threw something in the toilet bowl, and when I didn't hear a flush, I checked it. I looked in, and there was no cigarette nor water."

"The bottom of the bowl will open and close when it detects something there, so the cigarette is gone; as for the water, the bowl will not fill with water until you sit on the toilet. When you are finished, the toilet will flush automatically," Vincenzo finished his explanation with finesse, although he sensed that Luke had further questions.

So, he anticipated his next question and hence, answered the question that did not yet form properly in Luke's mind.

"During urination, the toilet will detect the fluid increase in the bowl, and it will also automatically flush."

At that, Luke began to laugh.

"Vincenzo, you are amazing. I didn't know you could read minds!" he said, between laughs.

For the first time, Vincenzo laughed along with Luke. "I can't! You're not the first man to wonder about that toilet."

"Vincenzo, you've made my day. Thanks, I'm going for a ride," he said, walking out of the hotel.

He waved to the four men playing cards outside on his way to the car, but he stopped when one of the men waved him over. "Are you Franco's boy?" he asked him in Italian.

"I don't speak Italian very well, not at all, really," he apologized, putting his palms up and spreading his arms.

"Franco Cassaro, you look just like him; you're his son, right?" the man tried again.

Vincenzo, who was now standing in the doorway, came to Luke's rescue.

"He wants to know if your father is Franco Cassaro; you look just like him." Luke turned to face Vincenzo. "Thanks, and yes, yes, he was. He passed a few days ago."

Vincenzo translated to the four men, and in unison, they made the sign of the cross and asked for God to receive his soul.

"Tell him that his father was a true gentleman, and if he allowed us, we would be honored to share a drink in his memory."

Vincenzo translated, and Luke accepted their kind offer.

The conversation continued without Vincenzo, who had disappeared after bringing out the drinks. Although it was lively, without a translator, it was hampered for Luke. After seeing a few hands of scopa, a game he recognized but couldn't remember the rules for, he thanked the men for the drinks and apologized, thus taking his leave.

As he climbed into his car, a profound feeling of pride crashed over his being, and for the first time, unconstrained by anger or doubt, tears fell liberally. He began to long for his father's presence. Unable to see where he was, he stopped several hundred meters away from the hotel and grieved until he finally exhausted himself.

Taking a couple of long deep breaths, he returned to a more stable state.

Not quite back to normal, he took a few shorter normal breaths allowing his heart to settle. He wiped his eyes with the back of his hand, engaging the retractable roof to let in the fresh air as he continued with his earlier goal.

He slowly rounded one of many gently sloping curves that lead out of Corleone proper, and he noticed two older women sitting idly by their front door. Intrigued, he slowed to a stop and exited the car with his camera in hand. Pointing to his camera and then to the women, they thankfully understood his gestures, giving Luca their approval with disinterested nods.

Luke had only taken a few shots before a younger man stepped out of the door.

"Who are you, and why are you bothering my aunts?" the man asked in Italian with an obvious confrontational tone.

"Hi, my name is Luke; I'm a photographer from New York," Luke answered in English, guessing what the man had asked him.

The man shook his head, obviously not understanding English.

"Photographer," Luke said, pointing to his camera. "America," he said, pointing out into the distance. "Luke, Luke Cassaro," he said, pointing to himself.

The transformation was swift. The older women's faces brightened and waved him closer. As he approached them, the young man shrugged his shoulders and went back inside his house.

Moving closer, Luke continued to take pictures of the women, their home, and the surrounding areas until he was only a few feet away from them. He concentrated on the two women, used to the subject matter as it was his preferred genre; he heard the women use his father's name several times. Although he took what he believed to be some keepers, the lack of clear communication hindered his M.O. and thus, the visit was cut short rather swiftly.

Thanking the women for their patience and co-operation, Luke slowly got back into his car and rode off. Checking his rear-view mirror, he saw the older women laughing and clapping. Shaking his head, he shifted a little till he was able to see his face in the mirror, and he smiled at himself as their voices followed after his vehicle.

Franco, Franco.

Continuing his gentle, curving climb, he noticed that the view, earlier lined with old and well-maintained buildings, now revealed some of the most magnificent cliffs and rocky hills he had seen. Indeed, the trees around the New York area were beautiful. In fact, he had often argued that Catskill Park, a 700,000-acre (2,800 km^2) state-protected forest, preserved some of the nation's most splendid trees.

But the trees that he was seeing now were somehow greener, lusher.

Sometime later, lost in this world of understated charm, the image of the mysterious lady in the window filled his thoughts. Slightly upset that she had invaded his thoughts without a formal meeting, he absentmindedly drove to Corleone towards his hotel.

Suddenly, he heard the siren and saw the lights of a police car in his rear-view mirror. Obeying the officer's request, he pulled over and parked in front of the hotel as he had done before.

"Boun giorno, la tua licenza per favore," the officer asked in Italian.

"I'm sorry, officer, but my Italian is not very good. I assume you would like my driver's license?" Luke said, searching for his documents.

"You were speeding," the officer responded in English.

"Was I?"

"You were going 30 km over the speed limit," the officer said, admiring the GT.

Noticing the officer's preoccupation with the car, he tried to chat him up.

"It's a beautiful car. It makes you feel like you're part of the road. I'm sorry; I guess I got carried away."

"I'm sorry as well, Sir," he responded curtly, "It's not a Ferrari, but it is a beautiful car. Unfortunately, you'll also get a beautiful speeding ticket. Your driver's license, please."

Luke handed over his identification while mustering as big a smile as possible. As the officer inspected his license, Luke noticed the beautiful lady from the window of the Corleone Historical Building had just joined them. Pleased that perhaps she would help him out of this jam, he couldn't help but wonder; why was his heart skipping a beat at her sight?

Happily, he greeted her with a broad smile, "Buongiorno!"

His pleasure quickly vanished as the beautiful woman leaned closer to his car and spoke curtly to him in Italian. Although the speed of her speech was too fast for him to understand even a word, her manner, one of confrontation and agitation, was not. Having said her peace to Luke, who could only stare at her with his mouth slightly open, she shook her head and turned to the officer. Saying something in Italian that Luke did not understand, they turned away from him and walked towards the officer's car. Each step she took moving away from him, he felt more alone. Unable to define this feeling, he exited the car wanting to confront her.

Halfway to the police car, Alessandra turned to the officer, and with a slight tug at his arm, she halted his progress.

"This has to stop; you need to do something!" she ordered him in Italian.

The officer looked at Luke's identification, and then all of a sudden, he started walking back to Luke's car. Alessandra waited a few seconds and then caught up with him.

"What now?" she asked in Italian.

The officer looked at her and then looked back at Luke. He then looked back at Alessandra and turned his back on Luke, handing her his driver's license. She had barely enough time to read it before the officer snatched the license back and walked to Luke's car. Alessandra closed her eyes, knowing exactly what was about to happen.

The officer gave Luke his license back with a big smile.

"I apologize, Signor Cassaro. Please have a good day."

The officer was obviously perturbed. He walked back to his car, shaking his head while he passed Alessandra.

"What did you expect me to do?" he asked rhetorically in Italian before getting in his car and driving away.

Not surprised, Alessandra slowly walked up to Luke, who was standing, carefully watching her.

"You people are all the same!" she yelled at him in Italian.

Luke had no idea what she had just chastised him for, but her bitter words, made considerably sweeter by her brilliant aqua blue eyes, hit him square in the middle of his chest. Extending his arms palms up in a sign of incomprehension but secretly wishing she would fall into them, he began to apologize.

"I'm sorry..."

Cutting him off with a wave, she turned and walked towards the Corleone Historical Building, leaving Luke to wonder what had just happened. But there was something else that was intensifying this feeling of incomprehension, something that, as her figure became smaller with each step she took away from him, made his heart a little heavier, a little sadder. He knew he had to get to know her, but the question was how.

Suddenly feeling guilty for these unexpected and unsolicited emotions that this interesting woman had triggered in him, exhaustion took him over. Sluggishly locking the car door with a touch of a weary finger, he walked into the hotel, where he found Vincenzo standing by the entrance.

"Mr. Cassaro, if you would allow me, I would be happy to park your car in our lot at the back of our hotel. Just let me know when you need it again, and I will bring it around for you." Noticing that Luke was still a little frazzled from his encounter with the officer and Alessandra, he explained further. "It's just that you've parked in a no-parking zone. I wouldn't want you to get inadvertently ticketed."

"Is that what that young lady was upset about?" Luke asked.

"Partially," Vincenzo agreed, raising his shoulders.

"What do you mean partially? What else is she disturbed about, and who is she?"

"That would have been Alessandra; she doesn't miss much and lets you know it. Perhaps it would be best if you asked her, Mr. Cassaro. She runs the B&B and the historical society building."

"I think I'll do that, but right now, I think I need to rest a little," he said, handing his car keys to Vincenzo.

Exhausted, he barely had enough energy to enter his room, flopped on the bed, and slept through the night.

CHAPTER FOURTEEN
Beautiful Narrow Streets

Not only had he slept through the night, but he saw that he had slept longer than usual after checking the clock. Now that so much time had passed, he was unsure if he should get ready and go for breakfast in town or have something to eat in the hotel. After fighting a battle within his own mind, his ultimatum was to call the front desk.

"Hi, Vincenzo?" his voice was groggy, albeit polite; he was careful not to offend the hotel staff with his morning mood.

"Yes, good morning Mr. Cassaro. How can I help you?" the man answered, his voice awfully vivacious for his ears.

"I think I'd like to explore your town this morning. Can you recommend a place where I can get some breakfast nearby?" As he asked this question, he reached out to his bedside table, rummaging in the drawers to find his little notebook.

"There are many café shops within walking distance; I'm sure that any of them would be pleased to serve you. But try Filomena; the grandmother still makes the best cannoli in town; it's just two streets down from us." Luke silently hummed, writing down the recommendation onto a notepad beautifully embossed with the hotel's logo.

"Great, thanks. I'll see you later today." After bidding each other adieu, Luke placed the phone back into its place and decided that he change for the day. So, he started his day with a cold shower that effectively woke him up from the effects of slumber, and then he shaved, making sure that he looked presentable and fresh for the streets of the beautiful city.

As Luke headed for the exit of the hotel, he realized that Vincenzo had not told him which way he must go. All he knew was that Filomena was within walking distance. Vincenzo's answer was sufficing, but for a tourist like him, he wasn't sure how much walking he had to do to reach Filomena. So, to get to the bottom of the specificities of 'walking distance, he turned to the front desk, but he noticed that the front desk was unattended, and when he couldn't see anybody nearby, he walked out of the hotel. Uncertain but hopeful for his journey to the café.

Looking to his right, he noticed the Corleone Historical Building. Suddenly a flurry of memories crashed against his reverie, causing him to turn his eyes away from the building, not ready to relive yesterday's confrontation with the pretty Italian lady that worked there. In finality, he chose to walk towards the left, and within a few hundred meters, Luke had already taken more than fifty shots of buildings and people with his camera.

Before crossing the street, he looked past the glittering tar and decided to take a quick shot of the scene. The street, a series of steep and gentle declines, appeared to stretch towards the end of town. No more than 10 feet across, with concrete stairs, dug out in the middle and worn-out cobblestones on either side, this narrow, colorful street with houses painted pink, orange, and tan made an interesting shot once he aligned the scene into his frame. In comparison, his home lacked the charm and nostalgia this city offered. *"Why was it,"* he wondered, *"that a town that could produce this subtle yet exquisite beauty was only famous for notorious reasons."* Not for the first time since landing in this country, he felt a conflict within his conscience. Shaking this fleeting though, he

continued to take shots of the area until his attention was attracted by a man smoking on his balcony. At that moment, the street was too narrow for vehicular traffic, so he peacefully positioned himself about three-quarters of the way down the steepest part of the road. During the attempt to balance himself with his camera, a sudden sound of a car horn interrupted his concentration. The sound was so shrill that he jumped, making his heart skip several beats from fear. Turning towards the startling sound, he had just enough time to look up the street and spot a car barreling down towards him, and he jumped out of the way with only seconds to spare. The young girl, who was driving the car, yelled something at him in Italian. However, he did not understand the curse but spotting the international sign of 'fuck-you' on her middle finger, he understood that the girl was not happy with his adventurous behavior.

Meanwhile, the man on the balcony was laughing so hard that he began to cough. His guffaw continued to shift from coughs to chortles till he could no longer breathe correctly. In the middle, he was forced to call for help from his house, and within the blink of an eye, a woman hurriedly appeared from the house. Luke clearly saw that the woman was worried; she said something to him and started to lightly slap the back of the man, holding his buckled form in her arms. With little effect, she palmed his back so hard that he was forced to defend himself from her panicked state in fear for his life.

Laughing at the comical albeit worrying spectacle, he observed the pair's windmilling arms and rapid exchange of words that he could not understand, but he could tell that both of them were panicking through its tone. But before Luke could be run over by another car, he decided to use the walkway as a throughway. During the journey, he was astonished to see that the tiny street could accommodate any vehicle, excluding the respect for the drivers' skills who could keep the car on the cobblestones while maneuvering through the concrete stairs. With this stray thought in mind, he quickly jogged to the next street and made a quick right, only to find himself in a narrower laneway. He observed that it could never accommodate a car, so he finally took a moment to rest, allowing his heartbeat to calm down before he moved on.

Then he remembered that motorcycles existed, especially Vespas, so, in a panic, his mind willed him to move from the area- *Vespa*!

Quickly looking up and down the laneway, he raced to the top with broken breaths.

Reaching the top of the laneway, Luke was completely out of breath. Groaning, he stretched his back and looked up to the sky only to spot the Corleone Historical Building. The building was directly in front of him, and much to his surprise, Filomena was next to him on the left. This revelation motivated him enough to recover from the fatigue quickly, but as he walked to the café, his thoughts drifted back to Alessandra and her intoxicating reprimand.

Instantly losing his appetite and gaining a pang of serendipity, his goal for the day changed.

Instead of visiting the café, he entered the historical building, determined to confront the beautiful but slightly impolite woman. Observant eyes would quickly scan the room, but there was no impolite woman to be found, so he decided to walk around the main floor, hoping to find her soon.

The first area he found himself in was the small library, where, surprisingly, there were more books stacked on the shelves than Luke had predicted. Checking several of the books, he noticed that there were no books of fiction, romance, or fantasy available; the selection was saturated with history books surrounding Sicily and Corleone. These books were arranged through centuries, starting from the early hundreds to the 21st century; Luke could have bet that this extensive encyclopedia of the island's history would satisfy even the most discriminating historians. Maybe he would ask the librarian about the number of books in the library; he was genuinely curious as he carried on his slow search for the woman.

As he walked toward the museum section, he heard a voice that sounded uncannily familiar, like his target's. Peeking about the shelves like a meercat, he confirmed that the voice belonged to the woman he looked high and low for. Surprisingly, she was speaking in English rather fluently as she explained something to a young girl regarding a picture of a Sicilian town hanging on the wall near them. Deciding that it was best not to interrupt, he spent his time wandering around observing some strategically placed artifacts in showcases amongst the rows of books and paintings.

His eyes were particularly enchanted by a small figure of the Egyptian God Anubis accompanied by an equally small cartouche, which according to the description, dates to the fourth millennium B.C. Upon reading that, he began to recalculate the estimates of the books along with the artifacts, so, as he moved on to new memorabilia, his mind instantly updated and rearranged the age of the various artifacts. Soon he found himself staring at a poster named; 'Mafia, Fact or Fiction,' and the section offered several posters of the wedding scene from the movie

'The Godfather.' Next to these were the photographs of real weddings taking place in Corleone in the early seventies. Luke was going to read the description of the weddings when he was startled by a voice behind him.

"Looking for relatives?"

"Pardon?" he said, swiftly whipping his head to her. "Sorry, Alessandra, right? I inquired about you at the hotel. I hope you don't mind. May I call you Alessandra?"

Luke couldn't control his tongue; despite his nervousness, he continued to speak without waiting for her answer, and he knew that he was going to feel so guilty for his behavior. "I'm the guy that was stopped by the police officer yesterday. Do you speak English?"

"I know you heard me speaking with that little girl. Do you think I was speaking French to her?" Her response was rather curt and sarcastic, but before he could utter an apology, she turned from him, forcing him to follow after.

"Yes, of course," he responded softly, following her. "It was a silly question; I apologize. I'm also sorry for parking in the wrong place; I didn't realize at the time that the parking was at the back of the hotel. The police officer was exceedingly kind to me."

"I'm sure he was," she quipped whilst walking to her desk without facing him.

Luke followed her for a few steps, then stopped to pick up a brochure from under his shoe. He observed the writing without much interest and walked to her desk, where he placed the leaflet next to her office supplies.

"I guess you're sick of tourists like me parking in the wrong place?"

Alessandra rolled her eyes and nodded her head, hoping that the action would be enough to shoo Luke away.

"Yes, I'm sure that's the problem," her words stretched on, dripping with sarcasm and disinterest for Luke's apology.

Meanwhile, Luke was genuinely unsure about her determination to avoid him. He didn't know where this rudeness was coming from, especially when it contradicted her usual pleasant countenance.

Finally throwing his etiquette out of the window, he pushed aside his attraction towards her to go on the offensive by forwardly asking her, "Have I offended you in any way?"

Alessandra looked at him but stayed quiet.

"Look, I'm sorry I parked in the wrong spot, but you don't need to be rude to me! I came here because I'm interested in learning about the history of Corleone," he lied, his gaze on her intense, as he continued carefully, "Actually, that is only half right; I came to Corleone to bury my father's ashes, I came here to your office to learn about its history, something my father probably had in mind all along for a proper burial. In any case, Vincenzo, the hotel manager, tells me that you are the one to see for such matters. But perhaps he was wrong."

Luke finally finished and turned away from her steely gaze; perhaps he would never be tired of that look she gave him. Though it was filled with negativity, he liked the fire behind them. Luke realized that Alessandra was feeling a little uneasy about her behavior by looking at her downturn look. He had seen her interact with many people so far, and she was never rude or uncaring; she usually went out of her way to make people feel comfortable; perhaps that was why her walls were crumbling upon his confession.

She shook her head and inwardly chastised herself; he could see it in her eyes once she looked up at him from her desk.

"Firstly," she began, causing Luke to blink and give her his undivided attention. "I'm being indifferent towards you; if you've interpreted that as rude, I apologize. Secondly, this is a terribly busy time of the year for us, so I don't know if I can help you."

Choosing not to address her rude behavior, he smiled at her. "Is it always this busy?"

"In the summer," she replied to him honestly, all the while returning his smile. "Our population is normally about 12,000 people. But in the summer, the population can double or even triple."

"Just from the tourists?"

"Yes."

"They come here because of the Godfather?"

"You're brighter than you look!" Alessandra's face lit up. Luke finally became a recipient of her kind nature.

"Well, thank you very much, Alessandra, and you're much more pleasant than I first expected."

The two smiled, their gazes locked for an uncomfortable amount of time, causing their silence to thicken. Alessandra began to feel slightly uncomfortable at this foreigner's strange effect on her; she didn't know how to continue the conversation, so she just looked away and fiddled with some paperwork on her desk.

Meanwhile, Luke cleared his throat, taking the opportunity to continue the conversation but on a different route, "I'm only here for three nights. I would appreciate it if you would show me around. I would pay you, of course."

"I'm sorry, but the tour is full, Luke," Alessandra said without looking back at his flabbergasted expression.

"You know my name?"

"Vincenzo told me about you."

"It seems that Vincenzo is the local press." Luke chuckled at the thought; it seemed that there was much more to that hotel clerk than he let on.

"There are plenty of tour guides around here. You could hire one of them; I can recommend a few." From her answer, he could tell that she was attempting to heal the broken bridge, but at the same time, she didn't want to yield to his words; it was her way of rebelling.

"That's very kind, but I think I would prefer your company," he said, smiling at her.

She gave him a perplexed look forcing him to backtrack. "I didn't mean it the way it sounded. According to Vincenzo, the reporter, you're the best, and I don't mind working according to your schedule. Plus, I owe it to my father," he said, hoping that mentioning his father again would extend the conversation.

"What does your father have to do with it?"

"It's his ashes; he wanted me to bury them here," he responded, thankful that his hopes were answered as she immediately retorted back. "Yes, you did mention that. Why here?"

"I think he loved this place. But he never told me. He just gave me an old coin purse that belonged to my mother's father and told me to follow the directions on this piece of paper. I guess it's because our family is from here. My father and mother were born here."

Once again, Alessandra's feeling of uncertainty about this man tried to take over, but she suppressed it by asking him a follow-up question rather candidly. "He never told you why?"

"He wanted to, in fact, we were going to discuss it at our next family lunch, but he died the day after he gave me the coin purse. He didn't have a chance to tell us."

Before confronting him with other questions, she scrutinized him. Standing only a few feet away from her, she has to admit that he was much more handsome than she initially thought. His tall, sturdy-looking frame interested her but what attracted her were his hazel eyes. Bright and intelligent, they seemed to emanate a gentle yet mysterious look that she sure had a challenging time holding.

"And that's the only reason you're here?" she asked him, hoping that he would shatter her suspicions.

This time it was his turn to look perplexed, and his answer reflected that sentiment. "That's a strange question. But yes, that's why I'm here."

Alessandra stood up and walked over to some shelves with various brochures.

"I'm sorry about your father," she said with her back to him, then looked directly into his eyes.

"Be here after lunch; you can join the afternoon group to which I'll be giving a tour." She quickly left to join another group of tourists; they were waiting at the far end of the museum.

Luke stood there for a few seconds and mused to himself with a smile.

"Thank You. Was that an order?"

CHAPTER FIFTEEN
At this Time of the Day

(Day Two)

Happy with the results of his interaction with Alessandra, Luke exited the Historical Building and enjoyed the pleasant warmth of the sun's beam on his face. As his eyes readjusted to the new environment, he saw a priest walking up the street, greeting people as he went along his path. The priest was undoubtedly a social butterfly; whenever he would see someone, he would acknowledge them with a simple nod or a lengthy and animated shake of the hand; the priest couldn't go more than ten paces without stopping.

At this rate, Luke estimated that it would take the priest the better part of an hour to reach his destination. After watching this for a few more seconds, he lost interest in the accommodating priest, so he finally succumbed to his craving for coffee, and knowing that they might offer him some, he decided to head there. Luke looked towards the hotel, where he spotted Vincenzo waiving at him.

"Hi Vincenzo," the man greeted him once Luke was close enough to the hotel.

"Hello, Mr. Cassaro. Did you find Filomena's?"

"No," he answered quickly, but then he thought about it and added, "Actually, I did, but I lost my appetite and went into the Corleone Historical Building."

"Lost your appetite?" For some reason, Vincenzo burst out laughing at Luke's escapade down the narrow street. Between chortles, he apologized for his outburst. Still, the ever-so cautious Vincenzo fired a question on Luke regarding the unusual driving habits of the Corleonesi and if he had met Alessandra.

"I did, and I think she finally came around. She invited me to join the afternoon tour," he said with a little too much enthusiasm.

"Very good. Is there something I can do for you now Mr. Cassaro?" Vincenzo spoke to him courteously, his mannerisms finally returning to a more professional state.

"Yes. First, please call me Luke, and second, I think I need a coffee."

"Certainly, I will bring it right out. Fortunately, I still have some of Filomena's cannoli. Should I bring you one?"

"Sure, thanks."

"Please, have a seat on our patio." Vincenzo directed Luke to the area where he looked around and headed for the first empty seat next to the railing. Before he could settle down, he called out to Vincenzo.

"Vincenzo, please, just chocolate and no cinnamon, thanks," he told him, finally settling down into his seat

Vincenzo abruptly stopped and turned, his eyebrows furrowing in confusion, "Sorry?"

"No cinnamon sprinkle on my cappuccino, just chocolate, please."

Vincenzo took note of the patio's status. It was filled with the hustle and bustle of visitors, so he had to walk close to Luke, whispering the question circling around in his mind.

"But it's almost noon." Vincenzo looked at Luke with a questioning look; he stood close by his side.

"Yes, I know," Luke said, a little confused.

"So, you'll want an espresso, no?" slowly he replied, still not aware of Luke's growing impatience.

"No!" Luke finally retorted, to which Vincenzo had back away, his professional façade overtaking the once-friendly face.

"I'm sorry Mr. Cassaro," Vincenzo apologized, visibly shaken by Luke's forceful response. "I apologize for my impertinence. Of course, a cappuccino it is," he finished, holding up a hand.

Feeling guilty, he was quick to apologize, "That's okay, Vincenzo. I didn't mean to be that abrupt. Is there something wrong with a cappuccino?" Still, he couldn't shake the questions he received from Vincenzo over a cup of coffee.

"No, a cappuccino it is," Vincenzo responded quickly and politely, but Luke knew he was withholding some information.

"Vincenzo?" Luke flashed him a knowing look before continuing, "You're not being completely honest with me. Please tell me what's going on?"

"I'm sorry Mr. Cassaro; I didn't mean anything by it. It's just that I didn't think you were a regular tourist. But that's fine, a cappuccino it is," Vincenzo said, turning away, but Luke caught him; he was now curious about Vincenzo's little insistence.

"Hold on, Vincenzo, now you got me curious. Please explain your insistence to me, and please call me Luke," he said with a big smile.

Resigned to having to explain himself, Vincenzo took a deep breath and began. "In Italy, cappuccinos are taken in the mornings for breakfast and perhaps late at night by old people and children. Espressos are for the rest of the day," he finished with a serious look.

At this revelation, Luke broke out into a hearty laugh, immediately apologizing to the man, "I'm sorry, Vincenzo, I have to tell you, and please don't take this the wrong way." Luke relaxed and looked to the sky. Behind the umbrella, he could see the blue skies of Sicily. "I think I'm starting to appreciate this Sicilian culture, but the people here are strange, in a good way, but strange nonetheless. Yesterday, I broke the rules by parking in the wrong place. The looks from passersby were less concerning than the look you had when I ordered the cappuccino."

Vincenzo appreciating the moment of honesty, laughed alongside Luke, "Yesterday, you broke the rule of law. Today you are breaking the rules of our culture! I'll bring you your cappuccino."

"Not on your life. An espresso it is," he said, extremely proud of himself, but Vincenzo shook his head.

"You don't have to say espresso; it's almost noon."

The two laughed happily when the priest arrived at the hotel's patio café, moving towards Vincenzo once he caught him in the distance "Boun giorno, Vincenzo. You're happy this morning," the priest said and saluted him.

"Ah, boun giorno, Padre Mario. This is Luke Cassaro. He's here visiting from America." Vincenzo stood aside as his hand subtly introduced the priest Mario to Luke.

"Yes, yes, buon giorno Luca." The priest regarded Luke with kindness, to which Luke couldn't help but stand in respect.

"Boun giorno, Father." The two shook hands before the soft-spoken priest continued, inviting the tourist to the Church.

"You must come and visit my church," the priest said in English, shaking Luke's hand.

"Yes, of course. I'm only here for two more days, but," Luke continued with a hopeful smile, "I will if I find the time, father."

"You must always make the time for our Lord, my son."

Duly reprimanded, he answered as if he were a child caught in the act of doing a bad deed. "Yes, of course, Father. I definitely will but will you join me for coffee, Father?" he asked, smiling at Vincenzo.

"Thank you, I think I will," he accepted, taking a seat next to Luke.

Following Vincenzo's silent departure, the two were left to their own devices, to which Don Mario addressed the passing of Luke's father.

"Luke, I wanted to offer my condolences on your father's passing; may his soul rest in peace," he added in tandem with respecting the Holy Trinity before praying for his soul.

"How do you know that?" Luke asked, his brows furrowed from confusion before remembering his manners in front of the sage priest. "Thank you."

"News travels fast here, Luke. Sad news travels faster, much faster, and I found out from my sister. Your mother talks to her occasionally. So how did it happen, exactly, some kind of vehicle accident?"

Before he could respond, Don Mario, who was looking over Luke's shoulder, called out to a familiar name, "Alessandra, please come, come, I need to speak with you," he spoke to her in Italian waving her over to their table.

"I don't have time right now, Don Mario. I'm preparing for the tour," the woman responded from the other side of the street, clearly manifesting her impatience by the sound of her exclamation.

"But it's almost midday; your tour doesn't start until three!" the priest answered softly, his hands resting on his abdomen, signifying his patience with the lady.

"Not that I need to explain myself, but I'm going home; I need to eat something and then prepare for the tour," she continued to speak as she covered the distance between them until her eyes fell upon Luke.

"Yes, yes, this will only take a few seconds, please." The priest was blind to the two's gaze, for he only sat back on his chair in satisfaction.

Luke, still not fully aware of the context behind the conversation, could piece it together by studying Alessandra's body language. Clearly, she compromised on something, thus being strung by the priest's request.

Just as Alessandra had stood beside the table, Vincenzo had arrived with the coffees. The two were quick to greet each other in Italian; the energy in their movements was contagious.

"Ciao Vin," Alessandra said, kissing his cheek.

"Ciao Ales," he responded, putting the coffees and cannoli on the table.

"Are you a waiter too, now?" she said in Italian, looking at him sideways.

"Marco is not here yet."

"Mom wants to know if you'll be home for dinner," she asked him.

"No, going to eat at Luciana's house."

Alessandra nodded her head and then turned to Don Mario, finally acknowledging the man who called her over in the first place.

"What did you need?" she asked the priest rather impatiently.

The conversation, which took place, was in Italian, so Luke was barred from it entirely. He could barely understand every third or fourth word; regardless, he noticed that there was something between Vincenzo and Alessandra. He couldn't accurately point out the nature of their relationship, but it did not feel like a 'boyfriend-girlfriend' type of relationship.

Although so many thoughts preoccupied him, he thought to make another mental note to ask Vincenzo about the two once they were alone. But for now, he decided to concentrate on the discussion between the priest and the historian, albeit his attention was solely on the historian.

"Alessandra, there's talk that you are going to try and restore the Arab Mill. I don't think that would be a good idea." Don Mario's voice was raised to the point that caused several guests to look up from their tables along with Luke, and he didn't expect the priest to have such vocal cords on him.

Then Alessandra didn't hesitate to match his gusto, replying to him without restraint, "Why not? That's a historical site. Are we not responsible for protecting history, as you do daily, Don Mario?" The historian seemed appalled at the connotations of the elderly priest, but he didn't back down. His brows furrowed as the man continued in a calm manner, "The Church protects our Lord Jesus Christ's holy life, Alessandra, not the life of an occupying nation."

"Occupying nations? Don Mario, the entire world is a museum of occupying nations. From the Pyramids to the Coliseum, do we not protect history? All I want to do is restore part of our history, our Sicilian past," Alessandra attempted to inspire the priest, hoping that her words would reach out to him, but the old man was stubborn.

"Then work on Christian monuments, not the ruins of an infidel's mill." His voice was sharp and his words venomous at the mention of the outsiders, but Alessandra was quick to put his rising demons to rest with her quick-witted reply, "Don Mario, please stick to saving souls. Leave the saving of history to the people that want to preserve our heritage."

"Alessandra!" he said, raising his voice, "That's sacrilege. And I'll tell you, I'm not the only one that thinks this will never happen."

"Really, who else thinks that it will never happen? The other criminal organization around here?" she accused, staring at Luke as the words had left her lips, "I need to go." She didn't waste her time taking her leave. She turned on her heels and clacked away.

Don Mario stood and turned to Vincenzo.

"Tell your sister that she can't fight everyone in this town." He did not wait for a response but turned back to Luke, his eyes communicating an emotion that he couldn't quite decipher.

"There's no saving that soul. Jesus, forgive me," the Don whispered his final words in English in tandem with crossing himself with his shaking finger. Afterward, the two finished their meal in peace; Luke finished his cannolo with clear delight, and Don Mario drained his espresso before standing up to offer Luke his hand.

"I hope to see you soon, Luca," he bade adieu and walked away.

By the reaction of the people that had a front-row seat for the drama, divisions were already being made as some of the people were shaking the priest's hand while others were looking away, shaking their heads at the sight of him.

Once the Priest was out of sight, Vincenzo was at their table, gracing Luke with a polite smile.

"Will there be anything else, Mr. Cassaro?"

Before he could ask Vincenzo about the previous squabble, he became aware of his rumbling stomach, so he turned to the waiting man with stars in his eyes, "I thought that the espresso and cannolo would hold me over to dinner, but I think it just gave me an appetite. I need something else."

"Okay, Italian or American lunch?"

"Are you kidding me?" Luke said, flabbergasted. He felt like an idiot. Surely, there was a difference between the two, but he was afraid to even utter that question in front of the kind waiter. "There's a difference, of course. Please explain."

"Certainly," Vincenzo said. Putting both his hands behind his back, he walked to the other side of the table, where he took a professorial stance before continuing his explanation, "The Italian lunch is usually the largest and longest meal of the day. It will start..."

"You're enjoying this, aren't you?" Luke interrupted him with a sarcastic laugh but was quickly stopped by the raised index finger of the serious man.

"It will start," Vincenzo continued, his sharp eyes piercing as he continued without addressing Luke's jab, "With a light antipasto, followed by a pasta or rice dish, then 'il secondo,' the main, can be a meat dish of veal, pork, beef or chicken, fish on Fridays of course, and lamb on special occasions, with sides of rapini or other greens, a light gelato, usually lemon for a palate-cleansing, followed by a coffee, espresso of course with a 'biscottino', a little cookie."

"Jesus, Vincenzo, I'm stuffed just listening to you." Luke's mouth began to salivate upon hearing Vincenzo's explanation, but he wasn't in the mood for a Kingly feast, and thankfully, Vincenzo had read his mind.

"A veal sandwich it is then," Vincenzo said, spreading his arms.

"After all, I am American!" Luke responded, spreading his own arms in the air.

"I'm not sure about that, Mr. Cassaro. But then, you've only been here a day!"

Behind Vincenzo's retreating form, his short but honest laugh ringing in the air convinced Luke that if not for his short stay, they would have become very good friends.

Alas, when the sandwich arrived, it was Marco that delivered it. Perhaps Vincenzo had something else to do, but it was okay. It gave Luke the opportunity to strike up a conversation with the other man.

"Your veal sandwich, Mr. Cassaro," Marco said rather professionally, letting his plate down in front of Luke, who took the opportunity to strike.

"Hi, you must be Marco," Luke stated in a friendly tone, much to the other man's unease.

"Yes, sir, you know my name?" Marco asked in a wary tone, to which it went deaf on Luke's ears.

"I think I heard Vincenzo mention that you were late. Did Vincenzo leave?"

"Oh, no, he is still here. Would you like me to call him for you?"

"No, that's fine," Luke said whilst taking his first bite of the sandwich, but as he chewed, he mulled over the information and then continued after gulping down his bite, "On second thought, would you please?"

Marco obliged his request, walking into the hotel to call for his superior, who soon emerged with a smile.

"Nice sandwich!" Luke yelled to Vincenzo as he took another bite.

"Thank you?" Vincenzo said with his tone rising, sounding uncertain as he came to a stop near Luke.

"No, no," Luke said, immediately recognizing Vincenzo's doubt. "I mean, the sandwich is great, but I wanted to ask you about that conversation between Alessandra and Don Mario. What was it all about?"

Vincenzo smiled and happily explained to Luke the context and the spirit of the heated confrontation before laying to rest the biggest problem in Luke's head. "And yes, Alessandra is my sister."

The smile between bites was not lost on Vincenzo, but he elected to ignore it.

"Mr. Cassaro, I'm sure you'll get more information about the mill from Alessandra during the tour. But you better not be late; she will not wait for you to start the tour."

"Thanks, Vincenzo," he said, eyeing the remaining half of his sandwich. "But please call me Luke!" he yelled after Vincenzo's retreating form.

Back in his room, with his hunger satisfied and time to spare before the tour, Luke decided that a shower was in order before anything else. Besides, he was excited to use the bathroom again. He quickly undressed and stepped down into the depression. Once he found his footing, he turns on the shower, ready to relive the marvelous experience in peace.

Extremely relaxed after his shower, he lay on the bed, intending to take a few minutes to reflect on the morning activities. Alas, in the middle of his musings, sleep took him over.

Once he awoke, he sat up in shock, his panicked body stumbling to check the time. With only minutes to spare, he hastily dressed, grabbed his camera, and rushed out of his room.

CHAPTER SIXTEEN
A Stranger in the Room

Entering the room without hesitation or trepidation, the man in black took a cursory scan of the suite before closing the door behind him. He took quick notice of a towel haphazardly left on the bed, which he picked up, folded it into a neat square, and rested it on a nearby chair; he inspected it a couple more times before he was finally satisfied with it.

Without turning his body, his eyes scoured the apartment before falling on a grouping of camera bags to his right. He slowly approached the bag noticing that it was zipped open; standing motionless for a couple of seconds, he took a deep breath and knelt over. He used his index finger to enlarge the opening, peeking inside it; a satisfied smile stretched across his features within seconds. Standing up straight, he turned and moved on towards his next target; picking up the pack of cigarettes, he smelled them and gently placed them in their original place of rest.

As he turned to face the closet doors, his true goal, he heard the front door opening and instinctively reached into his jacket's inner pocket to retrieve one of the most used tools of his trade. Extending his other hand towards the new arrival, he nodded his head and invited his accomplice to cross the apartment's threshold.

Cautiously walking up to the man in black without looking him in the eye, the much smaller man handed the other a small object; once his task was done, his nervous hand blindly accepted the envelope. Quickly stuffing his reward in his pocket, he silently exited the room.

Left alone, the man in black decided that it was high time to continue his plan. Placing his hands on both knobs of the closet doors, he pulled them open to reveal the objective; a safe tucked away into the safety of the closet. Using the newly obtained cloned fob, he opened the safe where his prize sat, waiting for his thick, long fingers to free it from its airless prison. With profound respect and measured strength not expected from a brute like him, he clutched the neck of the urn and slowly lifted it out of its confinement.

Ignoring the box that this prize used to travel this great distance, the man produced a large black velvet bag with drawstrings; he slipped the object within the bag, swaddling it perfectly. Putting the strings around his massive shoulders, the bag melted into his visage, camouflaging it with his black suit.

Boldly walking behind the front desk, he stood with the employee, confirmed the deletions of the past fifteen minutes of the video recordings, and walked out of the hotel's front doors.

Satisfied with the completion of part one of his assignment, he confidently transitioned to the next.

CHAPTER SEVENTEEN
A Tour

Alessandra was leading the afternoon group of tourists along the countryside, explaining the region's history to them. As they walked away from the little church in the San Giuliano district, she mentioned how its Patron Saint was the Madonna of the two Fortresses. Luke saw the group from afar and managed to wriggle his way next to Alessandra, pushing and brushing shoulders with his now angered fellow tourists.

"I can't believe the beautiful things I'm seeing here; I've taken more than 100 pictures, and I'm afraid I've missed many more." Luke was in awe; he was attempting to hide that he had napped after his shower, but he couldn't tell the stern lady that.

"Yes, you did, in the first ten minutes." Her response was candid, reprimanding him for his tardiness.

"I'm sorry I was late," Luke apologized sincerely, bowing in front of the lady to exaggerate his emotions, only for them to fall on her cold shoulders. The historian turned to face the buzzing crowd and continued to guide them with a bright smile, "Come this way, everyone, and be amazed at the next sight. Follow the path around the mulberry tree!" she announced to the group, ignoring his apology and directing the group by pointing to a tree about 50 yards away.

Afraid of being scolded again, he was the first to obey Alessandra's directions, taking the narrow walkway around the dancing mulberry tree, following the curve that gently slithered to his right.

Luke was impressed that this well-used interlocking brick path was not in need of any repairs, and in fact, it seemed to be out of place with the rough and deteriorating laneways that he had noticed earlier. *"Perhaps the historical society has something to do with this. I'll have to ask her later,"* Luke thought to himself as he continued down the path to the Mulberry tree; the closer he got to it, the more underwhelming it appeared, but he trusted Alessandra's belief and therefore followed her directions without question.

The ordinary view of bricks and stone was soon replaced by the most spectacular view he had ever seen. He had stopped in the middle of the trek, paralyzed by its marvel, causing a group of grumbling visitors to accumulate behind him.

"Le Cascate Delle Due Rocche," Alessandra announced with her arms raised, ushering the group to hurry their steps, "Move on, please."

Upon seeing Luke's frozen state, she walked to him and whispered in his ear. Her voice was forceful, albeit soft.

Alessandra's pleasant voice, the physical proximity, and vailed fresh scent sent a shiver down his spine, and for that moment, time had stood still. Stunned at the beauty of the land and the woman, he remained standing on his spot, stunned and awestruck by the overwhelming electricity of his emotions.

Seconds, minutes, perhaps even hours had gone by, and he had no idea where he was or why he was standing there, but he could care less, for the two natural wonders had stolen his breath away.

"All around the glauconitic rocks, you'll notice the rock vegetation. Look closer at the walls," she commanded, causing the man's consciousness to return to the present.

"You may notice the remains of an ancient aqueduct. The steam you see, caused by the cold water and the warm earth, is the catalyst to the sun's ability to generate these amazing rainbows that are characteristic to this sight."

Luke stared with his mouth agape. Noticing this unbridled and genuine look, Alessandra momentarily allowed her guard to drop, and as she passed by Luke, she closed his mouth with her index finger.

Awaken from his trance, Luke suddenly felt confused and questioned what really had affected him. Not wanting to face that question just yet, he raised his camera and began to shoot at the scene to his heart's content.

Maneuvering his way around the group, he politely shot a series of photographs of the magnificent waterfalls. Still, he was not shy of launching soft elbow jabs to get the perfect shot, and during this session, he managed to place Alessandra in the frame, taking a shot of her with the rainbow as her halo and the waterfall accentuating her beauty in the background.

"That's beautiful...." he said to himself, not realizing how loud his volume was; he mistakenly invited the group's attention onto him.

Alessandra saved him some embarrassment by attracting the group's attention.

"Yes, it most certainly is beautiful and inviting. Unfortunately, we cannot swim in the water. People have been polluting this pool for many years, and today it is forbidden to enter the water only to be given a heavy fine otherwise. But...," she continued whilst raising her finger, "...you can get as close as you want, without getting wet, and take as many pictures as you want," she finished the sentence by sending Luke a knowing gaze. She knew how much he loved taking pictures. The glimmer in his eyes turned brighter as he could see what she couldn't, the silent whispers of art forming out of the fountain. Its glaze branching into hues of blue with a tint of white. The shining dark waterbed, just waiting for him to lie near the fountain end and just above its belly, click pictures of its arms touching the sky and falling over fascinated onlookers.

As the rest of the group scrambled, Luke continued to take pictures until he spotted Alessandra approaching. Stopping a little too close, she confronted him.

"Did you take a photo of me?"

"Me? No!"

"Are you sure?" she asked again, holding his gaze with her own steely eyes.

Luke took a step back and fixed his shirt in nervousness; he gulped and continued, attempting to hide his stammer from her.

"I mean, yes..."

"Yes, no, what?" she asked, pressing her advantage on the nervous man.

"I mean, yes, I'm sure I did not take your picture," he lied, trying to hold her gaze.

Failing miserably, he lifted his camera to his face and turned to take a shot of the waterfall. Winning the stare-off, Alessandra smiled, knowing that his eyes would never deceive her. Deciding that she had her fun with him, she left him standing alone, to which Luke slowly turned to find himself well behind the slow-moving group. Luke wasn't particularly worried since the group was moving slow enough for Luke to catch up later. He would run after the group during the trip, take a break, take more pictures, and then repeat!

Reaching a clearing filled with what can only be described as rubble, Alessandra waited for the group to gather closer before she began.

"Here we find, 'Il Mulino Arabo' the Old Arab Mill," she said, facing the ruins whilst continuing her discussion. "I know, it does not look like much, only a lot of stones and debris, but there..." she pointed to her right, "...you can see part of the original left side of one of the mill's walls." She stopped and stood in quiet reflection for a while.

Luke continued to take pictures, mostly of the scattered remains, but often made sure that Alessandra was in the frame. Not surprised that she became the focus of his attention throughout the trip, he lowered his camera and looked at Alessandra in real-time. His fascination with this woman was real; her quiet confidence and sublime beauty had pulled him in when his eyes first lay on her, and the realization was making him feel a little uncomfortable.

Aware of his gazing, Alessandra was shaken from her inner thoughts.

"Sicilians will joke that we are not Italian, we are Sicilian, and there's some truth in that statement. You may not know that Italy is more than 100 years younger than the United States as a country. Yet, in all of Italy's different regions, you will find cultures and architecture that are more than 1000 years old; the most obvious and probably the most known is the Colosseum in Rome, built-in 80 AD, it is almost 2000 years old. Sicily?" Purposely stopping to gauge the group's interest, she smiled, examining their faces. Happily, most of them are looking back with anticipation; that was one of the most important aspects of the tour to Alessandra, as this was where she revealed the real Sicily. As she continued to scan the group, her eyes landed on Luke, whose look perplexed her. There was interest there, but there was more, so much more that she momentarily lost her concentration.

Hearing the clicking of Luke's camera, she regained her focus and continued with her commentary.

"Sicily? Sicily, a name that derives from ancient tribes known as Elymians, Sicani, and Siculi or Sicels, has a unique history in Italy."

"For centuries, the location being the major reason, we have accumulated traditions and cultures gathered from many occupying civilizations and made them our own. In Sicilian architecture, you can see Norman Cathedrals, Greek Theatres, Baroque churches, Arab monuments, and Mill," she said, pointing to the ruins again. "Some traditional Byzantine religious practices and Turkish traditions continue to this day. Many years of foreign occupations and conquests have influenced even our language. In contrast, the Italian language is almost entirely based on Latin. Sicilian has Greek, Spanish, French, Catalan, and Arabic components."

She moved closer to the well, causing the spectators to follow suit diligently. "You could say Sicilians are protectors of their own unique way of life that was assimilated from a blend of rich, distinctive, and rare cultures."

Alessandra moved a few steps ahead of the group, climbed a portion of the wall, and turned to face them.

"On a personal note. Since my childhood, when we played amongst these ruins, I have felt an intense sense of responsibility to restore this mill. As a child, I fell asleep wondering what this mill meant to the people of that time. Now, its restoration consumes much of my waking thoughts. We are far from restoring the Mill to its original state, but we are on our way. We have some hurdles to cross, not the least of which is the Church's ownership of this site, but the Historical Society committee has decided to be proactive and has just approved the setup of a crowdfunding.org account. We hope with a substantial amount of donations and a considerable amount of challenging work that, one day, people will come to Corleone to visit this Mill, which in the end, I hope it will stand as a symbol of Corleone's influence on Sicilian History."

Enamored by her extensive knowledge and passionate speech, Luke began to clap. The rest of the group was slow, but soon, everyone clapped, including Luke, who showered the historian with thunderous applause.

"Thank you. Okay, back to town we go." She pointed toward town. "Follow the narrow street behind you and to your right."

Staying slightly behind the group, Luke waited for Alessandra to reach him.

"Grazie," she thanked him with a caress on his shoulder as she passed by.

The shiver he felt earlier when she whispered in his ear is insignificant to the shock his whole body just experienced. *Shit, no! Why is this happening?* Tightly closing his eyes, he forcibly willed the feeling to disappear.

Alessandra led the group in describing and commenting on the various parts of the town they passed. The tour had taken on a ' private outing' feel with Luke beside her and the rest of the group a few steps behind. Recognizing this, Alessandra stood in the middle of the main street and beckoned everyone to converge near her. She spread her arms in the sky, directing the group's attention to either side of the street.

"This is our contradiction. To your left, you will see a bar called The Godfather. To your right, we see the Corleone Anti-Mafia Center. There is no denying that the Mafia is part of Sicilian history, but so is the effort to eradicate it from our current lives." Speaking to everyone but glancing at Luke, she continued. "I will say this. We have lived with this contradiction for many years. Understandably, we have become somewhat complaisant, not totally and not all of us." She stopped to look around the group, and then once again, she turned to Luke. "I will do whatever I can to educate people on the negative contribution the Mafia has made to our community. I hope that by emphasizing the amazing gifts other civilizations have left us, I will be a little closer to achieving that goal."

"And restoring the Old Arab Mill will bring you closer to that goal?" Luke suggested.

"Perhaps," she said, nodding her head, then noticing some questionable expressions around the group.

"I don't want anyone to misunderstand," she said, looking at Luke again. "The people here are extremely proud to be Corleonese, of their history, ancient and recent. We understand the effect that the Mafia has had on our town, real and the Hollywood version. In fact, we need to thank Mr. Coppola for putting us on the map. However, we need to educate as many people as possible on the real effects of the Mafia versus the real effects that other civilizations have had in Sicily."

Then turning her attention back to the group, she thanked them for their attendance and wished them all a continued pleasant time in Corleone.

Delaying his departure, Luke once again found himself alone with Alessandra. Pleased with the opportunity, albeit unsure as to why he inched closer to Alessandra, hoping she could shed some light on the strange actions of the people he had met thus far.

"I have to tell you, Alessandra, the people's attitude here is very strange..."

Before he could finish, an old lady walking by pointed at him crossed herself, cursed him in Italian, and continued walking past him, muttering to herself. Following her with a shaking head until she disappeared around a corner, he turned to rejoin the group. To his surprise, he was alone with Alessandra.

"What did she want?" He asked her.

Her response was a shake of her own head and a noiseless exit that left Luke isolated and bewildered once again.

CHAPTER EIGHTEEN
A Needle in a Haystack

The man in black drove along a well-traveled outer road of Corleone proper, where the trees encroached on the narrow but deep unprotected ditches. Purposely slowing down, he allowed the traffic behind him to pass and waited for the solitary oncoming vehicle to go by him and disappear around the curve that was visible from his rear-view mirror. Soon, the man was alone, so he drove the car another 50 meters, making a sharp right into a well-hidden narrow road that turned back onto itself, making it invisible from the main road. Leisurely he drove along the manicured, interlocking brick pathway where the tall evergreens shielded him from the elements.

Flanked by tall mature pine trees, the long winding driveway was beautiful. He rode on that path many times but was never tired of it; it offered him the opportunity to relax and the time to peek at the valued bag on the passenger seat. Reassured that the prize inside was safe and waiting for delivery to its recipient, he continued his drive.

At the end of the driveway, the man, like anyone else that had intentionally or unfortunately reached this point, was greeted by two stone archways. On the left was a welcoming, unobstructed entrance that ensured that whoever had chosen this entrance was met by two men. One would most likely be casually perched on a stone wall surrounding the main house, seemingly oblivious to his surroundings. The other would be leisurely pacing that same enclosure, looking sluggish in the afternoon heat. But both men were neither lazy nor disinterested, for they were a part of a well-organized private security team of six highly trained and handsomely paid Sicilian-born, former U.S. Navy Seals. These men guarded the villa with their lives if violence ever ensued.

Guarded by a heavy wrought-iron gate, a similar stone archway was to his right. Beyond this uninviting barrier, a pleasant and welcoming expanse was occupied by an olive grove, fig, and pomegranate orchards with a large pen holding eight prized goats. These goats were tended by an elderly man much older looking than his chronological age in the late sixties. Although the man looked as friendly and approachable as any grandfather, he was extremely dangerous, for his decisions, based solely on self and family preservation, were made without any regard for human life.

The transponder in the man's car opened the gate on his right, allowing him to pass unimpeded.

The man stepped out of his parked car and walked to the passenger's side, where he carefully lifted the black bag and carried it to a small wooden table where he relinquished his obligation.

CHAPTER NINETEEN
Reflection of a Tour

As Luke entered his hotel room, he was almost knocked over by a wall of frigid air. Pleased that he had the foresight to lower the temperature with his cell phone before leaving for his trip, he mentally patted himself on the back before dropping his camera bag on the bed. Soon his body followed after, arms spread wide, he pirouetted and plopped backward on the bed. The force of the dead flop caused his camera bag to fly into the air and land on his unprotected face. Despite the sharp pain, Luke laughed at himself, the force of which caused him to slide backward until his neck was hanging over the edge of the sheets. Although everything was upside down, he could discern the doors of the closet, and for some reason, he had the urge to check it.

'*I should check on the ashes,*' he spoke to himself, convincing his body to wake until it gave in. Unconvinced, he let out a deep sigh, looked up, and stared at the edge of the canopy. '*I should really try to figure out what's going on here, in this curious town.*'

Deciding that his latter thought should take precedence, he swung his body to lay his head on the pillow, resting his palms underneath his temple, and with a final release of his breath, he closed his eyes.

The first face that came into his empty mind was that of the flight attendant who told him about the upgrade to first class, but it didn't last long. Her face dissolved before Alessandra's features were introduced to his hazy mind's eye. Forced to refocus on the image, he visualized the people at Palermo airport, but their faces rippled in and out as soon as Alessandra's visage appeared.

Troubled that he could not concentrate on connecting the puzzles in his head because Alessandra's face kept interrupting, he quickly jumped up and headed for the closet, hoping to eradicate her from his thoughts. Although the attempt was futile, for each step flashed a different image of Alessandra; halfway to the closet, his phone rang, releasing him from the fever of that woman. He celebrated the distraction and peered at the caller display, and was hit by a tsunami size guilt wave.

"Tiff!" he answered, a little too excited.

"You must really miss me," she said.

"What? Ya. Ya, of course, I miss you," he said without enthusiasm.

"Is everything okay?" she asked, noticing his tone.

"Yes, it's just this place."

"What do you mean?"

"I don't know, it's strange; some people look at me with a distant expression on their faces, giving me the feeling that they would rather not deal with me, while others seem to like me, even go out of their way to try and please me. But Tiff, this town is enchanting; the possibility for amazing pictures is endless. The countryside is so picturesque; there's an old mill I saw today and a waterfall..." he stopped as his mind traveled back to his covert picture of Alessandra.

"Luke?"

"Sorry, I just thought that I needed to go back and take more pictures. Anyway, I still haven't taken care of my father's last wish. I think I've been..."

"That's great, Luke; I hope the pictures turn out fine," Tiffany interrupted and then continued in a nonchalant tone, "About your meeting with the Graf family, I rescheduled it. You can meet with them when you come back. Isn't that amazing?"

"What? Ya sure?" Luke answered, perturbed at her disinterest but slightly relieved he did not have to share his memories of the waterfall with her.

"It's so great, isn't it? Things will work out for you, for us. I can't wait for you to get back here; I do miss you."

"Yes," he responded in a tone that he hoped was satisfactory for her question.

Scratching his head in an inattentive state, he walked over to the balcony and looked out. The street and bars were alive, but unlike the party noises of New York, there was a sincere vibration to the sounds of the people enjoying their life. As the rumble of many conversations hit his ears and the smells of various dishes invaded his nose, he closed his eyes and inhaled deeply, allowing the aroma to attack his senses, making him salivate.

Tiffany's voice brought him back from his daydreams, "...and I feel sorry for you having to spend so much time in that Godforsaken place."

Luke laughed aloud and then took a deeper breath allowing more of the delicious odor to fill his body.

"Sure, but this needed to be done," he finished with a wide smile.

"What's so funny?"

"Nothing, just some kids in the street," he lied.

Their conversation continued for a while longer without Luke really paying attention until she brought him back with a closing remark.

"Okay, call me before you go to sleep."

"Okay. I will."

"I love you," Tiffany said to dead air.

Luke took a few steps into the room and threw the phone on the bed. The toss was so poor that he almost missed the bed entirely. He was holding his breath as the phone spun around. It teeter-tottered until it finally settled on the edge of the bed, allowing Luke to exhale loudly and go back outside.

Leaning on the balcony rail, he surveyed the street below, where he noticed a little girl running toward a man who had his arms outstretched. Reaching him, she launched herself into his open arms, buried her head on the man's neck and shoulders, and hugged him tightly. Sliding off, she reached for the man's hand and dragged him to a table where he bent down, tenderly kissed a waiting woman a couple of times, and patted the boy on his head. Although engrossed in his iPad, the boy stood and gave a bear hug, what Luke now believed to be his father. Tugging at his heartstrings, he recalled his own family's love.

"Did she say Godforsaken?" Breathing through his nose, he was staggered by the intoxicating smells of the food, and his mind wandered away from the words of his lover to the tender moments shared at his childhood dining-room table. *"I think I am hungry."* He thought to himself and decided to walk out; he was about to close the door when a muffled sound caught his attention. Looking towards the bed, he saw the phone on the ground.

"Thanks, pops. Was that you?" he said aloud to the emotion-filled air.

Silently thanking his father a second time, he went back to pick up the phone from the ground and his camera from the bed.

CHAPTER TWENTY
Food Clears The Mind

Something about the man-made him feel uneasy; perhaps the jacket he was wearing in the heat was questionable. Still, the man's serious and standoffish expression was out of place amongst these happy people that Luke found concerning. Nonetheless, as the man followed him with his eyes, Luke had no choice but to respond with a smile. Although the man's stone face caused a slight tremor to run up his spine, he continued smiling as he looked for a restaurant, eager to ease his hunger pangs.

Prior to entering the first restaurant in his path, he turned his head to see if the man was still behind him. Thankfully he lost sight of him, so he sat down outside near the patio, after which a waiter approached him immediately.

"Good evening. Can I start you off with sparkling water?" the waiter spoke in perfect English.

Luke looked up and waited a few seconds before responding, "Yes, thank you, but before I order, I need to ask you a question?

"Of course."

"I noticed that, like you, a lot of people here speak English."

"Yes, sir, the ones in the service industry certainly do. It helps with communicating with our customers," he answered with a wry smile. "What can I get for you?"

"Great answer; what's your name?"

"Sandro."

Surprised that Sandro did not ask for his name, he began, "Sandro, this is my first time in Corleone. I'll eat whatever you recommend."

"Excellent. Not to worry, we will fix something special for you."

As Sandro walked away, a young server walked to his table with red wine in a ceramic jug and a perfectly chilled mineral water bottle.

"This is carbonated, sir, or would you prefer flat?" he asked.

"This is fine, thanks."

The young man poured the water and walked away, leaving Luke to his fears.

Looking around the patio, Luke again felt a sense of uncertainty about the people he had met thus far. The man in black had unquestionably unnerved him, but the waiters and the people around him had raised his spirits once again.

"Contradictions are alive and well in this town," he said to himself as he waited for his food, but thankfully, he didn't have to wait that long. Placing the plate on the table, Sandro described the dish carefully, "Here we have, wild boar salami with pecorino cheeses, and lupini drizzled in olive oil and lemon. Bon appetite." He bade him adieu before walking away.

"Thanks, this looks great," Luke said, looking at the plate, he studied the food for a bit before digging in. He took tiny bites of each food item, making sure to try every dish commemorating the bursts of flavors onto his pallet forever. A voice in his head told him that he had eaten these dishes before, but he was amazed at the intensity of the flavors. There was no doubt about it that although their names were the same, the taste of each dish was very different.

"Wow!" His emotions were evident in his eyes and on his tongue. To others, Luca might have seemed like a famished man, but regardless, he didn't care whose eyes were on him.

Carefully placing a little cut of wild boar and cheese on a small piece of crusty bread, he devoured the item but didn't swallow the bite. Luke chewed it slowly, allowing each food's texture and taste to mix upon his tongue. He didn't know why but his lids fluttered to a close, and it enhanced the experience as he attempted to decipher and enjoy the food.

Chefs would taste and smell each article of food before incorporating it into their dish; it was like art. Perhaps, in the world of gastronomy, the eater or the audience also had a vital part in their artistry.

Why else would pompous critics exist? These men and people had the livelihood of chefs under the nib of their pens, albeit he was just a humble customer enjoying the food of a chef from another country. Finally, he swallowed the bite, and immediately a smile spread across his lips. Just like a kid who found a game for a mundane task, he repeated the process, purposely pressing his tongue to his palate in an attempt to make the taste last just a little longer. Before taking the next bite, he took a sip of wine and decided on the spot that it made an excellent pair with pecorino cheese.

Just as he was recovering from the antipasto, the main course took the place of the empty plate right in front of him.

"Bucatini Corleonese, homemade of course, with swordfish, pistachio, and fresh tomato." Sandro described the pasta dish with pride, but he didn't need to say a word because the very aroma of the dish testified to its quality.

Piercing the fork into the glossy pasta, the braids unfurled in between the twirling prongs of the cutlery. He scooped the perfect amount and took his first, thus, everlasting bite. Despite having his fill with the last meal, his mouth was salivating in anticipation before eating the pasta, and within the first three chews, he had ascended to heaven as his senses danced in tandem with his tastebuds.

"Oh my God!" Luke couldn't help but whisper out praises and words of fervor after each course, his mouth in the process of savoring the residual bits of pasta and sauce in his mouth.

The waiter, who had not left his side, asked for confirmation with a smile and tilted his head slightly, but Luke could only offer the same answer, although not so humbly as before, "Oh my god." His mind was unable to move forward from the taste. Similar to a man attempting to make sense of the divine, he was stunned and unable to form proper sentences, "I feel like I just discovered the purpose of life."

"I will let the chef know."

"Hum," Luke responded nonchalantly, for his hawk-like eye was affixed to his waiting bite of pasta.

Left alone with only a sly smirk on his face, it didn't take Luke long to finish his meal. Eyeing his clean plate with a slight sense of regret, he noticed the sauce remnants seemingly begged him to sponge them up. Remembering the crisp, crusty bread resting in the basket, ready to fulfill its ultimate purpose, his mind drifted to the many occasions this scenario was acted upon at his parent's dinner table, and he reached for the bread. He was about to clean up the remaining sauce off the plate but stopped mid-way when he felt eyes on him. Looking up, he noticed a woman at the next table.

"Fate come se state a casa di mamma," she told him in Italian with a smile.

"She said, do what you would do at your mother's house," Luke jumped a bit when Sandro magically appeared next to him, translating the lady's words with a smile.

Luke did not need to be told twice. With a shrug, he took the remaining bread and cleaned his plate.

Finished, he pushed himself a little away from the table, believing that it would enable him to breathe more freely. After cleaning his mouth with a linen serviette, he turned to his left and found the waiter standing there.

"That was out of this world. Thank you, Sandro."

"My pleasure," Sandro responded, nodding to the server to remove the used dishes and place the next dish on the table.

"As you are aware, Sicily is famous for our sardines. They are caught offshore every day and are the fattest and tastiest in the world. Baked, Sarde a beccafico, stuffed with pine nuts and raisins. The side dish is a small serving of caponata."

Moving closer to the table, he did not even try to protest against the server's words. He took several long breaths and dug into the dish without a second thought. Whatever he tried so far was delectable, Luke felt terribly full, but he continued excitedly. The second the sardines hit his palate, he was bombarded with an explosion of different sensations that suddenly teleported him to the Tyrrhenian Seashores; the scent of the ocean was almost tangible, and he could visualize the time when he started his voyage to Corleone in his GT.

Once again, the waiter's words rang true; the sardines were the best he had ever tasted. As an afterthought, he took a small sampling of the caponata. Although he was familiar with the dish due to his mother's cooking, he felt a little guilty, for, in comparison, his mother's caponata came in second. In his head, her dish was ahead of the Alitalia dish but behind this one, whose texture and flavor were much more vibrant and longer-lasting.

With the dishes void of any particle of the previous food, Luke was now content and sipping peacefully on his wine. Without him doing anything, Sandro appeared out of seemingly thin air! At this point, Luke was curious whether Sandro had telepathy or some sort of psychic ability.

"Thank you, Sandro. I didn't need that, but I sure loved it!"

"My pleasure, sir. Now for dessert, it's..."

"Oh! no, no, no, no, I can't!" Luke interrupted.

"We have strawberry gelato in our homemade brioche," he continued, waving to the server to clear the table.

"Please, Sandro, I just don't have the room."

But once the gelato was placed in front of his eyes, the personalities within his mind were locked into war. Inside the crystalline container, the light brown pastry filled with lemon gelato called out to him, and Luke looked at the dessert. Then he turned to look at Sandro and then back to the desert until finally, his conscience waved the white flag.

"Okay, maybe I'll get it to go."

"With all due respect, if this is your first time eating this dessert, I strongly recommend you eat it here."

"What's this called again?"

"Brioche."

"Brioche?"

"Yes, perfect."

"Okay, I'll take your advice. I'll eat it here. But could you please bring me the bill?"

Before responding, Sandro cleared his throat.

"No bill for you tonight, sir. We're happy to serve you."

"What! What do you mean no bill?" Luke did not know what to feel; he was never the recipient of such kindness and hospitality.

"The meal is our gift to you."

"Now, look, Sandro, there's no way I'm not paying for this meal. It's the best meal I've had since, well, since I ever had, and I'm happy to pay for it. I know that Sicilians are very hospitable, but this is crazy. I insist on paying." Luke stood to make his point more effective and concluded by taking out his credit card, but before he could, Sandro interrupted him with a gentle smile on his face.

"We cannot accept your money. Please Mr. Cassaro, it was our pleasure."

"How do you know my name? I never gave it to you. And you didn't ask." Luke's eyes shot open, his nerves shocking his entire system; then, he began to investigate the server's face.

"Mr. Cassaro, this is not such a big city; we all know who you are," Sandro responded, excusing himself before Luke could have questioned him.

Suddenly, he was left to his lonesome, where his thoughts became so loud that he could no longer hear the world around him. Luke was trying to make sense of what was happening to him from the moment he set foot on the plane in New York. As an artist and photographer, he tended to see the world as a snapshot, a fragment in time where his lens would capture the world reflected within his camera. Everything was so simple, albeit metaphysical when he held up his camera, but this was n*ot here, not now. I can't ignore the strange things that are happening to me.*

Forcing his mind to focus on the recent events, he sat back down and took a bite of the brioche, hoping to distract his mind. Fortunately, the brioche was able to help him relax; the explosion of new flavors attacked his senses stealing all his thought. Engrossed in this enjoyable task, he was oblivious to his surroundings, including the woman who sat with her girlfriend staring at him.

CHAPTER TWENTY ONE
A Napkin Saves the Day

Speaking in Italian, Giovanna was complaining again about her on-and-off relationship with her boyfriend. "There, Giovanna, there he is," Alessandra blurted in, her pointed finger catching Giovanna's attention to someplace else.

"What?"

"The Americano I was telling you about!"

Giovanna discreetly turned her head and saw Luke clumsily trying to eat his brioche. Silently watching him, Alessandra wondered why it was that each time she caught him in public, he was constantly stumbling around with something like at the moment he was attempting to bite into the brioche? Trails and stray squirts of the ice cream were flying everywhere, causing Luke to do an awkward dance to move away from the falling ice cream.

"My God, he's trying really hard. He's so sweet." Giovanna said, laughing, grabbing onto Alessandra's arm, steadying herself in the process.

"Don't make it so obvious!" Alessandra whispered to her friend, forcing her to turn around from the scene.

"Are you kidding? Everyone is watching!" She laughed, and Alessandra joined in, unable to protect herself from her friend's contagious energy, but something kept bothering her.

"And you think he's a Mafioso?" Giovanna asked, laughing harder at the display of Luke dodging a piece of ice cream falling onto his shoe.

"Yes, stop. He's going to notice."

"No way. It's not possible," Giovanna stated emphatically.

"Why not?"

Giovanna looked at Alessandra with raised eyebrows and then, with a nod of her head, directed her to look at Luke, who was far too distracted with his ongoing war with the brioche.

"Come on, Ales, look at the way he eats! He doesn't know what he's doing."

"He's American. What do you expect?" Alessandra said, shrugging, rolling her eyes so hard that Giovanna could swear that they could have popped out of her sockets, "I've been watching him trying to eat that brioche, and I can't stand it. I'm going over."

"So, you HAVE been watching him?" There was a mischievous smile on her face, her fingers intertwining, knowing that her sarcasm didn't bother the other woman.

"Yes, but apart from his pathetic attempt at eating the brioche, I wondered what he's really doing here."

"Sure, go tell it to someone else. I've known you since you were born. I see something else on your face," Giovanna said, her voice dancing to the cynicism to annoy her friend further.

"Yes, it's bile working its way out! I'm going over," she said again without moving.

Sighing at her friend's childish sense of humor, Giovanna continued the conversation, raising her voice to gain her attention. "Anyway, you told me he's here burying his father's ashes."

"That's what he told me. I don't know Giova, too many inconsistencies, and then there's his name and how everyone around here treats him. The police know him, the restaurants know him, and even the old people in the town know him. I'm not convinced," she stated flatly.

"Come on, Ales, there's lots of Cassaro's worldwide, and if people here want to treat him with more respect than he deserves because of his name, let them know he's not hurting anyone."

"Yes, he is; he's hurting us. Or at least his kind is. Besides, what they have for him is certainly not respect, it's fear. Jesus Giova, they're afraid of a name!"

"No, not everyone," Giovanna said, looking at her and smiling. "Plus, he's no Mafioso."

"Why not?"

"Look. He's got ice cream all over him. This American needs to carry a bib, not a gun." At this, Alessandra couldn't help but laugh along with her friend, the air between them became light again.

"Does he speak Italian?" Giovanna questioned.

"Not well, maybe not at all."

"Well, maybe he doesn't know?"

"Doesn't know what?" she responded, her brows furrowing at her friend's implication, "You think he's that clueless?"

"Why not? Wouldn't be the first time a man is clueless."

"The Mafia is many things, but clueless is not one of them."

They continue sneakily observing Luke, who was in a personal war with the desert that he was on the verge of losing.

"Perhaps this man is clueless. I think the brioche is winning. You'd better go see if you can help him," Giovanna said again sarcastically.

"You're a real bitch; you know that, right?" Alessandra responded, and without waiting for a reply from her smug friend, she grabbed a napkin and walked across the cobblestone patio to Luke.

"Here," she said, handing him the napkin rather roughly.

"Alessandra!" Luke responded incredulously, slowly taking the napkin which lay on his stained shirt, "Thanks."

She did not comment but simply pointed to his face.

"That's embarrassing," Luke said, wiping the ice cream off his face. Meanwhile, Alessandra shook her head at the display; it was like looking at a kid who didn't know any table manners.

"May I?" she said, gently taking the spoon out of his hand, "You must take the spoon and use it to take some of the ice cream off the top."

Although Luke's gaping mouth was an easy target for Alessandra, she was somehow lost in his eyes, and she wished that she hadn't connected her gaze with his in the first place. She found it hard to concentrate, forcing her to lower her eyes and carefully feed him ice cream with the spoon.

"Once the amount of ice cream remaining in the brioche is manageable," she managed to say, feeding him several more bites, "you bite the edges of the brioche, allowing some of the ice cream to enter your mouth."

She placed the brioche on his lips, enticing him to bite onto it, which he obliged, holding onto her directions as if he were mesmerized by her words, like a siren to a sailor.

"This process is repeated until your dessert is finished."

Luke watched her and forgot where he was.

"Aren't you going to swallow?" she said, holding his stare.

Blood tells no lies

CHAPTER TWENTY TWO
An Evening to Remember

Distracted by his stomach's selfish desire to be fed, the last forty-five minutes had passed without the thought of the sometimes rude, albeit fascinating historian. Their first meeting was etched in his head, and he clearly remembered the lioness within her. Now, looking at her vulnerable form, he was shocked that she had the magical ability to look beautiful, more so than she already was. She was gently holding the remaining brioche within her soft hold, and the sight of her peaceful features hijacked his thoughts with brutal force; memory upon memory, the photos he had taken of her in the past flashed into his reverie rather vividly. He didn't know if she was talking to him or not because Luke was frozen at the moment as time ticked by, but he was positive that she was able to detect the ruthless beating of his heart. It was threatening to leap out of his sternum, so how could she not hear it? Hopelessly looking for a distraction, he glanced in the direction she came from.

"There's someone waving at you," he told her, praising God that He had sent this stranger to distract him; otherwise, he would have kissed the girl and ruined the tender moment between them.

Clicking the tongue on the roof of her mouth Alessandra turned around to face her table, where she spotted Giovanna waving bye at her as she took her boyfriend's arm, forcefully dragging him away from the patio.

"Trouble in paradise?" Luke asked.

"There's always trouble when those two get together," she answered with a hum, her gaze followed after the two chaotic love birds.

Luke could not control himself.

"I can't believe how good this is," he said, gently reaching for her hand with both of his and guiding the remaining morsel of the brioche into his mouth.

"Can't believe I just did that!" His eyes widened from his behavior, but he didn't dare to say his thoughts out loud. Instead, he turned to look at her. Alessandra was licking at her moistened fingers, licking away a tiny drop of melted ice cream that trailed down her willowy digits.

"Corleone is full of surprises," she declared, looking slightly down and away. This otherwise insignificant gesture churned his gut with a myriad of emotions. The strongest of these emotions was a sense of loss.

"But at what? What I'm I going to lose." He was so overwhelmed that he decided this evening could not end.

"There's no doubt about that. You know I could use a long walk. Would you come with me?" He got up; one hand extended towards her while the other rubbed a bloating stomach.

Although her convictions were waning, Alessandra continued to believe that Luke was a Mafioso in hiding, but the longer she spent time with him, the more she leaned towards Giovanna's convictions. Luke was the only mafioso she had ever met. Convincing herself that she had to commit to finding the truth about this man or about her wavering feelings, she accepted, believing it would be a wise move.

Silently enjoying the cool mountain air invading the town square, they walked for several surprisingly comfortable moments. Suddenly, Alessandra stopped, turned to Luke, and looked him in the eyes.

"What do you do back in America?"

"I'm a photographer."

"Really?"

"Are you surprised?"

"No. That explains why you were taking all those pictures."

"Yes, I do take a lot of pictures, don't I?"

"What do you do with all of those pictures?"

"I keep the ones I like and delete the ones I don't like. There's only a very small percentage I would judge to be keepers."

"What do you mean keepers?" she asked, honestly.

"Pictures that I keep. I shoot hundreds of pictures, and then I go over them and keep only the ones that I really like."

They walked a little further in silence, then she asked, "Is that difficult?"

"Is what difficult?"

"Choosing the keepers."

"What a wonderful question!" Luke thought deeply about her reply. *"This is a woman that probes without prying."*

"Being a photographer these days is child play compared to the days before the digital age. Back then, you had to be selective before pushing the shutter release button; a photographer needed to spend most of the time in setup, lighting, poses, etc. It would have been impossible to take hundreds of pictures and then find the perfect picture using only the negatives, or worse, develop all the pictures and then throw away the ones you didn't like. Can you imagine the cost? Now," he said with a big smile, "The time is spent reviewing the pictures; you take hundreds of shots and delete the ones you don't like. The keepers are the ones that touch the realm of perfection. I've taken tens or even hundreds of thousands of shots, and I don't think I've kept more than a fraction. There's no question that we photographers of today have it much easier than the artists of the past. Choosing the keepers, I mean," he added, seeing as Alessandra looked slightly confused. *"Or is that something else I see?"*

Alessandra was impressed. His appreciation of the history of his craft and the talent of the photographers that preceded him shows empathy, something she was sure Mafiosos did not have. Still, she had some reservations, so she decided to continue with the same line of questioning.

"Do you have a gallery back home?"

"I hope to, someday," he answered honestly.

Something about his answer made Alessandra hope for his dream to be true; for now, all she could do was continue walking and nodding her head in agreement with each statement.

"Alessandra. I need to ask you something," Luke asked, continuing without her acknowledgment, "Some strange things are happening here that I can't understand. Even tonight, the restaurant didn't..."

He was cut short by a group of Sicilian monks in bare feet approaching them. Smiling, Luke reached into his pocket, pulled out a few bills, and handed the possessions to them.

Smiling back and shaking their heads in unison, the monks quickly refused and looked towards a now laughing Alessandra.

"What?" he asked, a little embarrassed.

"You can't give them money, Luke. These monks only leave the monastery to gather food."

"I already finished my brioche," he said, pocketing the bills. "I'm sorry," he said as they resumed their walking and laughing.

Luke was about to continue with his inquiry when coming around a corner, he saw the façade of a church. This clean, almost pristine structure looked peculiar amongst the old two-story apartments that were attached to it.

"Is that the church of Santa Rosalia?"

"You know about this church?" Alessandra asked, surprised.

"Yes, my mother told me a little about it. It's much smaller than she described it."

"It is small. It is also beautiful. Do you want to go in?"

"Yes," he responded, taking his camera off his shoulder, his finger ready on the shutter release button. However, steps away from the church, a man taking pictures of his family at the entrance noticed Luke and met him with a request.

"Excuse me, sir," the man asked in French, "would you mind taking a photo of us?"

"Sure. Can you hold this for me?" Luke answered without hesitation in French, handing his camera to Alessandra.

"You speak French?

"High school French, just enough to get by, not fluent," he admitted, turning to the tourist.

Yet again, slightly annoyed by this man's propensities to confuse her, she took his camera and allowed him to help the family without any obstruction from her side. As Luke began snapping pictures of the family, she looked at the camera, wondering if she should snoop. She knew it would be violating his trust, but it would be interesting to see what this man's newest project was about. Alas, she was a slave to her own conscience, so she reluctantly pushed the camera away from her gaze.

The man asked if he could take a few more pictures, and Luke happily accepted. Deeply engrossed at the moment, Luke directed the family to various locations he found interesting.

Finally, far enough away, with her heart practically beating out of her chest, Alessandra abandoned her reservations and turned the camera to view. Although she was not an expert, a quick scan of his camera role revealed his talent. Every picture was beautiful, picture after picture. His craft and practice were evident in each picture. She wondered how he could possibly find the 'keepers' from his library! She prudently lowered the camera and looked to see where Luke was. Reassured that he was still busy, her heart now at a more recognizable rate, she resumed her spying. A few more pictures in, she found the photo with the waterfall in the background. Mesmerized by the beauty of the picture, she lingered too long and missed Luke's return.

"See anything you like?" Luke asked, smiling sarcastically.

Appreciating Luke's friendly attitude after being caught red-handed, Alessandra answered him in kind.

"There are a few decent pictures."

"Really?"

"Yes, especially the one you lied about."

"And, which one would that be?"

"This one," she said, handing him the camera.

Wanting to add an element of suspense, Luke leisurely looked at the screen.

"Yes, I agree the waterfall in the background is absolutely perfect," he said, looking back at her. "But I don't think it's a keeper. The person in the foreground looks a little, oh, I don't know…."

Playfully slapping his shoulder, she gave him a tiny, crooked smile and walked away, not allowing him to finish. Luke watched her walk away and then looked back at the picture.

"Naturally beautiful, I would say!" he declared, loud enough, hoping she heard him

CHAPTER TWENTY THREE
Realization

After their playful exchange, Luke followed after Alessandra into the church and was immediately frozen in awe.

"This is beautiful...." His soft voice lingered in tandem with his gaze that followed after the skeletal ribbed arches to the painted cupolas above.

"If only I were here in the day, what beauty would I have seen," Luke mused absentmindedly until Alessandra's voice pierced through his thoughts; if it were anyone else, he would have ignored them, but the historian's voice was a pleasant distraction.

"Yes, it is, and it's not the only church in the area that is."

"How many churches are there around here?"

"One of our mottos, probably the most famous, is the city of one hundred churches."

"That's a lot of churches."

Alessandra stopped Luke in his tracks and looked up at him with a solemn face.

"We Corleonesi have suffered under rulers for many years, foreign and domestic. Where there is suffering, there are churches. One hundred churches may be too few." The way she grew silent made him feel as if she had more to say, and that rang true when she turned, gesturing him to follow after. "Let me show you something."

Leading him to an inconspicuous part of the small church, Alessandra stopped to face him and gestured with her thumb to behind her right shoulder, his eyes automatically followed the action to be met with a list of names engraved on a brass plaque. Nodding in understatement, he scanned the names, attempting to remember some names before refocusing on her hoping to receive an explanation for the memorial.

"There must be hundreds of names. Is this a list of past contributors, supporters, important people of the community?" Luke straightened his back, his eyes downcast towards Alessandra's head as she stepped closer to the plaque.

"They are certainly all important," she said, then looked at him, the sorrowful frown on her lips reached her gaze. "These are the names of all the people killed by the Mafia."

"Shit!"

"Watch your language!" she said, crossing herself.

"Sorry, I just can't believe that many people were murdered in Corleone."

"Luke, all the churches here have these lists. These names are just the ones that came to this church."

"Holy shit!"

"Really?" she huffed, her high-pitched tone reverberating in the church; once she rested her palms on her hips, he couldn't help but compare her to an angry teacher.

Luke only shook his head, crossed himself in the name of the Holy Trinity, and remained silent as he prayed for the souls lost in the needless massacre.

"This is real life, Luke. Corleone is not just a town in a movie. It's a real town with real people and real bullets that kill those real people. No actors, no fake guns, and no coming back from a bullet to the head," she explained with her eyes glued to the plague. For a while, she just stood there, the light from the rose windows reflecting on her somber features before she marched away from the light and towards the altar.

Flustered, Luke followed her wanting to know more about the bloody history of Corleone because, until now, all he saw were smiles and hospitality. Once he stopped beside her, he couldn't help but envision the two like a married couple, standing side by side; the only thing missing was a priest. Alas, life threw cold water on his dreams through Alessandra's voice.

"You have no idea, do you?"

"No, I never looked at it that way. To me, Corleone was a place in the movies. I always thought that my parents left this place because there would be more opportunities in the States, and they said as much when as children, we would ask, but now I wonder if there were other reasons. As beautiful and energetic as this town is, it's also perilous." He stopped and looked down at Alessandra and then continued, "It's only become real to me in the last couple of days."

Looking into each other's eyes, the momentary silence felt endless. For Luke, Alessandra was standing so close to him that he could feel the heat radiate off from her body; though their fingers were inches away from each other, her very presence accelerated the beat of his heart. Though she was unaware of it, she had him in the palm of her hand. His mouth was shut tight, the muscles of which taut due to his loyalty to Tiffany.

Fortunately, Luke wasn't the only one afflicted by the magic of the moonlit night. Alessandra was facing her own troubles; while her mind was feverishly trying to reconcile her feelings toward Luke, her convictions regarding his supposed relations with the Mafiosi forced her to keep up those walls.

She felt that Luke could hear her audible breathing; no matter how deep of an inhale she took, her lungs could not take in enough air to endure the constant action.

Once again hit with a sense of great loss for something he did not possess, he instinctively reached for her intending to stop her flight. Before grasping her shoulder, however, the entrance of a few faithful parishioners shattered the frail moment forcing Luke to retract his outstretched arm.

Recovered from her momentary lapse in judgment, she stopped mid-step to face him again.

"Luke, when I said you have no idea, what I meant was…Luke?" she asked, noticing that he was looking over her head, she tilted her head to a side, attempting to force a connection between their gaze, "Luke?" she called out to him once more.

"Sorry, excuse me. There!" He pointed over her shoulder with haste causing the historian to catch herself from her state of shock. "Alessandra is that a Valasco?" he asked as he started walking towards the painting with a massive smile on his lit-up face.

"I never thought I'd see his work here, most of his paintings are in Palermo."

Alessandra stood with her hands on her hips, shaking her head in unison.

"Incredible!" Luke said, staring at the painting.

Alessandra stepped up beside him, agreeing with his words whilst observing the painting.

"We are lucky to have it. You know the artist?"

"I do. I briefly studied 1700-era painters when I was in college. This guy caught my interest because he changed his name to Velazquez to honor his parents' Spanish heritage. I learned this during a time when I was thinking of changing my name because I was... I don't know, I was confused," he confessed, turning away from the painting to face her instead, "To be honest, I think I still am, although things are starting to become clearer. Alessandra I...I don't even know anymore," he confessed with fervor, shaking his head to avoid the myriad of dangerous thoughts running in his head. Turning back to her, he quickly continued, "I'm just a simple wedding photographer, and perhaps life is simpler when I stick to doing that. Let me take a photo of you," he asked, hoping that in doing so, he would give himself enough strength to reveal his feelings.

Alessandra had to admit that this complicated man, knowledgeable enough to recognize a Velazquez yet seemingly oblivious of the gravitas of his own name, did not act or think like a Mafioso. Yet, she was still not totally convinced that this was not an act.

"But, to what end?" Her voice lingered within her reverie.

She had always depended on her intuition to make choices; emotions were never a factor. As she negotiated the sharp curves on the road of her private argument, emotions took the driver's seat. She needed confirmation but did not know where she would get it or how. Hoping that he would reveal the real reason he was here. *"Is that all you are?"* She thought to ask him, but her lips formed another word, more so an exclamation.

"No!" she refused his request.

"Why not?"

"I'm not just a simple model. I can't allow a simple wedding photographer to take my picture. I have standards, you know," she said, smiling and giving him a slight pose.

"You are interestingly beautiful, Miss Alessandra. I do agree that I am a simple wedding photographer, but you're wrong on two counts. First, I don't think anyone has ever accused you of being simple, and two, being a model is an important job. Most beautiful paintings begin with a beautiful model."

"Did he say beautiful three times?" She felt her cheeks grow hot, but the woman continued to hold up the stoic mask, not giving the man the satisfaction of making her feel flustered.

Alessandra had not heard anything Luke had said but the word beautiful. There were no more curves on that meandering argumentative road. This mysterious man was driving straight to the heart and embracing her core, *"Shit! I'm in love with a Mafioso!"*

"I suppose," she finally answered him, hoping that her response reflected his statement. Taking that as permission granted, Luke snapped a photo. She crossed her arms and looked away as to feign anger.

"You know it's fine if you stay angry. It was the first expression I saw of you, and I still like it."

"Gesù aiutami…" she whispered in return.

CHAPTER TWENTY FOUR
A Palace

A Middle Eastern man dressed in native garb called thwabs walked swiftly through the kitchen doors, a veiled tray in his hands. He could see its metallic material glitter with a silvery light if he looked closely. He moved through the vast central hall, ignoring the left marbled staircase, for it was reserved for the use of women. It went up the right staircase, a twin of the left for those who are curious. He entered the theater room and placed the tray on the coffee table, making sure that he did not obstruct his master's view in the process.

Before leaving, he lifted the cloche off the tray, revealing an espresso and a few Italian cookies.

"Will there be anything else, Your Highness?" he asked, reverently stepping back, pressing the empty tray to his abdomen in a practiced fashion.

"Godfather or Don Zarif, Ahmad!" the prince reprimanded, keeping his eyes on the screen, "How many times do I need to remind you? In this room, you must call me Don! I hope it's not decaf, and yes, bring us some anisette."

"My apology, Don Zarif, of course! It is not decaffeinated; it is regular espresso. I will be right back with the anisette," Ahmad responded in a very high, wavering voice and quickly left the room before bowing to the man who called himself Don.

Dressed in a black tailored suit, the man in the chair reached for his remote and put the movie on pause afterward, and he began to speak.

"I particularly like this next scene. Apolonia is absolutely beautiful here!" he said, turning to Basri, his personal secretary who was seated next to him in an identical chair, "Do you not agree, consigliere?" he asked him.

Left alone, the friendly tone and flavor of their conversation filled the atmosphere in their private quarters with jest and wit.

"I most certainly do. May I remind you, Don Zarif, that two of your wives look like Apolonia and..."

"Yes, yes, Basri, you found them, and you negotiated, etcetera, etcetera." He waved his hands in the air, giving significance to his words. "You know Basri; you've made a career from that one task. If you..."

"Yes, yes, Don Prince," Basri answered him, purposely mixing up what his master and friend wanted to be referred to as, "if I wasn't your cousin, four times removed, and your closest friend since birth, etcetera, etcetera."

At his impromptu imitation of his cousin's last words, the two burst out laughing, which was then interrupted by Ahmed, who came in with the anisette.

"Thanks, Ahmad. That will be all."

"Of course, Prince Zarif."

Realizing he had again made a mistake, Ahmad closed his eyes tight and waited for his reprimand. Spooked by the deafening silence of his master, like a mouse seeing a cat from the lowered corner of his eyes, he dashed from the confines of his sentencing hall.

As soon as Ahmad was out of sight, their laughter continued to ring in the room.

"I think that man is a few camels short of a caravan!" the prince joked as the laughter resumed in earnest.

Once their bellies hurt and their vocal cords croaked, the two's voices had halted to broken chuckles. The prince cleared his throat and turned to his consigliere, asking him if everything was set for their trip.

"Yes, Don, we're leaving early tomorrow; we'll be landing in Palermo at 8:00 am local time and arriving in Corleone no later than 9:00 am."

"Excellent, Basri; I'm looking forward to finally seeing where my favorite movie was shot," he told his cousin again for the hundredth time in the last two weeks, but each time he said it, it seemed as if it was the first time.

"Oh! And Basri," he continued, smelling the anisette that he will never consume, "Don't forget my fedora."

CHAPTER TWENTY FIVE
The Note

Cool and rejuvenating, the morning air managed to enhance the experience of sipping a steaming cup of cappuccino. Luke also had a cannolo in front of him, made by the hands of the chefs from the renowned Cafe Don Corleone Amaro.

Luke was so lost in the taste that he didn't realize that he bit into thin air. Expecting his tongue to savor the flavor of the Italian pastry, disappointment finally settled upon learning that he had finished his cannolo. Hoping to weaken that feeling, he picked up the left-over crumbs with a wet middle finger, albeit he was still unsatisfied with the results, so he simply ordered another.

While waiting, his eyes turned to the nearby window where he spotted the attractive historian Alessandra as she was walking towards the Corleone Historical Building. Smiling to himself at her sight, the previous night's extremely sensual but sexless events began to overrun his mind. Deciding it was best to call her over, he stood up and waved to her, but during that quick flurry of confusing movements, he also reached for his camera in an attempt to snap a few pictures of her.

Alessandra smiled at his antics, but instead of her usual nonchalant response, she began to walk toward him. Just like Luke, the closer she got to him, the events of the night before began to flood her conscience, filling her up with butterflies that she couldn't quite explain, so instead of overthinking, she did what felt natural to her, she just passed him a beaming smile.

Meanwhile, Luke had his lens trained on Alessandra. The device hissed in response to Luke's practiced hands, its eye zooming in and out before a soft click was heard. Each click signified a successful shot taken of the woman who approached him with the sunniest of smiles, and with each click, his heart seemed to beat faster, and he was no longer able or willing to take notice of the line that was now blurred between his loyalty for Tiffany and his feeling for Alessandra.

Engrossed in the impromptu photo shoot, he suddenly noticed the man in black from the night before offering him his hand. Flustered, Luke took it only to be given a note by the man who suddenly left him in his state of confusion.

Seeing this, Alessandra stopped. She bit her bottom lip, and her eyes became sharp. If he were to look at them, then he would have seen the sense of betrayal pooling at the corners. The woman shook her head and spun on her heels, walking outside of the café in haste.

Everything happened with such speed that Luke didn't have the chance to absorb and compute the events. He wanted to race after

Alessandra, but he was also curious about the note that sat burning in his hand.

Who was that man, and why was he adamant about following him? Everything felt so compromising, so he chose the latter option despite the screaming voice in his head wanting to run after the upset historian. After reading the note several times, he decided to go after Alessandra, and since he knew where she would be found, he ran towards the Corleone Historical Building. Right on the nose, he found the forlorn woman sitting at her office desk, laughing to herself.

"Good morning?" he said in a pleasant and friendly tone attempting to catch his short breath.

"What do you want?" she answered him in a cold and distant tone.

"Were you laughing by yourself?" he asked her, ignoring her attitude.

Alessandra shrugged, said something in Italian, and looked down at some of her papers.

"What does that mean?"

"I'm laughing with the angels. They can be very capricious!"

"No kidding. My father said that all the time."

"Sure, he did," she said very sarcastically.

"Alessandra, what's wrong?"

"I don't want to talk about it, especially with someone like you!" She stood up abruptly, storming out of the building before he could answer her.

With stray pieces of paper flying about him, Luke looked about him. He shook his head and followed after her, but by the time he raced down the steps, Alessandra was gone.

Luke walked up and down every street within a kilometer radius but could not find her trace. Several times he was fooled by his desperate mind but taking those paths where he thought he saw a glimpse of her proved fruitless.

Finally, exhausted and discouraged, he was about to give up until he saw her sitting down on the steps of Piazza Giovanni Falcone. Taking a deep breath, his determination fueled his legs to run after her, and it wasn't until he was a few yards away that he slowed his pace. The closer he got, the stronger her aura became; she wanted to be alone, and the air around her spoke for her state of mind. So, like a puppy with its tail tucked, he approached her slowly and cautiously, his voice soft as if he would scare her.

"Alessandra. What is going on here? I thought we really connected last night; we didn't get home until well past midnight. Why this attitude now?" Despite the softness in his tone, it was also strained. He felt frustrated and annoyed like her but what she felt was tenfold compared to his fascination.

"Connected? I fell in love!" She thought to say it, but her mouth spouted out words much different from what she felt within her heart, "I had my suspicions, but now, I'm sure."

"Of what? What are you sure of?"

"I know what I saw. The man gave you reverence!" she said, raising her voice and turning away from him as if his very face had burned her skin.

"The man gave me a note! Here look!" Luke reprimanded, shaking the note in front of her face, but she ignored him, refusing even to acknowledge his presence.

"Why are you here, Luca?" she asked him with venom laced within the Italian version of his name.

"Luca? Why did you just call me Luca?"

"Why did you come to Corleone, the real reason?" she asked, ignoring his question, but behind that cold façade, he could see tears pooling within her glassy gaze.

"You know the reason. I'm here because I made a promise to my father."

"Exactly! And a promise made to the family must be kept." She stood up and walked away quickly before spinning back to yell at him, her hand extended towards him in an accusing manner.

"Don't follow me!"

Determined to understand the reason behind her anger, he ignored her demand and chased after her. Arriving at the Corleone Historical Building with only seconds to spare, he tried to push the door open; finding it locked, he knocked several times, but there was no answer.

"Come on, Alessandra, open up! Please!" he begged after her vanishing form.

"Suspicious? Of What? What the fuck is going on?" After several more unsuccessful attempts, extremely agitated, he for a moment gaped at the door, swore under his breath, and quickly turned to leave.

Unprepared, he ran into a Middle Eastern man in a suit and a fedora surrounded by a small entourage of large men in thwabs. Luke stumbled a few steps and then apologized.

"Are you okay, sir?"

"I'm not the one falling backward, but thanks, I'm fine, Mr. Cassaro. I am Prince Zarif," he introduced himself, extending his hand to Luke.

Taking his hand, he dived into memory for some light. Finally recalling who the man was, he briskly shook the prince's hand with a wide grin.

"Oh! Very nice to meet you, Your Highness."

"Believe me, Mr. Cassaro, the pleasure is all mine. I'm very excited to be this close to someone like you."

"Like me? What do you mean like me?" he asked as his eyes grew big in wonder. "Sorry, Your Highness, I didn't mean to be impertinent. It's just that I'm surprised that you even know my name."

"Your name says it all."

Luke found himself stressed to the point of collapse. There was a jigsaw piece missing from his board. He knew he had to get away to figure out what was happening to him.

"Please excuse me, Your Highness. I have an urgent matter to deal with," he apologized slightly, moving away from the familiar yet unfamiliar crowd.

"Yes, yes, the lovely young lady. I saw her going into the building. I hope we will have a chance to talk further, Mr. Cassaro."

"Yes, of course," Luke responded, walking away as fast as he could, trying to hide his panic.

"My name? A prince knows my name, and what the hell is an Arab prince doing in Corleone? I really need to find out what's going on here. Maybe a nice afternoon nap can help me solve my mystery. I need to catch up on the loose ends. Everything is getting too frizzy."

Walking towards his hotel while fighting with his thoughts in his head. Luke got startled by a very old lady passing him from the side with her two granddaughters. The girls giggled at his dazed reaction.

"You look like him," she said in Italian, stopping him from going any further.

"I'm sorry, I don't understand."

"She said you look like him," one of the girls translated.

"Like him, how?"

The girl turned to the old lady, "Like whom?" she asked her in Italian.

"What do you mean like who? Like his father, Franco."

"She said like your father, Franco."

"That's right; yes, my father, well, thank you." Luke smiled, recovering from his mental fog.

The girl translated to her grandmother and then turned to Luke. "She wants to know what you're doing here?"

"I'm here to bury my father's ashes," he explained with a gentle frown.

"My condolences," the girl offered and then turned to translate.

The old lady came close to Luke and took his hands. "God only takes the best ones." She let go of his hands and then touched his cheek with a soft motherly smile. The woman and the girls walked away towards a street, leaving Luke to ponder over his thoughts. He stood there, gaping, as they walked further and disappeared into a corner.

"This is incredible! First-class, bumping people off planes, bumping into a GT C Roadster? Finding a beautiful woman, making a connection, the connection breaks, then see a mysterious man. He vanishes and reappears to fuck everything up. Old ladies hate me or love my father, and the freaking prince who can forget him, his highness knows my name? I really do need a close eye, or else I will go insane."

He was about to make his way back to his room when he heard his name from a corner.

"Ciao. Mr. Cassaro, would you like to have a drink?" a man inquired in a thick British accent.

Luke, startled by a sudden question, responded rudely. "What?"

Noticing that Luke was still recovering from his sudden spook, he continued, "Sorry, I didn't mean to startle you. Please, Luke, may I call you Luke? I'm Johnny, the bar's owner," he said, stretching his hand.

"The drink is on the house," he added to lower the pressure residing in Luke's eyebrows.

Luke shook the man's hand, "Sorry Johnny, yes, please call me Luke, and yes, I was going to my room to pass out, but maybe a drink is better."

Johnny pleasantly escorted Luke to the bar, where he pulled out a chair and motioned him to sit.

"Can I surprise you?" he said, pointing at the bottles behind him.

"I don't think anything else can surprise me today, but please do try."

As Johnny fixed his drink, Luke re-read the crumpled note in an attempt to solve the mystery of the man in black. After constant revisions of memory and the secondary information he knew of, he surrendered with a sigh and stuffed the note back in his pocket. Luke looked up to see Johnny pushing a drink towards him.

"Thanks," he said before taking a small sip. "Oh, that's good!" he exclaimed, taking the drink and downing it in one gulp.

"Easy there, this drink will sneak up on you."

"That was really good. What was it?"

"It's an Aperol Spritz with a twist."

"That doesn't tell me much. I don't know Aperol."

"Come now. I know you have Aperol in the States."

Luke gave him a blank look, so he continued, "Three parts Prosecco, two parts Aperol, one-part soda or sparkling mineral water, and a splash of Campari."

"Johnny, it's wonderful!"

"Thanks. I'll make you another, and I think I'll join you."

"You're from England," Luke asked, watching Johnny go behind the bar.

"I studied in London," Johnny answered as he fixed the drinks.

"Thanks, so why are you here, Johnny?" he asked, accepting the drink.

"Close to retirement, my wife left, the kids are in Australia and Canada, I found myself missing my childhood. I was born here. I loved it here, so I came back," he answered, taking a sip.

"Yes, but why are you really here?" he asked, emphasizing the word 'really' and earning himself a sideways glance from Johnny. "Sorry, it seems to be to the recurring question around these parts."

"We are a curious bunch!" Johnny chuckled.

Luke took another sip of his drink, "Johnny, this drink is really good."

"You're right. It's really fine, but be careful of the splash."

"I thought the splash was Campari."

"No, the Campari is the twist. The splash comes after you have too many of these beauties," he chuckled at his own wit.

As lunchtime approached, people came into the bar, and for their welcome, waiters magically appeared in the room to direct the new arrivals to their seats and take orders. Luke saw the crowd emerging and filling in. He turned back to the bar to see two more special spritzes on the counter.

"Last ones, I promise," he said, clinking Luke's glass. "Luke, I couldn't help overhearing your conversation with Signora Parisi and one of her granddaughters. I'm sorry about your father. I knew him when I was very young."

Luke's inquisitive look prompted him to continue. "I left Corleone shortly before he did. But the stories still reached us in England. Good

Chap, as they say there. My best memory of him is the time this goat was loose in town. The goat was running all over the place, and then as the goat started running up the hill..." he stopped and waited for this attractive woman to come and stand beside him. "Luke, my wife, Rosalia. Rosalia, this is Luke. Luke Cassaro."

"Hi, Rosalia."

"Hi Luca, Cassaro? Franco's boy?" she asked, shaking his hand and turning to her husband. "Are you making up stories, Johnny?" she asked him in a Scottish accent.

"No, love, I'm telling him the story of the goat."

"Well, that's a great story and true. How is your dad, Luke?"

Luke and Johnny exchanged a look and remained quiet.

"What?" she asked worriedly, pushing a lock of hair behind her ear.

"Sorry, hon," Johnny apologized but sat quietly.

"What?" she asked again, but this time her eyes were targeting Luke.

"Actually, I'm here to bury his ashes," he finally answered, looking down at the carpet. He could feel the pain gently crawling up his spine.

"Oh, my God, I'm so sorry, Luke, I didn't know," she passed Johnny the 'you could have warned me' look.

"That's okay, Rosalia. The only reason he knows it is because he likes to listen in on private conversations," he jested with a smile.

"Anyway," Johnny butted in in an attempt to break free from the spotlight.

"So, as I was saying, Frank climbs up right behind this goat, grabs him with one arm, and brings him back down to Teresa, who was so impressed she planted a huge kiss right on the lips! And after seeing this, her mother was so mad she grabbed Teresa with one arm and repeatedly hit poor Franco with the other. As Teresa and her mother were walking away, he turned to us and said, smiling, 'Her lips are really soft!' I was seven years younger than he was, but I still remember thinking, 'Boy, I can't wait to kiss a girl.'"

"And you're still waiting," Rosalia joked.

They all shared a laugh until Rosalia asked Luke what his father ended up doing in America.

"He became a professor of ethics at Columbia University."

Johnny and Rosalia passed each other a look and silently agreed with a synchronized nod.

"Perfect. And what do you do, Luke?" she asked.

"I'm a wedding photographer. One day I hope to be a real photographer!"

"Very funny. I'm sure you're very good. Have you been taking pictures in Corleone?" Rosalia's eyes beamed with interest.

"Yes, I'm really interested in the Old Arab Mill," he answered, looking into the distance.

"Really?" Johnny asked but quickly excused himself after being called into the kitchen.

"That's Alessandra's project," Rosalia added as she got up from her seat and headed for the kitchen as the banging voice of her husband called out to her in a panic.

"I took what I think are some of the best pictures I've ever taken." He quietly said to himself, picturing Alessandra in cinematic scenes aroused by the magic of his mind.

Sitting all by himself and feeling the sensation of alcohol rising in his gut, he pushed his glass slightly away and surveyed the now busy bar. His eyes caught a nearby tourist reading an English newspaper. There was something odd about the headline, but partially due to the alcohol, he couldn't figure out the problem. He tried squinting his eyes to focus but nothing made sense, so he pulled out his camera and focused on the headline.

"NOTORIOUS MAFIA BOSS LUCA CASSARO HIDES CLOSE TO HOME"

Suddenly, realizing the implication of his name, all strength left his body, causing the camera to slip away from his grasp, landing loudly on the cement floor. Oddly unconcerned for his camera, he stood up and began to move toward the man with the newspaper. Although the effect of the alcohol made it difficult, he succeeded in reaching the unsuspecting tourist, where he rudely snatched the paper and turned away. As the man attempted to stand to challenge, a gentle yet heavy hand was placed on the man's shoulder rooting him in place. The huge man dressed in all black standing over him, shaking his head, stopped the tourist from going any further.

Blinking several times, Luke re-read the headline again, but like a wanted poster, the words remain highlighted in bold. Turning back toward the tourist, he noticed the man in black parting the beaded curtain and walking out of the bar.

His anger hid behind a fury of other emotions, and Luke, in his tipsy state, went after the man in black.

Guided by the sunlight bursting through the beaded curtain, he miraculously managed to stagger out.

Hearing the commotion, Johnny walked out of the kitchen and read the headline on the newspaper now lying discarded near Luke's camera.

"*Shit!*" He said to himself as he picked up the camera and rushed after Luke. Two steps out, he nearly tripped over Luke, who had succeeded in making it only to the first step.

"Luke, you need to know that's not who you are," he explained, putting a hand on Luke's shoulders. "Your father was a gentleman. What he did..."

"Not what I am? Johnny, I have the same name!" Luke flipped Johnny's hand off, stood up, and turned to him. "Is this what it's all about? Is this why she said it's about my name?" He started walking away.

Johnny went after him but was immediately called back.

"Let him go. He needs time," Rosalia told him as she saw Luke wandering deeper into the crowd of people.

"But he needs to know the truth!"

"He will, Love," she said, reaching for his hand.

CHAPTER TWENTY SIX

A Mother's Help

As Luke approached his hotel, he stopped mid-step, took his phone out, and searched 'Luca Cassaro Mobster.'

"Holy Shit! Seven thousand results?" he uttered aloud.

He clicked on the first article and read to himself, *"Luca Cassaro, the most notorious mobster in Italian history, is suspected to be responsible for the killing of approximately 800 people."* Shaking his head, he said aloud, "Jesus, 800 people?" He then continued walking and reading to himself, *believed to be still in hiding....*

Entering his room with a commotion in his chest. He suffered inwardly at the thought of belonging to a Mafia family. He sneered at the mirror affixed to the bathroom wall.

"Who are you?" he said, shaking his head, unable to make sense of his personal crisis. His hands shook as he played with the headline in his mind. Out of frustration, he grabbed the phone and dialed a number, placing the phone on speaker. He waited for the receiver to pick up and stared at himself in the mirror over the sink.

"Hello?"

"Ma?"

"Luke! Is this Luke?"

Her sarcastic, icy question did not deter him from responding in a kind manner. "Funny, ma. It's only been three days, and you forget the voice of your favorite son?"

His mother knocked his wit with her brimming anger. All he could do while she screamed was stretch his phone to an arm's length.

"Ma, I'm sorry I didn't call earlier. Please, let me talk." The phone went silent. "Ma, are you there?"

"Yes, I'm here," she responded, sounding hurt.

"Okay. How's everything?"

"Great, how about you?" she asked with a little more kindness in her voice.

"I'm good, Ma but the last couple of days have been really confusing, even strange."

"What do you mean, honey?"

Glad that he could once again hear his mother's honest concern in her gentle voice, he relaxed a little.

"Ma, people here…Jesus Ma, I don't know, they look at me, and they either see a monster or an angel. I never know what I really am to these people. It changes from person to person. Ma, it's kind of freaking me out."

"Freaking you out? Luke. You're not a local to them, that's all, nothing to worry about," she reassured him.

"No, Ma, it's weirder than that. I know I'm not making sense, but Mom, it feels like some people want to hug me and others want to kill me. I don't know, Ma, this is all so confusing."

"Luke?"

"Ma?"

"Luke, what's really on your mind?"

"Ma, have you and Pops been keeping secrets from us all this time?"

"What?"

"You know, secrets."

"Secrets? Luke, what the hell are you talking about?"

"You know what I mean, Mom! Secrets!"

"You've said secrets three times now. I know what secrets are, Luke." She uttered a short sarcastic laugh and then continued. "The only secret I can remember keeping from you was when your father built a treehouse. Do you remember the treehouse?"

"Sure, what about it?"

"Do you remember when you were little, standing underneath the treehouse, and you suddenly felt water dripping on your head, and you asked me what it was?"

"Yes. Actually, I do."

"Well, I lied. I told you it was raining, but it was your brother peeing on you." She laughed wholeheartedly.

"What? You lied about him peeing on my head?" He started laughing as well.

"Ya, I'm sorry, I didn't have the heart to tell you," she mused during the fits of laughter.

"Mom, that's so mean."

Luke's spirit slightly raised as he heard his mother's pleasant laugh resonating in his ears. Glad for the momentary repose from his crisis, he joined his mother's laughter.

"I know. I'm sorry, really," she chuckled in between her laugh.

Luke abruptly ended the laughter. "Mom. I didn't mean that kind of a secret. Ma, are we part of the Mafia?"

Resa resumed her laughter. "Oh, Luke. You're killing me! Why would you think such a thing?"

"Mom, Luca Cassaro? You gave me the same name as the most notorious mobster in Sicilian history. Everyone here treats me like I'm part of the mob!"

"Luke, there are plenty of people with our last name. Even in Corleone, not every Cassaro is a Mafioso."

"But the one with the same name is."

"Yes, he is. He was your father's best friend, and he named you Luke out of respect for him."

"Jesus, Mom, you're not making this any easier. His best friend?"

"He knew that once he came to the States, he would never see him again. That was his way to keep some ties to the town he loved but left behind."

"Ma, I've got to tell you, that's pretty lame! Dad was a professor of ethics. This man with my name is a real bad guy. Where are the ethics?"

"Now, hold on a second. That's not fair to your father. I can't argue that Luca is a bad man now, but that was not always the case. Your dad, however, was always a good man, a great man. Believe me, sweetie. His intentions were always good. I remember when we were very young. He almost killed himself, saving my favourite goat."

"Yes, and you kissed him!"

"How do you know that?"

"It's part of Corleonese folklore."

"And I'm happy it is! But Luke, that's not the only thing your father did for me, for others, for the town, really."

"What did he do? I need to know, especially now."

The conversation turned one-sided, and Luke respectfully remained quiet until she was finished.

"Thanks for being honest with me. This really helps, but Ma, why didn't you tell us this before?"

"Your father and I made the decision of not telling anyone about what he did because we thought it would influence the way people would treat us here. Perhaps we were wrong. We didn't realize that the people there would not forget. Luke, we always intended to tell you about it, but only when you were old enough to understand all of it. We felt that your attitude toward your heritage would cloud your understanding of what he did."

"That's why he said I needed to visit Corleone. Boy, he was right about the wine and environment."

"What wine, what environment?"

"Just one of Pops analogies that turned out to be right on. Ma, thanks for being you. I wish I could tell Pops how much I loved him."

"Luke, I think he knew…. In fact, I'm positive he did. Have you done what he asked you to do?"

"You mean the ashes? Not yet, Ma."

"Please, don't leave it to the last minute like you always do."

Realizing he had not seen the urn since he put it in the safe, he made his way to the safe while still staying on the line.

"Ma, I'm not putting it off to the last minute. There's still plenty of time, don't worry, I'll talk to you soon. Love you."

After hanging up, he reached into his pocket and searched for his key fob to open the safe. Unable to find the fob, he looked around the room, thinking about where he had left it. He scanned the side tables from his place, but nothing of importance caught his eyes.

Not worried yet, he looked at the bed, but still nothing. Dropping on all fours, he looked under the bed. Remaining in the same position, he looked under the couch and scanned the rest of the room with his sight, but nothing glimmered in response.

Disappointed, but still not in a panic, he banged his head on the floor, trying to remember where he could have possibly left it. When nothing came to his mind, he jumped up and decided to look in his camera bag. The fob was not there either, but his grandfather's coin purse was. Distracted from his fob search, he picked up the small purse, rolled it around in his hands a few times, then opened it and took out the note with the directions to his father's spot. Staring at the directions, he realized that he had no idea where to start. It did say 'from the Tabacheria,' (smoke shop/convenient store), but he had no idea which one. He had seen three so far.

He knew what he had to do; he folded the directions, took out his Adidas sweat shorts from one of his suitcases, put them on, and stuffed the note in the zippered pocket. As he grabbed his camera off the small coffee table, the fob, as if deliberately hiding under its shadow, fell to the floor. He calmly picked it up, shook his head, and left the room.

CHAPTER TWENTY SEVEN

Be Nice

Walking in his compound, the Don, after receiving confirmation that the message had been delivered, turned to the man in black and gave him his next assignment with the explicit instructions not to be rough. "Or a least not that much."

CHAPTER TWENTY EIGHT

Busted

Luke walked through the streets of Corleone with one purpose in mind, to confront Alessandra at the Corleone Historical Building. Focused on this task, he walked right past Johnny, who was standing at the entrance to his bar.

"Luke, Luke! Where are you going in such a hurry?" Johnny yelled after him.

Luke paused and looked back. "Sorry Johnny, I didn't see you there." He walked back to him. "I'm heading to the Corleone Historical Building."

"The building is closed now."

"Yes, I know, I just thought that maybe…"

Johnny interrupted him, "I don't think so, Luke. It's mezzo giorno (mid-day or lunchtime), for the next two hours if you want to find someone, and I think that's what your doing, they're either eating at home or a restaurant, or they're sleeping at home."

"I could try her house. You know her, right? Do you know where she lives?"

"Everyone knows Alessandra, Luke. Her uncle is the priest. Her father owns the finest pizzeria in Corleone, and her brother..."

"What? Don Mario is her uncle?"

"Yes, why?"

"Never mind, I'll ask her. So, the directions."

"Go down the street. Just past the church is her father's pizzeria. She lives upstairs."

"Thanks," he said, walking away.

"Hang on. I'll walk with you. I need to get Don Mario to sign some documents for me," Johnny said, taking a few quick steps to catch up with Luke.

"Won't he be eating or sleeping?"

"Probably eating, he would say that if God never sleeps, why should he?"

As they reached the church, Johnny asked Luke if he would like to come in. "No thanks, I really need to find Alessandra."

"I'm sure Don Mario would love to see you," he said with a smile. "Hey, listen, I don't mean to pry, and I know she's beautiful, but can't this wait? She'll be around all night."

"No, I mean yes, it can wait. She is beautiful, but I have a girlfriend," Luke explained in haste.

Johnny laughed and held up his hands, "Slow down. Really, it's none of my business, just the bartender in me coming out."

"I need her to explain some directions for me."

"Maybe I could do that," Johnny offered with a sly grin.

Luke hesitantly explained to Johnny the directions and waited for him to read them, "What are these directions to or for?" Johnny asks, studying the note.

"They are the directions to where my father wants his ashes buried. But they are more than thirty years old."

Johnny nodded his head. Knowing the direction very well, he purposely lied, "You're probably right. Luke, Alessandra would be the one to help you with this but come in just a few minutes."

"Okay, fine, I did promise him," Luke agreed, noticing that sly smile broadening.

They entered the church, dipped their fingers in the holy water, and crossed themselves. Facing the altar, Johnny bowed slightly, and they walked down the nave to the front of the church, hoping to find Don Mario. As they reached the crossing, they heard voices coming from a small chapel next to the south transept. Recognizing one of the voices as belonging to Father Mario, they inched their way toward the conversation. Closer now, it became clear that the two men were in a private but heated discussion.

They were about to turn back when Alessandra's name pulled Luke in, and he decided to lend an ear to the talk. He held off Johnny with one hand and moved closer. They now heard the conversation very clearly, but it was also in Italian, so Luke turned to Johnny and asked him to listen and translate.

Curiosity won Johnny over, and he agreed.

"Okay, let me get closer," he said as he inched nearer the corner of the entrance to the chapel.

Holding on to a wooden banister that ran along the wall before turning into the chapel, Johnny anchored himself and leaned in. After a few seconds, he began to translate.

"Father Mario said that he doesn't care for that kind of history. He says it took us 1000 years to get rid of the Arabs, and now she wants to bring them back by restoring a mill?"

"Alessandra?" Luke suggested.

"I think so. The other guy said that that is what he wants too."

"Who?" Luke asked.

Johnny shrugged and carried on. "The same guy also said that there's a lot of money to be made in the restoration, and he wants it. Don Mario said that it's not always about the money. The other guy said. Who's he trying to kid? He knows the church will get a generous part of that money, and the church can always use more money. At least it's what you preach all the time." Johnny stopped and let out a little laugh. "Hold on," Johnny leaned forth around the corner. "There's someone else!"

"Yes, I hear a different voice," Luke agreed.

"Holy shit Luke, that's the mayor!"

"Shit!" Luke whispered.

Johnny continued with his on-the-spot translation, "The mayor says the town council has already approved a building and renovation permit. But it needs his signature, and he won't sign it unless Don Mario gives his group the project?" He turned to Luke and shrugged his shoulders. "What project?" he asked Luke.

Luke answered him with a shrug of his own.

"Now the first guy told him that he's been compensated for the permit already and to sign it, for Christ's sake!"

Johnny grabbed Luke's arm and squeezed hard.

"Don Mario is pissed. He just told them to watch what they say, they're in the house of the Lord, and he does not want to know more."

Luke tapped Johnny on the shoulder and signaled him towards the exit with his head.

"No, now I want to know more," Johnny whispered, turning away from Luke.

"Come on. This is a private conversation. I don't think we should be snooping."

"You're the one that wanted to stay when you heard Alessandra's name."

Luke came face to face with an ethical dilemma. On the one hand, he felt that listening in on a private conversation was not right. On the other hand, he wanted to be a part of it. He thought if he could learn something that could help Alessandra, it might help him convince her that he was not in the Mafia. With his mind made up, he gave Johnny a gentle push forward so he could see what was going on.

"What can you see?"

"Okay, don't push! I see Don Mario pacing back and forth with his head down. He just said to let him think."

A few seconds went by in silence. Anxious for more, Luke put a hand on Johnny's shoulder, "Well?"

"Quiet, I can't hear!" Johnny swatted Luke's hand away.

"But they're not saying anything!" Luke said, just before hearing a voice.

"The mayor just asked Don Mario to ask God for guidance, and the other guy asked Don Mario if their father told him what to do. Don Mario said that he's already told them once that this is the house of our father and to leave the sarcasm outside His doors."

Johnny listened for a while without translating. When Don Mario finished, he leaned back against the wall.

"Shit, shit, shit. This is too much. Let's go!"

"What did he just say?" Luke asked, holding Johnny back by his shoulders.

Johnny looked at Luke, then looked down and exhaled. "The mayor just told Don Mario that if 50,000.00 euros was not enough, there is more where that came from. The offer is from a large hotel and entertainment group that wants to build a casino, so money is not a problem. Plus, a casino would solve Don Mario's problem of renovating an Arab mill."

They heard nothing more, and Luke inched Johnny forward with a gentle push to look again.

"Nothing. Don Mario is leaning against the wall again with his hands crossed and looking up."

After a few more long seconds, Don Mario resumed.

Johnny's expression turned pale, "What?" Luke asked again.

"Don Mario said that God has given him the answer and that they must leave it up to providence to decide. The first man just said that he could care less who or what has to decide, but out of curiosity, he wants to know what God told Don Mario."

"Quiet!" Johnny turned to Luke, who was trying to get his attention.

They remained silent for a few seconds, and then Johnny continued. "He's saying that for 250,000.00 euros, the Church will step aside, but if Alessandra is able to raise 200,000.00 euros in three months, she will be allowed to proceed with the renovations. If not, then the mayor's group will build the casino. But the 250 is non-refundable."

The laugh from the other man was long and loud, almost as loud as the mayor's protestations. "The mayor said there's no way that his group will gamble with those terms."

Johnny suppressed a laugh. "Don Mario said that that group is in the gambling business. Why not start with this gamble."

A pause occurred in the conversation, and Johnny turned to Luke, raising his shoulders in silence. The conversation resumed, and Johnny quickly turned to listen again.

"The other guy said it is settled. The terms are acceptable."

Luke had had enough, so he leaned forward to have a look for himself. Seeing the previously unidentified man, he immediately recognized him as the man in black that gave him the note. Without a word, he grabbed Johnny's arm and dragged him out of the church.

Outside the church, Johnny looked at Luke and spread his arms. "What the hell was that?"

"There's a man in there dressed all in black. I saw him earlier today. He gave me a note, and he also gives me the creeps."

"Yes, I saw him. I think I know who he works for, and it's not surprising. Luke, this is way out of my league. Let's go. I'll show you where Alessandra lives," Johnny said, walking away.

Before Luke could ask who the man worked for, Don Mario yelled out from the church's entrance. "Luke, I was hoping to see you. Johnny, don't you have some documents for me to sign? Come, come."

"Hello, Don Mario," Luke answered, walking up to the church and feeling Johnny boring a hole in the back of his head with his eyes.

Silently following Don Mario down the nave, Luke was trying to formulate how he was going to tell Alessandra about her uncle's nefarious connections. Realizing that he had to first find a way to make her talk to him, he followed Don Mario.

"Come, follow me, my sons," Don Mario demanded, nudging Luke away from his private thoughts. They pass the crossing and entered the ambulatory, where Don Mario stopped and faced the two men.

"So," he said, putting his hands behind his back and looking alternately at each man. "Would you say that listening in on a private conversation is a sin?"

As both men falter in speech, trying to make up excuses, Don Mario was having a difficult time trying to suppress a laugh. Finally, unable to hold it in any longer, he stopped them with a gut-wrenching laugh.

"Wait a minute. You knew we were there?" Luke asked, looking at Johnny and shaking his head in disbelief.

"You two were very good, but then I saw Johnny leaning around the corner."

"If you knew we were there, why did you continue with your conversation?" Luke asked.

"Because I don't think they knew that you were there, and I didn't want them to find out."

"Don Mario, with all due respect, you're not making any sense!" Johnny accused.

Before answering, Don Mario turned and walked over to one of the windows overlooking the courtyard. After a few moments, he turned back to face the men.

"Before I answer this, I want both of you to swear before God and man that you will never speak to anyone about this. Especially Alessandra. Luke?"

"I promise," Luke said.

"Johnny?"

"I promise as well, Don Mario."

Don Mario nodded his head, "Very well then. About ten years ago, right after the warehouse was donated to us, I approached Alessandra to run B&B. She was then, and still is to this day, the smartest and most tenacious young woman I have ever known." Noticing that Luke and Johnny passed each other a look, Don Mario deviated a little from his explanation.

"Yes, yes, I know she's my niece, but regardless of my favoritism, there's no denying it." Both men silently agreed by nodding their heads, and Don Mario continued.

"Anyway, I thought she was the best for this job. She accepted right away, but true to form, she accepted with one caveat. She was to use part of the building for the historical society, house a small library and museum, run a tour guide service, and I must allow her to restore the Old Arab Mill. I know that is more than one condition, but to Alessandra, it's all one," he finishe with a chuckle.

"Wow, Don Mario, that's…"

"Don't interrupt Johnny; I'm on a roll, as they say in America," he said, looking at Luke. "The Lord and I have had many battles over the years. But he does talk to me. Actually, I do all the talking, and He listens if and when He wants. Anyway, He made me realize that the restoration of the mill would be good for the church, and Alessandra was the best person to manage the project."

"So, what was that scene with Alessandra at the hotel?" Luke asked and then apologized for interrupting the priest.

Don Mario looked at Luke with a silent reprimand. "That was for the benefit of the mayor. He must continue to think that our interests, mine and Alessandra are contradictory. I will do whatever it takes to keep my promise to make her dream of restoring the Mill come true. The town, the mayor, and even Alessandra don't know it, but most of that money will go to her through crowdfunding. She will have 200,000 00 euros."

"What about the mafia?" Johnny inquired.

"Don't be so naïve, boys. Who do you think is behind the mayor group? Those two were on the same side and didn't even know it."

"No Way!" Luke exclaimed.

"Absolutely, that man never said as much, but his acceptance is confirmation enough. Plus, they will get the general contracting job and make lots of money anyway," he finished and stared the two men down.

"Now, on your knees!" Don Mario commanded. "Both of you." They obeyed without hesitation.

"May God grant you the strength to keep your mouths shut?" He finished the benediction with the sign of the cross over their heads. "In the name of the Father, the Son, and the Holy Spirit."

Reaching for the men's hands with his, he helped them to rise. "Now you, Johnny, give me those documents to sign. And you, Luke, come, let's look for what you really came to find."

CHAPTER TWENTY NINE
Heaven Laughs too

Don Mario silently invited Luke inside for a little chat. He walked ahead with his hands folded behind his back and a somber look on his face. Luke quietly followed behind, gaping at his stiff neck for a while.

"Don Mario, is everything okay…. Is there something else you wanted to tell me?"

Don Mario's somber eyebrows turned soft as he answered without passing a glance to Luke.

"Luke, I know who you are and what your father did for this town. But a name such as Luke," Don Mario put a friendly hand on Luke's shoulder, "can carry a lot of weight, and in your case, that name can mean different things to different people. Around here, people's memories are cither very short or very long, depending on what suits them best. Do not concern yourself with others' perceptions of that name that you may never be able to change. Who you are, Luke, will be defined by filling up that empty space you now carry in here."

He stopped and put a hand on Luke's chest and then continued walking. "But Luke, the trouble with empty spaces is that they can be filled through virtuous deeds or sinful actions. Once that space is filled, any added deeds or actions will overflow, infecting others with those same attitudes and purposes in life." He stopped walking and looked at Luke.

"Your father filled his heart with love and integrity, and I can see that he has infected you with the same disease. He did well," he finished, resuming his walk with a smile.

Touched by the sincerity of the man's words, Luke took a quick step ahead of Don Mario and stopped to face him.

"Thank you, Don Mario, those are very insightful and moving words, you remind me of another man that I once loved, but now I'm beginning to admire."

"That is a great compliment, Luke, but there is something else that you should be aware of…."

Don Mario's words were cut short as a gust of loud voices welcomed the two conversing men from the opposite side. Their eyes fell on a fuming Alessandra, having a vocal battle with the Mayor and his wife.

"Can you hear them?" Luke asked.

"Half of the town can hear them!"

"No, I mean, can you understand what they're saying?"

"Not if you keep on talking," Don Mario said, holding up his hand.

Alessandra turned on her heel and walked a few steps away from the mayor and his wife but only to return to their faces with a blow of audible anger,

"You, you should be ashamed of yourself, putting your interests ahead of our town and this island."

"And you? You don't have any self-interest in restoring an old mill?" the mayor countered.

"Not a one!" she responded, shaking her head. "My sole interest is to bring to light the wonderful history of this fascinating town, that there's more to this place other than the Mafia. The Arab Mill is but one of the many ruins that are scattered around here that will attract tourists. I plan to begin with the Mill. Hopefully, I'll do more. What will you do? Or you?" she demanded, turning to the mayor's wife, who instinctively took a step backward.

"Leave my wife out of this, Alessandra. This is between us."

"That's where you're completely wrong, your highness! This is between all of us, all of us," she finished, emphasizing the 'us' with a sweep of her arms and looking around.

As she did that, she noticed Luke and Don Mario looking back at her. Frustrated, she turned and stomped away, disappearing amongst the narrow laneways of the nearby homes.

"Well?" Luke said, looking over to Don Mario.

"Come," Don Mario responded, grabbing Luke by the arm. "I'll explain as we go after your prize."

Luke quickly followed him as they trekked towards the place Alessandra had disappeared into. As they turned the corner, they ended up in an empty laneway. It truly seemed as if Alessandra had disappeared into thin air.

Don Mario apologized to Luke for needing to go back to the church but gave him specific instructions to Alessandra's home.

"Thanks, Don Mario, but I have Johnny's direction right here."

"Oh, let me see them," he entwined his brows to read the directions and let out a muffled laugh.

"Just as I expected. These directions will get you there, but mine will get you there quicker. I've been here all my life; my directions are much more direct."

"Thanks, Don Mario."

A bit disappointed that the priest could not accompany him any further, Luke shook his hand and then, on impulse, gave him a hug.

"I hope you don't mind," Luke said.

"A hug is a sign of trust as well as friendship. I accept it willingly. Good luck, son," Don Mario answered him with a smile.

As Luke watched him turn the corner, his heart filled with a feeling of satisfaction. He felt as if something had lulled the creeping anxiety within him. Still looking at the street the priest had vanished into, he could tell that the priest had many parishioners who came to him not only for advice but also for a glimpse of his calming presence. For Luke, the priest could put to rest any sufferer's worries with his peace radiating energy.

CHAPTER THIRTY
Pizza Puts Everything on Hold

As he followed Don Mario's directions, he could not help but feel a sense of awe for the man in the garb of a priest. Until today he never had imagined that there could be people in this world that truly had a spiritual calling, but the more he thought about it, the more he was certain that today he actually met one.

With a smile on his face, he continued to follow his friend's instructions until he stood looking up at a balcony and the windows beside it that Don Mario described perfectly.

He took out his phone to call her but put it away, realizing he did not have her number. Looking around and then down, he picked up a pebble and gently tossed it at the window.

"Alessandra!" he called out. When there was no response, he tossed another pebble. "Alessandra!" he called her a little louder. *"I feel like I am in a 1940's romantic movie."*

Still, the window glimmered in her absence. Smiling at his old-fashion method of getting someone's attention, he chose a slightly bigger pebble and threw it with a little more force. "Alessandra, will you just talk to me for a minute? I'm not who you think I am!"

An old lady opened the window and yelled at him in Italian.

"Alessandra," he asked in a gentle voice, not understanding the old lady.

"Luke?" Alessandra called him from a balcony window across the street.

Luke turned and saw Alessandra looking back at him. He turned back and tried to apologize to the other lady in Italian, but he made a mess of it and turned again to Alessandra.

"What are you doing?"

Before he could answer, the Lady at the other window yelled at Alessandra in Italian to tell her boyfriend to stop throwing rocks at her window.

"He's not my boyfriend! I don't even know him," she yelled back, slamming the window shut.

Luke looked over to the window with the blue sill, for that was where Don Mario said Alessandra's bedroom window was located. Although upset at his failure to communicate with Alessandra, a huge smile crossed his face, followed by a laugh. *"I can't believe that man. A priest and a prankster. I'm sure he's falling all over himself trying to get back to the safety of his church. God, if you're witnessing this, give me the opportunity to get him back!"*

Still smiling, he went over to the door under the other window and knocked several times.

"Alessandra! Will you please come down? I need your help. I'm not who you think I am! There's been a huge misunderstanding. Alessandra!" He lowered his head. "I need your help," he said softly.

Little misunderstandings can lead to never-ending dead ends. If only she gave him just one chance to explain himself, he knew he would win her over.

Luke felt relief as he heard the door emitting the sound of a lock opening. When the door finally opened, an older, softer version of Alessandra looked back at him. Surprised on several levels, he stayed silent.

"I'm Alessandra's mother," she smiled, introducing herself in Italian. "You must be Luca."

"Yes." "Wonderful! Come in," she uttered in Italian and tugged at him with another smile.

Before following Alessandra's mother up the stairs, Luke took a quick look to his left, where he found the back entrance to the restaurant. The opened door revealed several tables that were set with white tablecloths, black serviettes, stemware, and silver settings. A stark contrast to Johnny's bar, it made him wonder where he would be more comfortable.

The older version of Alessandra yelled for Alessandra as she reached the top of the stairs. She looked back down, inviting Luke with her hands to come up. This, obviously, was the back entrance to their home, which led directly to their dining room, where the family was sitting around the table.

Lively, happy, and talkative, it reminded him of his Sunday dinners with his family. How fun it was to be around family and share a laugh or two. A gentle nudge in his heart depicted his whispering pain. Was he really missing home? Suddenly recalling why he was here, he looked in to see if Alessandra was there. When he couldn't see her, he fought the urge to turn and quickly run back down the stairs, but he stayed put and politely greeted the family with a loud ciao.

The group turned in unison and waved at Luke, making him feel welcomed and less anxious.

"Come! Sit down! Eat with us," he said in Italian, leading him by his arm.

"Oh no, Grazie, I can't," Luke responded, guessing her intentions and resisting her pull.

"Sure, you can," she insisted, still speaking in Italian.

"Alessandra!" She called out again, "Don't be rude. There's a guest in the house."

"Ma, Alessandra left," a young man, who Luke assumed to be her brother, answered her.

"What? Where did she go?"

"Where's Alessandra?" Luke also wanted to know, again guessing what they were talking about.

"I don't know," the young man responded in English and then added, "Who knows what she does. She left in a hurry and was very upset."

"Did she say at what?"

"Something about an Americano."

"Shit!"

"That would be you, right?" The young man smiled at Luke.

"That would be me."

Alessandra's mother watching this conversation in English, finally stepped in.

"He's looking for Alessandra. Good! She needs a boyfriend. This is a good one! I knew his father."

"What did she say?" Luke asked the young man.

"She said that she knew your father, and if you want to marry Alessandra, that would be fine."

The rest of the family, a young woman who looked like she could be the young man's twin and a much younger girl, laughed aloud.

"What?" Luke said, turning red.

"No, she just said she knew your father. I just made the second part up."

"Very funny!" Luke laughed, making everyone feel at ease.

"So, she knew my father? Seems like everyone knew my father."

After the young man explained to his mother what Luke had just said, she turned to Luke and once again grabbed his elbow, pulling him a little harder towards the table. As she offered him her condolences, she directed him to sit in the empty chair beside the young man, and she sat at her usual spot to talk to Luke.

"She says your father was born not far from here. She also said you look just like him."

"Thanks, Signora?"

"Laila, prego. And these are my other children, Eugenio, Vittoria, and Lina."

"Hello everyone, I'm Luke," he said with a big smile and then turned back to Laila. "Laila, I'm sorry I don't want to be rude, but I need to speak with Alessandra right away."

"Eugenio, go see if she's downstairs," Laila commanded after the translation, "And bring up the pizza."

"Ma, send Vittoria. I want to talk to Luke about the United States. She's probably at Johnny's Bar anyway."

"Eugenio!" Laila said, looking at him the way all mothers do when they have been disappointed.

Eugenio and Luke stood up and began to leave the room.

"Where is he going? He must stay and eat. Your father just made a fresh pizza," Laila said, gesturing with her hand.

Eugenio turned and held up his hand.

"Wait. My mother says you must stay for dinner. We're having pizza, fresh, homemade. I'm going to get it right now and see if Alessandra is there."

Before he answered, the smell of the freshly made pizza made its way up the stairs and into Luke's nostrils, making it very difficult for him to decline the invitation.

"Thank you very much, Laila. You've been very kind. I would love to stay. Unfortunately, I really need to find Alessandra and resolve this," he finished, swallowing and licking his lips.

Laila's look made him realize that although she was acknowledging what he was saying, with numerous nods of her head and a bright smile. She had, in reality, no idea of what he was talking about, so he turned to Vittoria and nudged his head towards her mother.

"Ah, yes, you want me to translate," Vittoria said, turning to her mother to translate.

"She said that not having a piece of pizza is not going to make Alessandra appear any faster."

He turned to see Eugenio come through the door with the pizza but without Alessandra.

"She is not there. But the pizza is!" Eugenio laughed, placing the pizza on the table.

"There's more. Just let dad know when you want it," he told his mother in Italian.

Disappointed, he started to head down the stairs. After taking a few steps down, the aroma of the pizza overwhelmed him, and he turned back.

"Okay, well, maybe I'll just get a slice."

Everyone clapped and cheered, welcoming him back to the table.

CHAPTER THIRTY ONE
The Search Continues

Luke was always very disciplined. As a child, he often refused to play with other children if his mother told him to stay clean before a special occasion. As an adult, discipline now came in the form of punctuality, meeting deadlines, and fulfilling customers' requests. But when it came to food, discipline was a word foreign to Luke. Fortunately, he not only looked like his father but also had inherited his metabolism, for he could and would eat anything, anytime, without gaining weight. A blessing the rest of his family envied. So, when the second pizza arrived, it did not take too much convincing for Luke to indulge in the heavenly experience.

Now, with only a few pieces of pizza left, he pushed himself away from the table, intending to thank the family and excuse himself. Unfortunately, pushing away from the table did not remove the pizza from his view, and he unashamedly reached for one last small square.

"For the road," he said before thanking Laila and the rest of her family for their hospitality, great company, and, unsurprisingly, the best pizza he had ever had.

"Wonderful, wonderful, bravo, take the rest," Laila offered.

"Thank you. I can't, but thanks."

Laila quickly crossed the room and gave Luke a tight hug, then caressed his face with both her hands and told him in Italian to try and laugh with the angels occasionally.

As Eugenio translated, Luke hugged Laila and simply said, "Grazie."

The moment his shadow was out of the room, Alessandra walked in from the main stairway, where she was met by her mother.

"That was very rude of you," Laila scolded her.

"Do you know who he is?"

"I do. But you sure don't!"

"What?" she questioned, frowning as she waited for her mother to explain.

"Let me tell you about his father, and then maybe you'll know who the son is."

The story was neither short nor shallow. Thanking her mother with a long silent hug, she left to find the man she had mistakenly hurt.

Alessandra walked forward in search of Luke, yet in her mind, she was indulged in another journey of self-reflection and criticism. Why did she do it? Why did she let her scorn control her actions? Luke didn't deserve this.

Entering the restaurant chewing on the last bite of his pizza, he quickly scanned the room for Alessandra. Unable to spot her, he navigated the packed restaurant, ignoring the invitations from the locals to join them for dinner or a drink. Finally, hoping that Eugenio was right about his sister's whereabouts, he headed for Johnny's Bar.

Walking into Johnny's bar, his hopes were immediately lifted as he saw Giovanna sitting with her boyfriend at a nearby table. Blurring out the rest of the bar, he quickly approached them.

"Mi scusi. You're Alessandra's friend. I saw you with her at the restaurant. I need to speak with her."

"Hello to you too," she responded sarcastically.

"I'm sorry, that was very rude of me. I'm Luke," he said, extending his hand.

"Hi, Luke. I'm Giovanna and this is my friend Gianni," she said, taking it.

"Piacere," Gianni said, standing and shaking his hand.

Giovanna reached for Luke's arm.

"That's alright; I can see you're stressed. She just left. I'm sure she'll be right back. Please sit with us." she said with a pleasing smile.

"No, thanks, I really should be going to find her."

"Whoa! This guy is really cooked!" Her boyfriend said in Italian, earning him a playful slap on the arm from Giovanna.

"Giovanna, I really need to talk to her. I think she's a little confused as to who I am."

"I think we all are, Luke. She'll be right back. She just went back to her house to get something."

Reluctantly, Luke sat down and took a deep breath with his back to the entrance. He didn't see Alessandra walking in to stand beside him. Feeling her closely looming presence, he stood up to look at her and the extended hand that she was offering.

Refusing the hand, he hugged her tight and whispered in her ear, "I'm sorry."

Alessandra felt as if a boulder within her had perished. She could feel the cool air caressing her cheeks as she remained glued to his chest for a while.

"At least he is a bigger person than I am. Even after what I made him go through, he accepted me with an embrace…"

Taking his hand, she guided him out of the bar. Giovanna's boyfriend took her hand and looked her in the eyes.

"See, it's not always up to me to make the first move."

"Shit head!" She said, slapping his shoulder and kissing his lips.

CHAPTER THIRTY TWO
Waiting For a Guest

The old man pensively sat on a chair outside in his courtyard. As he twirled a glass filled halfway with wine, he looked at the urn on the table in front of him and wondered what could have been.

A very pragmatic man, Luca realized that his survival was a result of Franco's altruistic actions. But necessary as they were, those actions also had committed him to a future that, although he did not choose, he embraced non the less.

"Welcome home," he said, gently placing one hand on the urn and draining the glass.

CHAPTER THIRTY THREE
Limited Confessions

Walking silently down the street, each occupied by their own thoughts, Luke and Alessandra didn't feel uncomfortable in the awkward silence that often surrounded newly formed relationships. There was something between them that kept pulling them closer. Each hurdle that came forth would somehow vanish, and they would be back together, beside one another. Having formulated his thoughts, Luke inhaled the fresh evening air, stepped ahead of Alessandra and stopped her.

"This whole time, I couldn't understand why you were being so mean to me."

Alessandra gave him a cross look.

"Luke, please stop I..."

"Wait! Please just let me finish. The last three days have been filled with a series of misunderstandings because of my short-sighted beliefs about my heritage I did not manage well. I now know that because of my name, you, like many others here, believe that I'm a Mafioso. But there is no connection with that other Luca Cassaro. I'm not a Mafioso," he said, reaching for her hands.

In his eyes, Alessandra could see the truth. How did she miss it? He never lied to her. It was her trust that was playing games with her. Looking down, feeling a little guilty that she did not stop him, she tried again.

"Really, Luke, I know that…well, I know…"

"Look at me, Alessandra. Do I look like one of them?" He interrupted her again.

"Well."

"Do I act like one of them?"

"No. You're too clumsy."

"Exactly! Wait, what? Anyway," he said, shaking his head, "Besides, your mother knows all about my family, I mean the Cassaro family, the one that is not Mafia-related. My father was born around the corner from where you live. Can you believe that?"

"Yes, my mother knew your father, and that is what I..."

"Luca? Luca Cassaro?" Someone asked, stopping her again.

"Yes, but no..."

"Luca Cassaro? Ay! Vieni qua!" Another person commanded him, reaching for his hand.

Seeing that Luke was very uncomfortable, she grabbed his hand and pulled him away.

"Luke, let's go. I need to confess something..."

Before she could finish, another passerby interrupted them.

"Luca! Una foto!"

Luke had had enough. He held up his hands and yelled out, "Look! Everybody!" He tried to climb on a nearby chair.

Alessandra grabbed his arm to stop him, but he reached gently for it and removed her hand from his arm.

"No, Alessandra, I think I need to do this."

Interested where this was going, Alessandra deferred to him, and Luke climbed onto the chair.

"Hello everyone, my name is Luke, Luca Cassaro..."

Everyone gasped. Holding up his hands to calm everyone down, he began again, "Yes, my name is Luca Cassaro, but I'm not related in any way to the Cassaro that you all think I am. My father, Franco, and my mother, Teresa..."

The spontaneous cheering and clapping from the people around him at the mention of his parents' names forced him once again to put both his hands out to stop them.

"Please, please," he said, successfully quieting down the crowd.

He looked at the many faces of the curious crowd and continued, "My father, Franco, and my mother Teresa were both born here. Although they now live in America, they are proud Corleonesi. Yes, we carry the Cassaro name, but not the history of the Cassaro family you all think I belong to. For those of you who knew my father, you would know the kind of man he was. For those that don't, ask around, and you'll quickly come to understand who he was and what he means to this town."

A gentle bustle in the mids of the crowd took place, where to and fro, moving heads depicted a trailer-like glimpse into my family history and my parents' tale. Luke felt a bit strange that how many people actually knew his parents and remembered them up till now as if they were some characters of a folk tale kept alive by generations.

"When I came here to Corleone to bury my father's ashes, I considered myself to be a proud New Yorker. Along the way, I've gained respect for my heritage and my name. I have fallen in love," he said, giving Alessandra a penetrating look, "With the city of my ancestors and the people of Corleone. My name is Luca Cassaro, and I'm honored to carry my family name."

Complete silence.

A man looked at a woman and said in Italian, "I can't understand a fucking word he said!"

"Me neither!" she responded.

Luke saw the blank looks on the people's faces. Shaking his head, he realized his mistake. Perhaps the to and fro head movement was an act of confusion.

"Oh, that's right. Most, if not all of these people don't speak English," Luke said aloud to Alessandra as he stepped down.

"I'm so embarrassed. Can you translate?"

Impressed with his emotional explanation but overcome by his statement about his love, Alessandra stared at him with her mouth slightly open.

"Alessandra?"

Alessandra stood stunned to the core by his emotional outburst. She felt as if there were some invisible strings attached to her body and the little string end was in some way attached to the reel which was now in his hands. She could tell that her will had signed her up to Luke. The realization was a bit troublesome, yet the truth, so she continued to stare at him blankly in utter disbelief.

"Alessandra?" He touched her with a gentle shoulder rub.

Finally, snapping out of her trance, she turned to the crowd and spoke to them in Italian, "He's not related to the infamous Cassaro," she said in a loud, proud voice.

"We know that!" A man responded.

"We just wanted to show him some respect for what his father did for this town."

"It seems that I'm the only one that did not want to see the difference," she said softly.

"What?" the man asked.

"Never mind. I'll let him know what you said, thanks."

"Thanks, it means a lot to all of us," the man said, gesturing to the now dispersing crowd.

Understanding her explanation of the crowd's intentions, he looked intensely into her eyes before closing in to hug her tight.

"Come with me," he ordered, taking her hand and leading her away from the still busy piazza.

Away from curious minds and prying eyes, Luke stopped and turned towards her.

"Alessandra."

Holding his hand a little tighter, expecting him to say something romantic, she answered him in a soft murmur, "Yes?"

"Now that you know who I am. Will you help me find the place my father wants me to bury his ashes?"

"What?" she said, looking confused.

"Will you help me?"

Although a bit disappointed, she understood that perhaps her previous attitude towards him had caused him to be guarded, and he may need a little more time.

"Sure. What would you like me to do?"

Luke took out his father's directions and showed them to her. She took the paper and scanned with her eyebrows slightly narrowed.

As he waited for her to review the directions, he took a step back and began to examine her closely. Beginning with her long wavy, coffee black hair, one side of which cascaded softly below her shoulder blades and the other side falling gently in front, brushing one of her perky breasts, making it a perfect focal point. He was transfixed.

With her hand, Alessandra slowly flipped her hair backward, giving Luke a full and unobstructed view of her chest. Realizing that perhaps he had lingered a little too long on her breasts, he shifted his eyes to her bare shoulders, where the contrast between her olive skin and the thin canary yellow strap of her sun dress projected a picture of exotic beauty.

The photographer within Luke wanted to record this wonderful image, but the man in him froze his body. Unable and unwilling to look away, he resorted to taking a mental picture. His eyes lingered over her features for a while. How magnificently was she created!

Alessandra unexpectedly looked up from the directions catching Luke in a trance. Unwilling to release him from his daze, she lowered her eyes back to the piece of paper, smiling to herself. Sensing that she had caught his pensive stare, he asked her how she was doing.

"Almost there," she said, wittingly giving him just a little more time.

Purposely shifting her weight from one leg to the other, she exposed a little more of her thigh, holding Luke's attention further. Enjoying a moment of self-pride, she allowed Luke to gaze for a few more seconds.

"Would you like to take a picture?" she asked in a friendly, sarcastic tone.

"Sorry, Alessandra, that was rude of me. I..."

"No need to apologize. I know where to go," she said, letting him off the hook.

Luke cleared his throat and asked her to show him.

"I'll take you there. But Luke, don't you need to get the ashes first?" She asked with a sly smile, hoping that he had not totally cleared his head of her.

"Yes, sure, I'll get them," Luke said, turning away.

Wondering why he had not asked her to go with him, he turned back, a bit embarrassed at his awkward behavior.

"Unless you want to join me."

"What? To your hotel room?" She asked, looking at him sideways.

"No... I mean, yes...I mean my room...but I mean just to get the ashes," he stammered.

"Yes, of course, the ashes. Do you have another reason in mind?"

"No, just the ashes," he said, taking a few steps away from her. Then in a much lower voice, he said, "For now!"

"Pardon?" Alessandra asked although she had heard him perfectly well.

CHAPTER THIRTY FOUR
Your Ride Is Here

Using the fob to open the door. He invited Alessandra to enter first.

"Wow! I like what you did with this room," Alessandra said, scanning the room.

"Sorry about the mess."

"I've always loved this suite. The bathroom is my favorite room," she said, walking in further and running her finger along the edge of the couch.

Watching her pace around the room and seemingly recalling an earlier experience, Luke felt a pang of jealousy. Disappointed at this feeling, he tossed her the fob and asked her to open the safe while he changed the lenses on his camera.

As Luke began to change the lenses, he heard his name faintly called by Alessandra.

"Luke," she called again.

"Yes," he finally answered.

"Luke, the urn is not here."

"What? What do you mean it's not there?"

"I mean, the safe is empty."

Luke left the camera on the bed and walked over to the closet.

"Shit!"

"Luke. I'm so sorry."

"Shit," he said, slowly walking back to the bed. Sitting at the edge, he began rubbing his temples with his fingers and then hardened his knuckles. Joined by Alessandra, they immediately dropped flat on their backs, silently staring at the canopy.

Suddenly, Luke jumped up and told her to stay there. "I think I know who stole the ashes."

Alessandra watched him unzip his back pocket and take out another piece of paper.

"Alessandra, do you remember this morning when..."

With her dress riding slightly up her thighs and her legs dangling flirtatiously off the side of the bed, Luke momentarily lost his train of thought.

"How can someone look so amazingly sexy just resting on their elbows?"

All he could do to stop himself from launching on top of her was to swallow hard and continue, "...When this man in black came over to me? Well, the guy gave me this note," he said, handing the note over to her and quickly turning away.

After reading the note, Alessandra quickly stood up. "It's just about 5:00 pm now, and this place is right around the corner. But Luke, if I'm right, it's probably best if you leave it alone."

"What? I can't do that. It was my father's dying wish! I have to get it back."

"Luke. Listen to me. You don't know what these men are like. And believe me. You do not want to know."

"Alessandra, I'm not going home without... Wait, you believe me now?"

"Yes, but I still think you should not go."

"Alessandra, you have just made my day. Finally, thank you," he said, reaching for her shoulders and pulling her in an embrace.

With their bodies finally touching, an act that they both had been anxiously waiting for, they looked into each other's eyes for a few seconds in anticipation of what they both craved.

Closing her eyes in frustrated realization, a look that made her even more irresistible to Luke, she whispered, "There's no time."

"No," he huskily responded, unwilling to release her.

He smiled. A silent confirmation that there would be other opportunities for their desires to be consummated, he released her and took a step back.

"I understand if you don't want to come along. In fact, I think it's best if you don't. Just tell me where this place is, please."

"Okay," she said, extremely disappointed at God's invention of poor timing.

They exited the hotel and walked about 100 meters from their desired location.

"It's just around that corner."

He looked at Alessandra one last time.

"Thanks," he said and turned away.

Shortly after walking away, Alessandra stopped and looked at Luke, who was almost running.

"Wait!" she yelled.

Luke stopped and anxiously waited for her to catch up. "I'll come with you."

"Alessandra, no, you don't need to do this. It's safer if you stay."

"Why were you running?" she asked, ignoring his protest.

"I heard some footsteps."

"You're a very brave man," she said sarcastically.

"Shut up and run!" he yelled, grabbing her hand and pulling her away.

Running to the first cross street, they blindly turned the corner and ran into the man in black, knocking both of them to the ground.

"What's with people blocking my way and knocking me down?"

"What?" She asked.

"Nothing, I'll explain later."

Reaching into his jacket, he ordered them in his car with a turn of his head. The man's demeanor left them with no choice but to follow his directions without a word of protestation.

CHAPTER THIRTY FIVE
Luca

The rear-view mirror reflected Luke and Alessandra sitting quietly in the backseat. What the man in black couldn't see was Alessandra's hand resting by her side, silently inviting Luke's hand to engage. Impulsively Luke looked down at her hand.

"I'm sorry," he softly apologized, reaching for her hand.

Alessandra looked over, smiled at him, and gently squeezed his hand. There was no need to respond in words. Her actions confirmed that she completely understood him and would stand by him no matter the situation.

Parking in his usual spot, the man in black exited the car and opened the rear door. He motioned them to get out with a wave of his hand.

They walked up to an old man sitting at a table beside a plate of goat cheese, fresh figs, and crostini. A liter of red wine rested perilously close to the urn. The man in black approached the old man and whispered something in his ear.

"That's fine. It's better if she's here," he told the man in black in Italian.

Alessandra could feel Luke tensing up, so she reached for his arm and held him back.

"The urn is yours. Indulge this old man's possession for a few more minutes," The man told Luke in perfect English, sensing Luke's agitation.

Without waiting for his approval, he turned to Alessandra.

"You don't like me, do you?" he asked her in Italian.

"Like you? I don't even know you. But I'll tell you this. It's what you've done to this country, this town, that I hate."

"What I've done to this country is no more or no less than other nations and empires have done for centuries. But my dear Alessandra, either way, it is not for you or, for that matter, even me to judge, for we come from different perspectives. Historians will record it for posterity, and God will judge it for eternal life," he finished, inviting them to sit with his hand.

"You're wrong, Don Luca. It is for us to judge and fight for what we believe is right. After all, we live in this world here and now. Thanks, but we'll stand."

"I like this one. She's got attitude, and that's good. You shouldn't like a man like me," he told her honestly in English.

Then turning to Luke, he continued, "Now you. Luca Cassaro, my namesake." He smiled at Luke's expression. "You're wondering about my English. Not long after your father left for America, I went to Canada and graduated from the University of Toronto with a B.A. in Business. One of my greatest achievements." He nodded his head several times, confirming his pride in his accomplishment.

"But family called, and I answered. Perhaps we will have more time for that tale in the future, or maybe not," he quickly added after a short pause.

"You're also wondering what I'm doing out in the open like this," he said, motioning towards his estate with his hand.

"Do not believe everything you read, young Luke. There are many ways to hide. One of the best is to tell everyone where you are, especially the authorities that require your help from time to time. Isn't that so, Alessandra?"

Although the question was directed to Alessandra, it was Luke that answered.

"That's why you did not take our cell phones. The people that don't know don't matter. The people that do will not reveal anything for fear of retribution or perhaps loyalty. As for my knowledge, whom would I tell, like you say, the authorities already know."

"Like your father, you are a very perceptive man. He's a keeper, Alessandra," he told her.

"Like I need your advice," she responded in Italian.

"Now, do you know why I took this from you?" He asked, ignoring Alessandra's remark.

Luke shook his head.

"I wanted to meet you, Luca, so I could give you my sincere condolences in person. I apologize for the cloak and dagger, but you can appreciate that a formal invitation may not have gone so well. This," he said, gesturing to the urn, "was my insurance policy. Anyway, you are here now, and I formally offer you and your family my condolences."

Luke remained silent, holding the old man's stare.

"I can see that you are not convinced about my motives. Perhaps, based on my reputation, your doubts are justified, but Luca, my feelings are sincere. Your father was my best friend at a time in my life that was free of responsibilities and judgments. If you allow me, I would like to tell you who your father really was."

Luke's silent and unemotional look prompted Luca to continue, "Even after all of these years, I don't think Franco would have changed. In fact, I will bet that he never shared with you why he left his home."

"I know he wanted to, but he passed before he could."

"I'm not sure he ever would have. It wasn't in his nature. But it is in mine, and I think you should know. Would you like me to continue?"

"I do. Very much," he said, looking to Alessandra for support, which she granted with a slight nod.

"Great. Please sit, both of you." He pointed to the two empty chairs.

Once he saw them comfortably seated, he began. "We were both in our early twenties at the time. Young, full of great ideas and expectations, we thought we could change the world. Well, our town and perhaps our province, but we set our sight high. Always ahead of the crowd, your father and mother being deeply in love, had already talked about their future, and in fact, I think they had already set a wedding date. As for me, although I was interested in several of the girls in town, there was one that caught my attention. That was your mother, Laila," he said, looking at Alessandra.

Alessandra put her hands on her mouth.

"Oh, come on, Alessandra, don't be so dramatic. Anyway, as Franco, your mother, and I walked down the main street on a beautiful Saturday afternoon in September, we saw Laila coming toward us with my cousin Mauro. You must understand that my cousin knew how I felt about Laila, and yet there he was with that stupid smirk on his face as they walked by us. He didn't say a word, just looked at me sideways. Recognizing how upsetting this was for me, your father grabbed me by my arm and led me away."

He looked over to the man in black, showed two fingers, and pointed to his glass.

"We walked around for a while longer, then took your mother home and headed to our favorite hiding place. It wasn't much of a hideout, just a place behind some boulders where we smoked cigarettes and drank some wine or grappa we had stolen from our fathers' cellars. We both knew Mauro would be there, and he was. After a few verbal shots back and forth between my cousin and me, we got into a heated argument that escalated into a fight.

"Your father tried to break it up, but we wouldn't have any of it. After what seemed a lifetime but was probably a minute or two, Mauro started to get the better of me. I remember seeing him on top of me with a rock in his hand and thinking, 'he's going to hit me!' As he lifted his arm in the air, your father pushed Mauro off, knocking the rock from his hand. I didn't hesitate. I picked up that same rock and hit him on the side of the head. I didn't mean to, but I killed him," he said, looking down at his glass.

"As you can imagine, the shit hit the fan," he said, looking up again.

"Although the wrong was done to my uncle's family, my father, being the head of the family, had the responsibility to make sure that my uncle got his vengeance. My father did all he could to find out what really happened, but even with some intense interrogations, no one from this town came forward. After about a week, Franco told me that he could not let the people in town be treated this way and that he needed to speak with my father. I tried talking him out of it, but he would not hear it. He just told me he would handle it. The next day, he came to our house and asked to see my father about the death of Mauro...." He stopped for a while to ponder on his words, then continued,

"My father was not an educated man. However, being extremely cautious, suspicious, street smart, and relying heavily on intuition made him very good at what he did. So, when my father asked me to join them, I was not surprised. I had it coming. What I remember the most about him were his eyes. I swear they could penetrate rock. Anyway, in less than two minutes, he had figured it all out. He asked Franco to repeat what he had just told him, to me. Your father then turned to me and said that, although he wasn't the guilty party, he would take the fall for the town. He did not say that he was doing this for me, but the look in his eyes certainly was unmistakable.

Then turning back to my father, he went on to explain that although what he was proposing looked like an altruistic deed, he actually used the word 'altruistico'. He was always the smartest amongst all our friends. Anyway, I digressed a bit. He went on to tell my father that this was actually a selfish request. He and Teresa had been planning to go to America for some time, and knowing the atmosphere in New York at the time, he wanted assurances that whatever he chose to do, he, the family that they would build, and the rest of his family here, would be left alone.

Luca's face looked at something in the distance as if he could see all of it repeating right before his eyes. He then cleared his throat.

"Before giving him his answer, my father turned to me and then turned back to Franco. In that fleeting moment, I saw something in my father's eyes that I had never seen before. I could only stare at him as he gave him his word. You should know, Luke, that the story does not end there. When my father told my uncle that the matter was taken care of, my uncle wasn't satisfied. He wanted to be the one to take the pound of flesh. My father held firm, and the ensuing arguments between my father and uncle turned ugly. In the end, my uncle could not defy the head of the family, not openly anyway, so he backed down. But, being fashioned from the same cloth as my father, he did not give up. He tried to enlist help from others around this area, but my father's tentacles had reached a very long way, and my uncle finally had to give up."

Luke looked at Alessandra, who was lost in her own thought, as if she could feel what Luca was feeling. Luca, on the other hand, had paused for a quick breath. "A few weeks later, my uncle invited me to go hunting up some nearby hills. There, after several hours of pleasant conversation about family and my plans for the future, he finally asked me what he had brought me there to ask. He wanted to know if Franco's sudden departure had anything to do with the murder of his son. Like my father, I also held firm. I told him that Franco and Teresa's departure had been planned for a while and that I had no idea why my father was doing what he was for your parents in America. He smiled and told me not to worry, but his eyes told me otherwise. As fate would have it, on our way home, my uncle slipped down a rocky patch of the hill and was killed, an unfortunate accident, but one that quieted the family squabble," he finished, giving Alessandra a quick glance.

"I owed your father a great deal for what he did for me. I regret I wasn't able to thank him properly." He turned and reached for the urn.

"You honoured the deal he made with your father, Mr Cassaro. My father would have recognized that as the ethical thing to do," Luke flatly mused.

"Very well said. I won't offend you by offering you my hand." He picked up the urn from the table and handed it over to Luke.

"I've had my glass of wine with him. Now make his last wish come true."

"Thank You."

"He's going to take you to where you need to bury the ashes," he tells them, looking at the man in black. "To make up for the inconvenience."

"You know where he wanted his ashes buried?" Luke asked, surprised.

"I could be mistaken. But I doubt it. Give me your father's note."

Luke looked at him with uncertainty. Recognizing this, Luca reassured him.

"Please. I'll give it right back to you."

He read the note and nodded to the man in black after handing the note back to Luke.

For the first time, Luke saw a tiny sign of humanity in Luca. *Perhaps it's the boy he was when my father was here with him,* he thought and held up his hand.

"Please, you keep it. I'm sure my father would approve."

Luca looked at Luke, took a long deep breath, turned and walked away, folding the note.

Luke felt a gentle nudge underneath his ribcage. How strange life can be. One wrong step and you are forced to lose something which is dear to you. A gentle caress on his arm made him turn his head to Alessandra, who was also looking at Luca leave.

Luke's eyes softened. Life can be really unpredictable. *You are bound to leave something you get used to at its wish.* He held her hand tightly, and they walked away.

CHAPTER THIRTY SIX

Rest In Peace Pops

Just at the edge of town, around a gentle bend and behind some enormous boulders, was a clearing. In the middle of this clearing was an olive tree. Alessandra, Luke, and the man in black were standing over a hole under that olive tree.

At this time of the day, the dying sun had produced an array of amazing colors on the mountains it had invaded. Vivid and bold in some peaks, eerily subtle in others, this strange mixture of cloaking in combination with Alessandra's fascinating profile made the perfect picture. Instinctively, Luke reached for his camera to capture the moment. Unfortunately, his hands only felt emptiness as he suddenly realized that he had left the camera back in the room. Disappointed, he took a deep breath, focusing his eyes completely on Alessandra. He could only stare for a few moments before being caught redhanded. He tried to etch this amazing view into his memory.

His daydream was interrupted by the man in black's first words.

"Luca. This is where your father's fate was sealed," he said in perfect English and in a voice that was rather soft. Ignoring Luke and Alessandra's open mouths, he continued pointing between two rocks.

"If you look between those two boulders, you will see Corleone. This view has been described in many ways. I suppose it depends where the looking glass is aimed and who's doing the aiming, but its beauty can never be denied," he submitted, looking at Alessandra.

"It will grab on to your heart and never, ever let go." Then turning to Luke, he shrugged. "You must submit to it and enjoy it," he finished, walking away, leaving Luke and Alessandra looking at each other in astonishment.

"Well, I never would have expected that!" Luke said, picking up the urn and carefully unclasping the two locking hinges that held the lid in place.

As Alessandra watched Luke cautiously spread some of the ashes around the tree prior to burying the urn, a little breeze blew a speck of ashes into Luke's nostrils, making him sneeze.

"Sorry, Pops," he said with a slight laugh.

He looked over to Alessandra, who was trying hard to suppress a laugh which resulted in both breaking out into a peal of full laughter.

Luke's eyes glimmered as he watched her conceal her mouth behind her hand.

Once their laughing had subsided, Luke inspected the hole, saying, "You enjoyed that, didn't you, Pops?"

After a few silent moments, resigning to the finality of his actions, he took a few long breaths and lowered his head. Moved by Luke's sincere emotions, Alessandra reached out and placed her hand on his shoulder.

"I thought I knew him, Alessandra," he said, slowly reaching for her hand and turning to face her. "But not even in my childish visions of him as a Superhero did I imagine the magnitude of his strength." He looked back down the hole and continued, "I hope I can be one-tenth the man you were, Pops." His gaze shifted to Alessandra and he finished, "I can only promise that I will spend the rest of my life trying."

Wiping her tears with his thumbs, they turned and walked away from the olive tree, tightly holding hands.

As they reached the main street, still holding hands, he turned to her and reached for her other hand.

"Before this goes any further, I need to tell you something, Alessandra."

Anticipating he was going to reveal his feelings and wanting to have no secrets between them, she lowered her head a little and took a step toward him.

"I need to tell you something first. I was wrong about you," she confessed, looking up. "That story Luca told us about your father was true. My mother told me a few hours ago. It has gathered some exaggerations within the Corleonese people, but effectively they have it right."

"You knew this before I stood on that chair like Abraham Lincoln?" he said, taking a small step backward but not letting go of her hands.

"Mia colpa," she mused with a wicked smile.

"It seems to me we can depend on our mothers to set us straight no matter how old we are. I knew about it as well. I had a lengthy conversation with her, and she told me everything. I didn't say anything because I wanted to see if the story this Luca was telling would be the same. In fact, it was pretty identical."

Encouraged by her tight grip, the amazing view of the city, and a Frank Sinatra song coming from a nearby balcony, he decided that he must tell her about Tiffany. He took another small step toward her.

"But Alessandra, I need to tell you about..."

Before Luke could finish, she reached for him and kissed him. Letting go of his reservations, he tightened his hold and kissed her with a need and fervor that he had never experienced. Her response was generous, yet Luke felt it was but a scintilla of what she had to offer. Grasping the last lingering strands of his unraveling moral rope, he disengaged.

"Alessandra, I really should..."

Again, she kissed him before he could utter another syllable. But, steadfast in his convictions, he pleaded,

"Wait. Please wait. I need to tell you something."

"What?" she asked, a little annoyed.

"I have a girlfriend back home that I need to..."

The lightning-fast slap, strong, almost hateful, left Luke gently rubbing the affected area and wondering if he had finished his explanation.

"No, wait, what? No Alessandra, please let me explain," he yelled, running after her.

She turned around and stared him down. Her eyes glowered in ache and a feeling that was blurred on the hinges. Luke could see her gentle frame turning firmer with each second she glared at him.

"Don't!" she responded, pointing the finger at him and walking away.

"Fuck, I hate my life!" he yelled, unable to move his feet.

CHAPTER THIRTY SEVEN

Open Your Eyes

Hot, tired, frustrated, and above all, disappointed at the way he managed Alessandra's emotional revelation, he finally made it back to his hotel.

Walking down the steps to the small main foyer, he noticed the prince and his entourage gathered in the sitting area to the right of the elevator. Wanting to go to his room and trying to process what had happened in the last three days in Corleone, he quickly called for the elevator, hoping that he had not attracted their attention.

"Mr. Cassaro, the prince would like you to join him for an espresso," one of the prince's bodyguards informed him.

Obligated to respond, he looked over to the sitting area making eye contact with the prince.

"Come, Mr. Cassaro, join me for an espresso," the prince requested, waving him over.

Luke made his way over to the prince but remained standing.

"Thank you, your highness, but I'm very tired, I'd like to get a good night's sleep, and I'm afraid the espresso would keep me up."

"A nightcap then," the prince insisted. "Please, Mr. Cassaro, I'm fascinated with your lifestyle. I would appreciate your company."

Luke looked at the prince and shook his head. He knew the man was educated and intelligent, so why was he so fascinated with the Mafia? He wondered as he studied the man a little longer and realized that the prince was ignorant.

Not a boorish ignorance, but ignorance that often invaded the rich and powerful. The Prince, Luke recognized, was ignorant of the true beauty of Corleone and, more importantly, ignorant of the true selfish ruthlessness of the Mafia. Feeling sorry for the man's ignorance, he abandoned all reservations for self-preservation and decided to set him straight.

Deliberately, he nodded his head and sat next to the prince.

"Your Highness, please call me Luke." He smiled and continued, "I would love to discuss my family, but I beg your indulgence to release your entourage, so we can talk in private."

Giampiero D'Angelo

The wave, almost indistinguishable, cleared the area quickly and silently, leaving them alone.

"My family, your highness," he began, "is a typical immigrant Italian American family. We have kept a lot of our Italian traditions and customs and live a comfortable, quiet life in the New York area. My father was a university ethics professor and my mother, the glue of our family, raised what I would like to think are three loving, if somewhat argumentative siblings. All we share, your Highness, with the most wanted man in Italy is the last name. We are not involved in organized crime and never have been.

"I came here to bury my father's ashes, reluctantly, I would add. Back in the States, although I participated in our traditions and customs, I never really felt that they were a necessary part of my life. In fact, especially because my family comes from Corleone, a place made famous by a movie, I was ashamed and tried to suppress my Italian heritage. I even considered changing my name to Larry Cassy at one time. If it wasn't for a promise I made to my father," he stopped to take a long breath, "I would never have come here. I unenthusiastically came here to release his ashes, but I leave here proud of his legacy, a legacy that has nothing to do with the Mafia." The prince remained quiet, observing Luke.

"With all due respect, your Highness, I would recommend that you investigate the true history of this beautiful place embroidered in contradictions, not what a talented writer has etched in the minds of so many moviegoers. What you find will surprise you. Good night, Prince Zarif," he said, standing, "I hope you find what you're looking for."

With a slight nod, he turned and headed for the elevator, hoping that he would not be garrotted by one of the prince's bodyguards.

CHAPTER THIRTY EIGHT

Leaving Town

Luke pulled his car around to the front entrance of his hotel, where Vincenzo was waiting for him with his suitcases. Before getting out of the car, Luke opened the trunk lid allowing Vincenzo to put his bags in. Joining Vincenzo, he offered him his hand and a one-hundred-dollar bill.

Vincenzo held out his hand in a stop motion.

"No, I couldn't, Mr. Cassaro," he said, looking more hurt than respectful.

Luke got visibly upset.

"Look, Vincenzo," he said, looking as serious as he possibly could, "you've got to stop this. You know that I'm not related to that Luca, and you must by now know that I'm definitely not a Mafioso, so you need to accept this token of my appreciation and, for the fiftieth time, call me Luke!"

"I'm sure you're not a Mafioso, Luke."

"Finally! Great, thanks, Vinny!" He said, giving him a spontaneous hug.

Vincenzo returned his hug with a smile and a couple of pats on his back.

"But I still can't take that."

"Why not?"

"For one thing, I own the hotel," he said, shrugging, "and for the other, I really like you and would like to consider you my friend. I would never take a tip from a friend."

"Wow! I'm honored. I would love to be your friend. And wow again! You own the hotel? I was wondering why you didn't work with your father at the pizzeria. It's now clear. Congratulations, you have a magnificent establishment here, and I'm not saying this because I'm your friend."

"Thanks, Luke," he said, shaking his hand this time. "I'm sorry you have to leave so soon. It was a pleasure meeting you." He started to leave but then turned back to him.

"By the way, did you find what you were looking for last night?" He said with a knowing grin.

"Very funny! You know very well that I did. But then I lost her."

"What do you mean you lost her?"

"I found her, we got kidnaped, we spoke to the most wanted man in all of Italy, he turned out to be indebted to my father, he gave me my condolences, and we buried my father's ashes. I think I'm in love with your sister...."

"Wow! Full day, and does she love you back?" Vincenzo asked Luke, who was looking right through him. "Luke, you here?"

"What? Yes, you know Vinny, I think she does," he said with a smile that quickly disappeared. "But when I tried telling her I had to go back to the States and that I had a girlfriend there..."

"You what?"

"I what, what?"

"Tell her you had a girlfriend."

"I had to, Vinny. Sorry, can I call you Vinny?" He asked but didn't wait for him to answer, "I really think I've fallen in love with her."

"Yes, you said that. And that's how you showed her, by telling her about your girlfriend in America?"

"What? Are you going to hit me too?"

"Maybe."

"I didn't want to tell her about my girlfriend," he said, a little perturbed that Vincenzo, like Alessandra, did not get what he wanted to say.

"What I wanted to tell her was that I was going home to tell my girlfriend that it's over between us. I think I owe Tiffany that much. But now, I don't know, maybe it's better this way," he finished, looking disappointed.

"Listen, Luke, I'm the last guy you should be talking to about how to land my sister, but it seems to me that Alessandra should hear you say that."

"It's too late. I have to catch a plane in four hours, and I'm already running late."

"Non è mai troppo tardi per trovare quello che eri destinato a trovare."

"Seriously, you too? What does that mean?"

"It's never too late to find what you were destined to find. Go back, Luke. I'm sure that destiny is not finished with you in the States, my friend. Now go," he said quietly, "before you miss your plane." Vincenzo turned and walked away before he became too emotional.

Luke looked at Vincenzo for a few seconds, got in, and drove away.

"It was very nice meeting you, Vinny," he said, leaving Corleone behind.

Vincenzo heard the car pull away, and then he heard his mother.

"He's leaving?" she asked him in Italian.

"He was only here for three days."

"I thought he was interested in your sister. I'm disappointed."

"Ma, I don't think he was interested. He's in love with her!"

"San Antonio. So, he left?"

"As usual, ma, your daughter's lack of patience does her no good."

CHAPTER THIRTY NINE
Seeking Home

Directed to his seat by a middle-aged competent-looking American Airline flight attendant, Luke was almost disappointed that his mane held no weight with this company. Almost, because as he made himself comfortable in the no-frills economy section, he was glad that he would have this time to process the incredible events of his now completed obligation.

As he slowly played, rewound, and replayed the events in his mind, some things became clear. His blood, no matter how much he had tried to deny it was fully Sicilian, and he was now proud of it. And he had fallen in love. To be sure, he had fallen for the beauty of the people, and the amazing sights, sounds, tastes, and smells of Corleone, but the physical pain he now felt was due to his ardent desire to be back with Alessandra lingering forever in their kiss.

Giampiero D'Angelo

"There was no doubt that I had fucked it up. I should have told Alessandra about Tiffany right away. Telling her as I was cheating on my girlfriend was a cowardly act. I was doing it to make myself feel better, not for Alessandra's benefit. In her eyes, I had lied to her, and if I lied about that, I could certainly be lying about my connections to the Mafia. My selfish confession had cost me both women. Tiffany because my heart now belonged to Alessandra and Alessandra because she thought I was a moron.

Anyway, as I lay in bed the next morning next to a sleeping Tiffany, I wondered if I was so shallow that a beautiful body next to me was all it took for me to ignore my feelings for Alessandra. However, after a great deal of self-debate, I justified my actions in two ways. Firstly, Tiffany's welcome home was so overpowering and endearing that I did not have the heart to end the relationship right away, and secondly, Alessandra was a flesh burn that hurt like hell but would heal with time.

So, I decided to try and make it work with Tiffany. I tried to make her happy by accepting the position with the Graff's, but after a couple of days, they bade farewell to the company. I made it a point to be more interested in her circle of friends, but I would often find myself socially Isolated and uninterested, thinking of Alessandra and what could have been if I had only been smarter or clearer earlier in our relationship.

I began visiting my family more frequently than prior to my father's death, but those visits only made me desire Alessandra more and value Tiffany less.

To her credit, Tiffany tried to appreciate my visits to my mother or sister, but what she could not understand was the frequency and length of those visits.

We were living but not alive. The daily routine of our lives took over, and we settled back into the pleasant relationship that we shared prior to my trip to Italy.

But pleasant is not what I wanted. I wanted to feel what I felt in Corleone, where my pictures seemed to have more focus and definition. My palate jumped with joy in anticipation of a new taste or a rediscovery of an old one. I wanted to see people appreciate the simple things, where their laughter was genuine, not manufactured for the benefit of fitting in, where people would go to restaurants to enjoy great food and company and just not to be seen. Experience new dishes that look great but lack substance. Yes, I wanted all those things, but above all, I wanted my heart to ache with the anticipation a single kiss had brought. She was 4,500 miles away from me, but she was never more than 45 seconds away from my thoughts. I couldn't leave her behind. She was always with me, within me.... my normal life was starting to feel dim without her near me. Little pokes in my chest, again and again, reminded me of the mistake I had committed.

So, when I walked into our apartment a few seconds ago, and saw suitcases near the door, I was not surprised."

Silently he walked to the couch and sat beside Tiffany, who was slowly twirling her glass of wine.

Without looking at him, she stopped this nervous gesture, took the bottle of white wine out of the ice bucket, and poured him a glass. She then smiled at him with a raised eyebrow and resumed twirling her glass. There was no acknowledgment of the suitcase, for the meaning was clear to both.

"I'm sorry, I've been preoccupied. The trip threw me on a loop. I'm still trying to process what happened there," he apologized, taking a small sip of his wine.

"As am I. But Luke, you're very conflicted. I would even say confused," she began while still twirling her glass. "When you're going through something like this, I would think you would want me there to bounce things off of or just to comfort you. The fact that I was not there, and if you were, to be honest with yourself, you don't want me there. I think it's time to rethink our relationship," she finished, draining her wine.

Instinctively he leaned over and refilled her glass, taking a little more time than usual to formulate a proper response. He knew he was conflicted. The question was, was this the right time to shed his emotional armor and bare his true feelings knowing that his relationship with Tiffany would end. Taking a big breath, he began, "Tiff..."

"I want to apologize to you, Luke," she said before he could continue.

Stopped in his track, he curiously asked, "Apologize for what?"

"For not realizing how much your photography means to you." She held up her hand, predicting his objection. "I certainly know of your talent, but it's your passion for the art that makes you who you are. Mostly I'm sorry for trying to make you fit in my world, my world, without even asking you if you wanted to," she concluded, her last few words barely audible.

"You were thinking of us," he responded, trying to comfort her.

Tiffany removed one hand from her glass and stroked Luke's face.

"I promised myself I was not going to cry. But no, Luke I was thinking of myself."

"Tiff, please..."

Moving her hand from his cheek to his mouth, she smiled.

"Luke, you're a wonderful man, you're kind, generous, and when you're fully engaged, you're, well, you're perfect." She looked into his eyes and then looked away, afraid that she would cry again, "But you're not fully involved in this relationship, and that's not good enough for me. We love to be with each other, Luke, but we're not in love with each other. We both deserve to have a blissful life. I hope that whatever you found in Sicily will give you that," she said, looking at Luke, who now lowered his head, confirming that she was right. She smiled to herself and continued, "I think we'll always be friends. In fact, I know we will."

Slowly placing the empty glass on the table, she stood up then bent and kissed him on both cheeks.

There were no further words or looks exchanged. She quietly grabbed the suitcases and walked out.

He knew she had more class than to confront him about what he had found in Corleone, and he realized that she let him down gently, saving him from embarrassing himself with a self-servicing and disingenuous confession.

Luke's insides felt hollow. If only he had been honest with both the women. In fact, if he had been honest with himself, things would be better.

Vacantly swirling his half-full wine glass, he was jarred back to reality by the muted clang of the closing door. Patiently waiting for the wine to stop its revolving journey around its glass confines, he silently thanked Tiffany for her inner strength and wished her a happy life.

Confident that she would find it, he brought the glass to his mouth and drained it. The deep, noisy exhale was genuine.

CHAPTER FORTY
Settling The Scores

The flight was simply amazing. The business class ticket was a treat that Don Mario would never have thought possible, but as a gift from Luke, he was more than happy to accept. Of course, it did come with a request, and that was that he must personally bless the opening of Luke's upcoming exhibit.

As instructed by Luke, after picking up his bags, he looked for his name on one of the many signs that were being held up by the limo drivers. Correctly assuming that the sign would not say 'Don Mario,' he headed for the sign that read 'Father Mario.'

"Good afternoon," he said with a smile, "I'm Father Mario."

"Hello, Father," the driver said, folding the signs and stuffing them in his jacket's inner pocket. "I'll take your bags for you."

"Thank you."

"Please follow me. Is this your first trip to New York, Father?" The driver asked as they walked forward.

"Actually, no, I've been here several times. The last time was for a conference on working with the government to form laws and policies that will influence religious freedoms."

"How did that go, Father?"

"You tell me," Don Mario chuckled, "that conference was three years ago, and the only correspondence I've received is a new invitation to the next conference in Venice next year!"

They were both still laughing as they reached the limo. "Please make yourself comfortable, Father. I have the address. We should be there in less than 45 minutes, depending on the traffic, of course."

The rest of the ride was, in fact, very comfortable and interesting. It seemed that the driver was married to an Italian woman whose family, many generations ago, came from Sicily. His many questions, although probing, were asked with what Don Mario thought was a genuine and respectful interest in Sicilian history. It was, therefore, with a slight twinge of disappointment that they arrived at their destination.

As the driver opened the door, Don Mario noticed a placard with his name on it and the heading:

'The Virtues of Revenge'

'Keynote Speaker'

Don Mario

Confused, Don Mario looked at the driver for clarification.

"This is the address, Father," the driver answered as he shrugged. "There's a man waiting for you at the entrance."

The man at the entrance waived and called him over. "Don Mario," he yelled, walking towards him, "come, we've been expecting you. I'm Rabbi Shmuel, welcome," he said, extending his hand.

"Expecting me?" Don Mario asked, shaking the rabbi's hand. "But I know nothing of this. What is this all about?"

"What do you mean, you know nothing? Are you not ready to speak?"

"Speak? I'm…I'm…"

"Are you not Father Mario, from Venice?

"No! He's Don Mario, from Corleone!" Luke said from behind Don Mario.

Don Mario turned and quickly recognized the gag. "You scoundrel!" He said with a great big smile, then joined the others in their laughter.

After embracing and looking at each other and embracing several more times, Luke made the introductions.

"Don Mario, you've already met Rabbi Samuel."

"I apologize for the ruse Father," Rabbi Samuel said, shaking his hand again, "but he told me about your deception, and I thought you would appreciate the irony."

"I do, very much, but it seems like you went to a great deal of trouble to get me back."

"We had plenty of volunteers. And this," Luke said, directing Don Mario to the driver, "is Sal, my brother."

"Sal, my condolences on your father's passing," he said, shaking Sal's hand.

"Thank you, Father."

"He was a true gentleman. I'm glad that at least one of his sons has taken after him. I'm sorry that you have to put up with him," he said, turning to Luke.

"We all have our crosses to bear, Don Mario. Mine is a little heavier than most," he finished, slapping Luke's shoulder.

"Nosay b'ol im chavayro." Rabbi Samuel interjected.

"Yes, Rabbi, very well said. 'To share the burden with one's friend,'" Don Mario translated as they all looked at Luke.

"Amen," the Rabbi responded.

"What can I say, good friends, are hard to come by," Luke retorted.

CHAPTER FORTY ONE

The New York Exhibition

BLOOD TELLS NO LIESBY: A PROUD SICILIAN

GRAND OPENING BY INVITATION ONLY

Within minutes of the door opening, the gallery was full of invited guests. He had doubted that all the invitees would attend, but by the look of the turnout, he was wrong.

With 'Frank Sinatra's Greatest Hits' lightly playing in the background, one of three demands Luke had made to Mr. Barry Grander, the gallery's owner and curator. Luke worked the room doing his best to accommodate his guests' requests for his personal attention.

Noticing Barry in deep conversation with Sal, he smiled to himself as he recalled the events that had brought him to this night.

Giampiero D'Angelo

The first call came six months ago today. The call was neither long nor friendly. Mr. Grander's personal assistant simply requested a meeting, gave me several dates and times, and asked me to check my calendar while he waited. I knew that the Grander Galleries had spaces in New York, London, Paris, Rome, and other major cities around the world. I also knew a great deal about the man, for although I had never met him, Tiffany's parents would often refer to him as 'Barry, one of our dearest friends' when they would share a story about one of the many evenings they spent in his company. Still, I had many questions, not the least of which was how Grander knew of me, but if this very influential man in the exposition business wanted to meet, I would make myself available.

The first meeting was at one of several Grander's galleries in New York. First to meet me was Roland, who refused to shake hands or give his last name. Again, the meeting was short and cold. Roland showed me some photos, asked me if they were mine, and upon my affirmation, set up a meeting with Mr.

Grander. When I asked him how he got the pictures, Roland said that Mr. Grander would explain.

A week later, at 8:15 a.m., I found myself in Barry's Manhattan penthouse having eggs benedict and French fries. Barry explained that the first time that he heard of me was when he read my article 'Blood Tells No Lies' in Vanity Fair.

"I found the story about your three days in Corleone to be interesting, but what I found exciting were the photos that came with the article. I will exhibit your photos," he commanded, not expecting a refusal.

I certainly was not going to disappoint the man, but I did have some requests that became demands during many negotiation sessions, with and without Barry. In the end, I agreed with the terms of the contract, with three additional caveats. I would have the final say as to the pieces exhibited. Frank Sinatra must be played in the background. The opening night was for my invited guests only, and I would be allowed to open my own gallery in Corleone at my pleasure.

The exhibit was divided into three sections, New York, Corleone, and Faces. New York and Corleone's photos were of attractions and sites of the respective places, the Faces exhibit was a myriad of portraits, but unlike the pictures of the cities, these portraits were untitled and unnoted. Luke had left it up to the viewer to speculate where the photos were shot. Everyone he had spoken to had commented not only on the beauty of Corleone but also on the unique character of the town that he had been able to capture.

Although the most talked about photos were the portraits of what people had been calling, Scarred face and Little Lady. Especially because the subjects were in attendance and were personable enough to converse with any guest that approached them, the most admired was a portrait of the mystery woman amongst the ruins. No one could seem to put into words the power of the shot.

One of the first to take their leave was his cousin Lisa and her husband, Chris.

"Luke, this is amazing photography. I always knew you were the best," Lisa complimented without a hint of resentment. "But we have to leave. Little Christopher here," she said, holding her enormous stomach, "is pumping my kidneys like an oil well."

"And there you have it," her husband added. "Eloquently put, from my highly refined soulmate. But I agree, Luke. Your pictures are outstanding. My favorite is that of the United Nations. That ray of sunshine bursting through the overcast sky. It gives me a sense of hope. Love it!"

"It's yours, congressman."

"Chris! What the fuck," Lisa reprimanded her husband in a low voice.

"That's alright, Lisa. It's the least I can do for the man that made an honest woman out of you."

"Thank you, Luke. You're a very generous man. But I think you have it backward. It was your cousin that made me an honest man. And what's with this congressman shit?"

"I like to remind myself that I actually know an honest politician. Seriously Chris, I really want you to have it. I was actually thinking of you when I took that shot."

"Luke, thanks, man. You're going to make me cry."

"He wouldn't be the first in this family to make you cry," Lisa said to her husband.

"I told you, you didn't make me cry at my brother's wedding. It was my allergies. Luke, you were there. Did you see me cry?" The congressman protested.

"No way!" Luke said, holding up his hands. "I'm not getting in on this recollection."

"Either way," Lisa said, moving towards her husband, "you've been weeping for my love ever since," she finished, tenderly kissing his cheek.

"I can't argue with the truth." He embraced her and kissed her back on her lips.

"Okay, cut it out," Luke joked. "I think that's how you got that way in the first place," he said, pointing to Lisa's swell.

Lisa gave a false laugh.

"Very funny, Luke and very original," she said, taking her husband's hand and walking away. With her back to Luke, she flipped him the finger.

Laughing, and finally, with no one approaching him, Luke walked over to join Laurie and Sarah beside their portrait. Spotting Sal at the other side of the hall, he waved him over. After the introductions, Sarah excused herself and turned to closer examine Laurie's portrait.

"Do you know anyone that doesn't have or need bodyguards?" Sal asked, placing a hand on Luke's shoulder.

"Only you, Sal, and these two," he responded, looking over to Sarah, who was in a trance admiring Luke's use of a single sunray in Laurie's portrait.

Perfectly timed, the ray rested on Laurie's scarred side of his face revealing his beauty and openness and yet capturing his tortured soul. She had expressed this to Luke several times, but inevitably Luke always claimed that it was a lucky shot.

"I would say it was luck, but you use the sun's rays in more than one of your photographs," Sarah disagreed.

"I guess I've been lucky more than once," he said, still not wanting to agree with her.

Sarah seemed to have lost interest in the discussion as she looked at the portrait and then looked back at Laurie. She did that several more times as the other three continued to look at her in silence.

Laurie suddenly spread his hands toward Sarah. "You know, you're making me feel a little self-conscious."

There was not even a tiny sign from Sarah that she felt that she was being rude. In fact, she was the one who felt offended.

"Really?" she said, putting her hands on her hips. "This is coming from a guy that can't even look me in the eye when he's accusing me? If you didn't want people to stare at you, you should not have agreed to be photographed."

Not a shy person, Laurie responded, "First, it's not an accusation. It's a feeling. Second, you don't see me looking at your picture and checking 100 times to see if you're still short."

There was an uncomfortable stillness that was broken by Sarah.

"You want to grab a coffee? Starbucks is right across the street."

"Sure," he responded, turning away from the group.

As they walked away, Laurie looked at Luke and Sal, shrugged his shoulders, and followed Sarah out of the gallery.

"What was that?" Sal said, looking at the now empty front door.

"I'm not sure, but I'm glad they love their portraits."

Sal reached over to Luke and squeezed his shoulder. "Luke. I'm so proud of you. You are truly an artist. Dad would've loved this."

"Thanks, Sal. I know he would have. He was so proud of all of us. You know, he called me the day that you got that cinematographer job at the new Tom Cruise movie."

"You sounded so surprised when I told you," Sal said, adding a light slap to Luke's shoulder.

"No, I was. He called me after you did. He wanted to know if you'd called," Luke revealed, accepting a glass of prosecco from a server.

"Of course, he would never have told you before I did."

"No way!" Luke concurred with a smile, making Sal laugh.

"Would not have been ethical." Then turning to Sal, he offerred his glass for a toast. "To pops, he always made us feel important."

"You got that right," Sal agreed, taking a drink of the prosecco. "He always made a big deal out of our accomplishments no matter how small, and always played down our..."

"Mistakes, no matter how big," Luke finished, draining his prosecco. "I really miss him."

Sal nodded his head a few times.

"You know Luke, after you moved out, Pops and I got a lot closer. To the point where he confessed that his one wish was for you to understand your history and appreciate your heritage. Looking at you now, with this newfound appreciation for Corleone and in love with one of its citizens, I can feel him smiling down on us."

Luke's throat locked up, and he could only manage to look at his brother and hug him hard.

"Alright, alright," Sal managed.

As Sal opened his eyes while still hugging Luke, he noticed Tiffany walking in.

"Have you spoken to Tiffany?"

"Yes, just yesterday. Why?" he asked, knowing precisely what he meant.

"Everything cool?"

"Very cool."

"She's here, you know."

"Yes, I know."

"With her new boyfriend."

"Fiancé, I think?"

"Here they come. Oh man, you're so cool," Sal whispered as the couple got closer.

"Can you stay cool? Jesus, look at this. They're perfect for each other."

Walking towards Luke and Sal, Tiffany, in her very expensive, very stylish pearl white Vera Wang pant suit, radiated wealth and subtle beauty without being ostentatious. Bradley, her fiancé, looked like he had just stepped off the cover of GQ. He walked with such grace and power that his energy matched perfectly with Tiffany's. Confidently, they both walked toward Luke and Sal stopping just short with a smile that only old money can produce.

"Hello Tiffany," Luke greeted her, kissing both cheeks.

Tiffany accepted the kisses graciously as she presented Bradley.

"Hello, Luke. This is my fiancé, Bradley."

"Bradley Graf, pleased to meet you, Luke. Your photographs are incredible. I love the way you bring landscape and portraits together," he complimented him, holding out his hand.

Luke took his hand quickly, looking at Tiffany. "Thank you, Bradley, as in Ignat and Steffi Graf?"

"Yes, you know my parents?"

"I know your dad well. I worked for him for a week. I've also met your mom a couple of times. Very nice people."

Tiffany stepped in before Bradley could answer. "So, Luke, are you going to show us around?"

"Follow me," he commanded, offering a bent elbow to Tiffany.

Tiffany took his elbow and they began walking to the first exhibit with Sal and Bradley in tow. Creating enough space between the groups, Luke turned to Tiffany.

"Graf?"

"Shut up!" she said, refusing to look at him. "He's perfect. He adores me, and I allow him to!"

"A match made in Society Heaven."

"You're such an adorable prick!" she teased, pulling him a little closer.

They continued to walk around the gallery until Tiffany stopped in front of a picture of a beautiful woman with some ruins in the background. Quickly turning away from the picture, she faced Luke.

"We're getting married next September. Are you coming?"

"Are you inviting me?" He responded, looking over her right shoulder at the picture.

"You'll be the first," she mocked. "Beautiful ruins," she critiqued without looking at the picture.

"Very beautiful," he responded with a crooked smile. "Italian food?"

"She's also nice," she commented further, still not looking at the portrait. "Only if you cook it."

"Nice would not begin to describe her," he confessed, still looking at the picture.

Tiffany finally turned to the picture and then back to Luke.

"She's a lucky woman," she told him honestly.

"She doesn't even have my number, Tiff."

"No, but she has your heart. And that's priceless." She reached for him and gave him a short but wet kiss on the lips.

He hugged her tight and then looked at her holding both her hands.

"Thanks for coming and for being you, Tiff."

"Luke, are you kidding me? It was my pleasure. Your pictures are utterly amazing. I'm happy I could play a small part in your amazing world."

"Small part? Tiff, I know it was you that sent my photos to Barry."

Tiffany detached herself from his hands.

"Luke, I told you before, you were just another rung in the social ladder for me," she lied, looking over to Bradley.

"Bullshit Tiff, I know you better than that! Plus, you would never have started that low!" He said, earning him a gentle slap on his chest.

Tiffany turned half away from him and smiled. She then walked over to Bradley and held his arm with both of hers.

"I think I could spend half a day here. But we're expected for dinner at Bradley's parents. Aren't we, darling?" She asked, kissing him on the cheek.

"Yes, we are," Bradley confirmed with a smile. Tiffany turned back to Luke and shrugged.

"You know, cocktails and all," she said, smiling at Sal. "Come, Bradley. We need to stop at my parents to pick up a bottle of Boerl & Kroff Brut Rose. You know how much your mother loves that champagne."

"I'll show you out," Sal offered.

Making sure that no one else heard him. Bradley leaned closer to Luke.

"Like my mother doesn't have ten cases of that champagne in the wine cellar!" Then offered Luke his hand and continued in a louder voice, "it was a pleasure meeting you. I hope to have more time to enjoy your pictures next time."

As Tiffany and Bradley walked out of the gallery, Luke was confident that they would make the perfect society couple. He could feel nothing but a warm feeling for Tiffany. She had been quite kind to him, an ex that didn't end things on an ugly note.

Smiling, Luke turned to see a man dressed in thwabs approaching him. Recognizing him immediately, Luke extended his hand.

"Prince Zarif. Thank you for coming."

The prince took Luke's hand with both of his.

"Thank you for inviting me. Would you show me around, Luke?" He asked with a smile.

"It would be my pleasure."

They began walking around the gallery, followed by the prince's bodyguards. Occasionally stopped in front of a picture the prince simply admired or had a question about, they unhurriedly made their way around the gallery with light and pleasant conversation between frequent laughs.

As they entered the Corleone exhibit, the prince looked around at the bodyguards and held up his hand. Immediately the bodyguards stopped, allowing them to continue alone until they came to the Mulino exhibit, where they stopped to contemplate the photo in silence.

"You once told me that I should look at the history of Corleone," the prince broke the silence, looking at the picture.

"Yes, I'm sorry about that, your highness…"

"Please, Luke." The prince interrupted, putting a hand on Luke's forearm, "you were right, and please call me Jack."

"Jack?" Luke almost yelled, trying to suppress a laugh.

"I like the name. But please only call me that when we're alone, I wouldn't want the servants to get any ideas," the prince said seriously.

"Of course," he agreed, inclining his head.

"I took your advice Luke, and I've looked at the history of Sicily, Corleone, and specifically the Mill," he said, pointing to the picture.

Taking Luke's arm, he invited him to walk further. After a couple of steps, he continued, "actually, I've had a few scholars in my employment look into the history of Sicily. But regardless, I now know some interesting things. Would you like to know them?" He asked, continuing without waiting for Luke to agree.

"Early in the 9th century, the Muslims-Byzantine wars had reached a fever pitch. Ibrahim ibn al-Aghlab, founder of the Aghlabid dynasty, and by imperial decree of the Abbasid caliph Harun al-Rashid, emir of Ifriqiya, was concerned about the numerous scrimmages his armies had to deal with. Low in manpower and rations, he negotiates a truce with the Byzantine governor of Sicily. To celebrate this welcome truce, the two factions co-operated in the building of a new mill."

Luke looked back at the picture of the mill.

"That's right, that mill. Anyway, Ibrahim supplied the funds and plans. The Byzantine governor supplied the labor." He paused for a breath.

"Now, this is where it gets interesting. Charged with designing this symbol of peace was Hosni al-Qasr, the prominent architect of the day. The project took 14 months to complete, a feat that by the standard of the day was considered incredible." The prince stopped and looked at Luke, who had a perplexed expression. "No, that's not the interesting part. The interesting part is this. Did you know that your family name, Cassaro, derives from the Arabic word for castle?"

"No, I did not."

"Then it would also follow that you are unaware that the Arabic word for castle is Qasr. Therefore, Mr. Cassaro, you are a very distant relative of the builder of this mill al-Qasru." He finished with a hearty laugh.

"Prince Zarif..."

"Jack," the prince interrupted.

"Jack, that's a nice story but hardly believable."

"Then you'll never believe the rest."

"There's more?"

"History tells us so," Jack shrugged. "Remember I told you it took only fourteen months to complete the mill. The reason is that al-Qasru hired the best builder in all of Sicily, a Byzantine, by the name Aldus

Bonifatius. Mr. Bonifatuis is an ancestor of your friend Alessandra Boniface."

The men looked into each other's eyes, and together, they broke into a noisy laugh that gathered the attention of most of the other people in the gallery. Slowly reducing the volume and frequency of their laughter, they were finally able to speak again.

"Before you say anything, Luke," Jack said, snapping his fingers and bringing one of his guards to him with a small leather attaché case. "Here are all the documents you'll need to verify this fantastic tale. Enjoy." He nodded his head at the bodyguard, who handed Luke the case and retreated.

After the bodyguard left, Jack continued in a tone Luke noticed was a little more serious.

"Over the next few hundred years, the region was conquered many times. The mill, producer of the essential ingredient for bread and cakes, stood solid in perpetual motion observing every celebration and servicing the population in the precarious peacetime that followed, which lasted for almost 1000 years. Eventually, due to modernization and people's lack of interest in the part it played in history, the mill lost its purpose and quietly faded into a fable told late at night to young children." He turned back and stared at the picture of the mill for a few more seconds and then looked at Luke directly in the eye. "I've decided to restore the Mill."

"Prince!"

"But not only the Mill, and not only in Corleone, Luke. I want to restore as many of our buildings and edifices as possible in all of Sicily. My greatest wish is to see many of my people visiting Sicily for the rich and beautiful history our civilizations contributed to this island, not for the Mafia, a silly and erroneous conception I previously harboured. As for the Mill in Corleone, it will always hold a special place in my heart, for as it turns out, and to further make this story more incredible, Ibrahim idn al-Aghlab was my ancestor."

Silently staring at each other for several seconds, Luke tried to process what had just been revealed to him. As he was about to respond, the prince held up his hand.

"There's something else, Luke. I want Alessandra to head the project in Corleone, and I want you to tell her."

"Prince Zarif, this is truly great news for Sicily, for the town of Corleone, and especially for Alessandra, but why me?"

"Two reasons. One, you are truly a talented photographer, so I would like you to document the restoration project through your artistic eyes. Two and more importantly, your blood requires you to do so. Three..."

"I thought there were only two reasons," Luke interrupted with a chuckle.

"I'm adding a third," the prince responded, accustomed to changing his mind. "This is a great exhibition, no doubt, but by the look on your face, your pride is muted. I believe that there is something missing in the exhibit, a very personal piece, a 'pièce de résistance' Alessandra?"

"I did want to move the exhibit permanently to Corleone," Luke mused, not answering his question directly.

"Yes, Luke, I'm sure that that is the only reason you will accept this assignment," Jack retorted in a very sarcastic tone.

"You're a very perceptive man Prince Zarif, and a closet romantic, Jack."

The prince's infectious laugh was loud enough to get the attention of his bodyguards, but once again, a slight wave stopped them from approaching him. The laughing subsided, and Jack whispered in Luke's ear.

"Yes, I am. Just don't tell any of my twenty concubines. My chamberlain already has a tough time keeping them in line."

Their laughter resumed in earnest.

CHAPTER FORTY TWO

Corleone calling

The sparsely-filled bars, light walk-in traffic in all establishments, and half-empty piazzas not only indicated the end of the tourist season but also introduced a mixture of relief and regret in the citizens of Corleone.

Not immune to this yearly exodus of visitors, the Corleone Historical Building was void of daily activities. So, Alessandra unhurriedly unlocked the front door and casually walked over to hang her jacket on her antique Byzantine coat rack.

The rack, a gift from her uncle Don Mario on her twenty-first birthday, was her most treasured possession. She had seriously thought about not putting it up for fear that it would be stolen, but in the end, she decided that everyone visiting the Corleone Historical Building should have a chance to admire this unique piece of Byzantine art.

As she approached the desk, she noticed a small package on her desk. *This is odd.*

She thought, inspecting the parcel from her place.

The mail is not delivered before noon.

She picked up the package and rolled it in her hand. Noticing that there was no return address, she checked again to make sure the package was addressed to her. Satisfied, she slowly opened the package.

Carefully secured on top of yellow tissue paper is a memory stick with a tag attached to it saying: 'View this first.' Intrigued, she followed the instruction.

She inserted the stick into the computer and anxiously waited for something to happen.

She was surprised to see a picture of the Mill with the tagline 'our history ties us.'

She hit 'start slide show' and was treated with beautiful photos of her beloved town until the final picture of Luke holding a piece of paper further instructed her to look once again in the package.

Through her glassy vision, she looked back in the package and noticed a light blue picture frame peeking out from under the carefully placed yellow tissue paper.

Gently removing the tissue from the package, she exposed the backing of a framed picture with a handwritten note; 'To Alessandra, From Luca.' And one word, 'Beautiful' underneath.

She turned the picture over, revealing the picture of her at the waterfall. A glimmering pain rose within her, a nudge that she had silenced under the heavy hand of her ego.

With the image of Luke constantly in her mind, her emotions ran amuck. Sad, happy, longing, and other emotions that she couldn't explain filled her body, causing her legs to turn to jelly, and she looked around for a chair as she felt her will deflating.

Alessandra had no idea how long she had stood in this comatose state, only that the knock at the front door snapped her trance, and she was not happy about it. There was another knock. Annoyed, Alessandra walked to the door,

"I'm sorry we don't open until 10:00. Please come back," she said without opening the door and walked back to her desk.

She had not taken two steps back to her desired place when there was another knock at the door, a little louder this time. Upset that she couldn't go back to her desk to continue with her sad recollections, she exhaled and opened the door to her smiling brother Vinny.

"What are you doing here? And what's with that stupid smile on your face?" She asked in Italian.

"I just wanted to be here for posterity," he answered, broadening his smile.

"You're an idiot!" She yelled at him and turned to leave.

Her noisy gasp and sudden stop in her rumbling, combined with Luke's face as he stood at her desk, reassured Vinny that he could quietly exit, leaving it to destiny to complete the moment.

Her slow, methodical walk toward him left little doubt in Luke's mind that happiness was imminent.

There were no words exchanged, only a soft, moist kiss that defined their future.

Giampiero D'Angelo

EPILOGUE

Next to the Corleone Historical Building was the new 5000-square feet Art Gallery purchased by Luke a year ago, right after the wedding. Due to its overwhelming success in New York, it took Luke the better part of two years to move 'Luca's Exhibition,' as it has become known internationally, to its new permanent home.

Only a few short hours ago, the gallery was a grand assembly of who's who. Knowing that the media would be well represented, politicians, entertainers, sports stars, and high-ranking clergy from various religions lobbied extensively for an invitation to this highly anticipated opening.

The opening did not disappoint anyone.

Now, finally alone, they enjoy the serenity of the empty gallery sitting on the only backless bench in the exhibit.

"You truly are beautiful," Luke said without looking away from the picture that had interested the world.

Alessandra responded with a gentle kiss on his forehead.

"You say that as if you are surprised."

"I'm only surprised that you're still with me," he said, letting out a short laugh.

"So am I." She moved a little closer to him.

Locking her arms around his waist, she rested her head on his shoulder while still looking at the picture.

"Are you ready to go home?"

"Just about," he responded, smiling to himself as he recalled his attitude towards his heritage, this place, and how this picture changed his life.

It took an adventure to change who he was and what he thought himself to be. His push only pulled him within, and only when he let his roots consume his soul that he could finally feel someone who knew where he belonged.

Forcing himself to look away, he gently lifted Alessandra's head from his chest.

"Less than two years ago, I would have gone out of my way to downplay my culture. Look at me now, a beautiful Sicilian mayor as my wife, a new Sicilian life growing inside her," he said, tenderly touching her swelling stomach, "and together with his wife, living in and promoting a town his parents lovingly abandoned, it defies comprehension."

"No, it doesn't, my love. It defines it!" She corrected him.

They turned to face each other, and together, they said, "La vita e un viaggio, chi viaggia vive due volte."

"Okay, I'm ready. Let me check the side door. I'll meet you at the front entrance," Luke told her.

Reaching the side door, he noticed that it was slightly ajar. As he reached for the door handle, he was startled by a man's voice behind him.

"He's dead," the man said, triggering Luke to quickly turn and hit the door hard with his shoulders.

"What the fuck!"

"Luke, he wanted you to have this," the man in black said, handing him an envelope. "He wrote it in English," he added, gently pushing Luke aside. "I'll see you around, Luke," he finished, walking out the side door without an apology.

Trying to recover from the sudden blow, Luke stood motionless, staring at the side door until Alessandra called him back to reality.

"Yes, I'll be right there," he answered, opening the envelope.

Inside was a small handwritten note:

Giampiero D'Angelo

Luke,

I tell you this for the love of my family.

If you need confirmation, it is available. The one that brought you this note will have it. When my mother revealed this to me on her death bed, I needed no confirmation.

I finally knew what that look on my father's face was when your father took the blame for Mauro's death.

It was pride, pure unbridled pride.

For, are you ready for this, Luke?

My father and your grandfather were the same person.

Your loving Uncle,

Luca

ACKNOWLEDGMENT

This book would not have been possible without the valuable contribution of some individuals.

Salvatore Riina, my friend, whose wit, sometimes obvious and loud, other times so subtle and silent that only our 30-year friendship affords me the pleasure of understanding, was a witness to an event that eventually led to this story.

Pablo Petrucci, a young and energetic screenwriter who was able to understand two old men's incoherent prattle and produce some relevant situations that have made their way into the final draft.

Finally, to my loving and supportive wife Christa, who patiently listened to my blurred thoughts and cleared them with gentle suggestions, my eternal gratitude, and love.